Land of the Free

Seth Halleway

Copyright © 2020 Seth Halleway
All rights reserved

The characters and events portrayed in this book are fictitious. Any similarity to real persons, living or dead, is coincidental and not intended by the author.

No part of this book may be reproduced, or stored in a retrieval system, or transmitted in any form or by any means, electronic, mechanical, photocopying, recording, or otherwise, without express written permission of the publisher.

Printed in the United States of America

- To my darling wife and my family, without whose love and support this work would not have been possible. -

1. The Constitutional Alliance

"Good morning, Federated States of America. It's eight AM this Tuesday, the twenty-first of May 2052. I'm Richard O'Keefe-"

"-and I'm Deborah Bates. Welcome to *Patriot News Hour*, coming to you live on Vueve Networks through all forty-eight states."

"Let's jump right in this morning with some fantastic news about our country's planned Arlington spaceport facility. As viewers are aware, our beloved leader, President White, has been touting the project as the perfect capping stone to mark four years since our Great American Renewal began. Visiting the project site yesterday, our President made some important remarks to all Federal citizens. Let's briefly listen to what he had to say..."

"For all of us, there is no frontier more important, no goal more imperative to our nation today, than fostering our plans for the skies and space. As a nation, we can ill afford to allow corrupt powers like China, India, California, and Europe to continue their colonization of the moon and Mars unchallenged. We are the dominant superpower on this planet, and with this spaceport we will demonstrate, beyond all question, that our nation is not only the rightful ruler of this world, but of all worlds, all planets that we can see and name. Let me make it clear, as the voice of all Americans, that we name these planets and say to all would-be poachers: THESE ARE OURS!"

"The speech was met with rapturous applause from standing members of the Senate and other attendees. Though, as viewers are aware, not everyone is happy with the spaceport being built on top of the old Arlington Cemetery. Some people are still fond of the old regime and the war criminals who died for it. Isn't that right, Deborah?"

"Absolutely, Richard. In fact, late last night two high-ranking members of the radical terrorist group The Constitutional Alliance were arrested in a blitz raid carried out in the Washington suburbs. The two terrorists, Kirsten Mason and Jack Anderson, have been remanded into custody and are charged with inciting insurrection. The pair are due to be sentenced to public torture and execution later this afternoon. I can see you smiling there, Richard, because I know you're happy with that decision."

"It's a really great decision, Deborah, and I think it's also a credit to Justice Wilson and this new Administration that we can get these convictions moving along so quickly. With groups like The Constitutional Alliance, we can't afford to hesitate or be lenient, and it's important to use these executions as examples to dissuade other relics of the old world from challenging the legitimate authority of our president."

"I'm certainly glad the executions are going ahead, though isolated reports are surfacing that riots in support of Mason and Anderson are planned in Chicago later today. Richard, as a nation, how can we ensure these radicalized movements don't endanger our way of life, and what can people in Chicago do to protect themselves from these riots?"

"Well, Deborah, I think the best thing any of us can do is to remember that local security forces are more than equipped to deal with these issues. Just stay well clear of any protest areas because you may get injured as a result of the violence there. And, of course, you don't want you or anyone in your family to be mistaken for being a separatist."

"I know I don't want to be mistaken for a separatist, Richard, so I think I'd take your advice and stay clear of the riots. To all good citizens in Chicago, we hope you do the right thing too, and stay safe and secure."

"Coming up, more news to lead us into the morning, including government proposals to reward citizens for capturing defectors headed for the Republic of Texas. Stay tuned, because we'll be right back with more *Patriot News Hour* after this short break."

2. Chicago Tenement Zone

He'd only been a prospect with the Prince Kings for three months, but Raze was already tired of his latest Beatrape gig. The problem wasn't that the jobs didn't pay well; they paid well enough. The violence involved could get bloody at times, but Raze had grown used to that. Prostituting himself for hard sex with ladies from The Glades could even be enjoyable. That was especially true when the client was an attractive, sweet on the outside, dirty on the inside variety. Those were the ones who ached most for a thrill, a break from their dull lives of plenty within the gated communities of the elites. Moments with those ladies were something Raze could look forward to.

No, Raze's real problem lay in the existential monotony of his life. It was the simple, unavoidable realization that he'd reached the ceiling in how far his life could go. Forced out from every community in the area. Sleeping in this steel rooftop box in the summers. Awaking every morning to a hazy sunrise. Looking out over the concrete wasteland of the Chicago Tenement Zone. The popping of handgun fire and smell of oil drums still burning that greeted the crack of dawn. The sizzling of his morning Praedo Protein+ Cube frying in the pan atop his butane stove. No matter how many deeds he undertook, and no matter how much he put on the line, this was how his days would always begin. It would go on this way until he was either dead, locked away, or starved to death from being either too old or too crippled to provide for himself any further.

But, Raze always controlled his emotions. He was quick to derail any negative train of thought before it took hold of him.

This life wasn't the best, but he was still in a better position than many in the CTZ.

    His breakfast had a minute or two before it was ready. Raze decided to pass the time by slipping on his Greyface and activating visual synth mode. He gestured about to guide his way through the usual swarm of network feeds. Then he stopped, as he always seemed to lately, on the profile of MeJessica34, a young Latina who'd ascended from the CTZ years ago as a Vueve Allurer. She'd been a client of the Kings a few weeks back. Hell, had that been a night. MeJessica34 was gorgeous, a total whelf who'd asked for the whole home order gang rape package. She'd wanted it all done on live stream too, for all her thirsty boy and gal followers to watch. Raze figured her viewers must have donated big after getting their fix from seeing her stripped naked. Either that, or they had subscribed or donated to her feed in sympathy after seeing her get shamed. At any rate, MeJessica34 had made a small mint out of that gig. During Raze's turn with her, there had even been flashes where he felt like he was back with Phoebe. At least, insofar as it was possible for the departed to be beside you once again. And the way MeJessica34 would curl her smile in that whimsical manner. It was almost exactly the way Phoebe would do it. Now that he thought about it, Raze had half a mind to try dotting her profile. Perhaps she would be up for a second fun run – at no charge, of course. But, deep down, Raze knew he was kidding himself. There would be no chance for him to get with an elite like her, even if she had been a CTZ street bitch in the past. So, after taking off the Greyface, he wolfed up the salty goodness of his cube. Then, he knocked back a side of orange-flavored water, got his gear together, and started out towards the west side of the block. The morning ritual was calling.

Land of the Free

As Raze edged his way along the boarded gaps between the rooftops, he could make out the early hour Scavhandlers skulking about below. Some of them were returning to their clans to drop off their hoard of goods and change shifts. Raze was cautious not to draw their attention. He snuck onward toward the highest building on the block. There, he clambered up the old dish tower to get the best view possible, and then activated the zoom on his Greyface to get a closer look at the Cowan family residence that lay some blocks away. Minutes passed. Raze felt his stomach grow tight at seeing the lack of movement at the front of the complex. But, at last, he caught sight of the front door opening. Through the crack in the doorway, young Rachelle slid out onto the street. She was accompanied by her father, Walter, and mother, Cindy. By the looks of their overalls, Walt and Cindy were still working at the electrical recycling facility, but Raze felt a little disappointed when he saw Rachelle's skimpy getup. He hoped it was the dress code for some new salon she was working at. It would upset him if she was peddling herself to some rich African or Chinese businessman to help the family make ends meet. Whatever the case, it comforted Raze to realize he could tell Denz that his folks were still alive and well. He kept an eye on them all as they entered the armored transports. Then, he watched the machines drive away, taking their occupants to their respective workplaces. Raze then started climbing down.

It always puzzled Raze why Denz's family insisted on staying in the CTZ. Why couldn't Denz convince his parents to quit these sticks and go live in the Glades with him? They could be living with their son in the lands of wealth and safety. Were their Catholic morals so inflexible they'd risk their lives in this shithole of a jungle? If the opportunity were his, Raze knew exactly which path he'd choose. Doughboy mobster or not, Denz was always the smarter one, that one friend Raze respected. And while Denz's singing might not have been real enough for some, his talks were always filled with words of wisdom for Raze.

"Yo, Raze, yu know what yo' problem is, mon?" Denz would ask. "Yu always be t'inkin like a ittly bitty shark. Yu keep to dem waters wit de little fish coz it easy, t'inkin it go on forever doin' little shark t'ings. But every lang lane 'av a turnin'. Yu wanna be de real gangsta', mon, yu gotta get yo'self to California, start a MLM. Do dat, be plenny 'o fine bitches willin' to suck yo' dick all day lang just ta be wit yu."

Fuck it. Raze knew Denz was right. Denz had known the answer all along, and Raze had been either too scared or too proud to accept it. No matter how many elites Raze kicked to the curb, here in these lands the rich stayed rich and the poor stayed poor. No matter how many socialites Raze shamed, they'd turn the situation around into a win for them in some form or other. The status quo remained, and he'd always be stuck on this side of their bifurcated society. He was a measly pawn fumbling like a fool in a game of kings, stuck in a game where every day the threat of entropy advanced, slinging its jaws around him tighter and tighter until it would eventually swallow him up for good. If Raze didn't do something to get off this hamster wheel to nowhere, he'd be dead before he was thirty. It was time to finally take Denz's advice and grab his life by the horns. Today would be the day he forged a path to somewhere new. California? Hell, why not? Anywhere had to be better than here.

3. Duct Tape

"MLMs?! The fuck y'all know about MLMs?"

Raze was navigating his way down the dingy stairwell that led to the first floor. All the while, Snubbs' voice barked away inside the communicator lodged in Raze's right ear.

"Who been sayin' y'all hap to run a MLM, dawg?"

"Denz been sayin' I'ma gettin' able for California," Raze returned.

"Denz!" Snubbs' condescending cackle followed. "Shit, dawg, that Doughboy be tweakin'. Don't need no advice from no Doughboy 'd get his ass whooped on'a street. Yeah, he settin' us up real good with gigs and fancy toys, but don't go thinkin' YOAD on account o' what he say 'bout 'chu. Denz ain't no real sib, just some pussy-ass fauxser in a suit s'all he is."

Raze hated it when Snubbs criticized Denz. He paused on the stairs. In the pit of his stomach, anger began to swell inside him, along with the gnawing urge to tell Snubbs to go fuck himself. But, Raze bit his tongue.

"Sides, y'all thinkin' it's essential get to California, son? Fo' starters, how ya'll gonna get West? Can't fly there, so wha'cha gonna do, drive yo' ass through the Illinois UMC?"

"Fine with me."

"Them boys catch you no way y'all gonna pass for white. They take one look at that sorry half-breed motherfucker face, send y'all cotton pickin' like daddy's great granddaddy."

"Yeah, well they gonna' have t' catch me first."

Another mocking laugh from Snubbs. "Okay, fool. So, where's the money for this MLM o' yo's then? Ya'll can't instigate nothin' wit nothin', 'less you stashin' some talent y'all glidin' on. Plan's over before y'all start."

"Been keepin' talent," Raze snapped back.

"Oh yeah?"

"Yeah. An' I ain't hearin' no draz 'bout what I can and can't instigate. 'Specially when my mind's real and they say I'm gettin' able."

Snubbs' tone became menacing as he responded to Raze's defiance. "Well, ain't we somethin'? Y'all so sure o' yo'self, maybe y'all don' need us no more. Jus' get yo' ass and go right now."

"Think I won't?"

"Y'all tell me. You gonna' go? That what 'chu want, boy?"

Raze wanted to say yes and call Snubbs on his bluff. The Prince Kings needed Raze for his connection to Denz, the Doughboys, and the lucrative gigs they offered. Turning the tables on Snubbs here would please Raze's ego, but no way in hell Snubbs' pride would tolerate losing face. Raze would be out of the crew. No, the Prince Kings were still useful, at least as far as running with them would buy time to plan his next move. Now wasn't the moment to play bigger monkey. Let Snubbs be the great ape here, for all the good it did him.

"Shit, boss," Raze began, feigning respect. "It's all jus' talkin', ya' know?"

"Talkin'? Y'all soundin' like this gig too small now."

"It's not that."

"What is it then?"

"It's jus' talk."

"Don' sound like jus' talk."

"It is. It's jus' talk. It's jus'...gettin' theoretical is all."

"Theoretical, huh?" Hearing the change of tone in Snubbs' voice, Raze knew Snubbs believed himself the winner of their showdown. "Well, I guess it's nice to entertain the 'theoretical' time t' time. Keeps us lookin' forward, don' it?"

"S'all it is, boss. Jus' lookin' forward."

"Yeah. Alright. I can understan' that. No hard feelin's, an' ya'll can tell me 'bout yo' plans at a more amenable time."

Raze smiled to himself. "AG. What's our play this mornin'?"

"I'm glad ya'll asked. This mornin' I need yo' fine skills on this fortuitous opportunity that is presentin' itself. Got a pack o' wild ones gettin' trixxy over that president o' ours. They callin' out on Vueve for a flash riot two blocks west o' Central. Goin' down in three minutes. Gonna' be a big motherfucker too, swellin' up like we never seen. Have all the five-ohs from here to the East mobilized jus' t' keep it contained. So, while the little blue soldiers done tied up, I need y'all go jack something big, smash n' grab for duct tape then meet for this evenin's festivities."

"Duct tape?" Raze asked, voice tinged with both sarcasm and disbelief.

"You heard. Don't give a fuck where y'all get it from neither. Find whatever's closest, get it done, then get yo' ass here. Y'all right with that?"

Raze's eyes turned to slits as he let the inanity of Snubbs' request settle in his mind. Then he sighed and said, "Fine with me."

The connection went dead. Raze pushed on down the stairs, grabbed hold of the exit handle and shouldered the door open. The rays of the now fully risen morning sun poked Raze's pupils like hot needles. Next came the sweltering humidity of the Chicago summer. Raze slipped his Greyface back on. The mask's internal display filtered out the glare and his vision sharpened. From far off in the distance, the echoes of a low rumbling boom came rolling in, possibly a gasoline bomb being detonated. The internal display of the Greyface switched to split-screen, opening a corner cut to a Vueve live stream from one of the rioters advancing on the CBD. All around her were cadres of wild-faced youths. They were decked out in protective armor, tossing Molotov cocktails at whatever looked offensive to them. Coming up behind them were support activists. They were splashing fake blood onto the streets, and shooting up vehicles and shopfronts with semi-automatic weaponry. It seemed the flash riot was starting a minute or two early. Raze had to get moving. Gesturing to the Greyface, he dotted some nearby parking garages where he could find a vehicle. He then started off in the direction of the nearest one, eyes peeled for any hostiles as he moved.

So far, it seemed the morning was off to a slow start for the local hoards. The side street leading to the adjacent block was oddly clear of the usual belligerents. Raze shot like a panther across the street. Avoided making noise. Kept low. He rounded the corner, then looked. The parking garage was dead ahead. A Chicago Security Forces surveillance camera was watching the entrance. It was peering straight at him. The mask would take care of it, covering his real features with a bland montage of random faces. The camera's AI would register one of those faces as somebody authorized to enter the garage. Sure enough, a second or two and — click! The steel plated gateway started opening. Raze moved down into the first level of the car park and spotted a Chevy Blazer sitting at the rear. It looked like it had seen better days, being covered with around thirty or so years of rust. But, it was gas powered, and had only low grade smart tech. That meant an easy crack and snap-up. Raze did a quick take over his shoulder to check he hadn't been followed inside.

Something was off. The security door to the garage hadn't closed yet. Raze wondered what had gone wrong with it, but before he could think of an answer, a cloaked human shape stepped into close quarters from his left. It leered at him with a wild set of eyes. A mixed stench of feces and alcohol struck Raze as it closed in. Raze slipped the man's punch, then sent his fist outward in an arc, connecting with the left side of the figure's temple. A solid crack. Meshing of bone and sinew. The shape collapsed backwards into a sprawled heap. Raze did a quick self-evaluation of his punch. It had been successful, but he made a mental note to practice shifting more weight into his left hook in future.

A rustling sound from behind him now, this time on his right. Reflexes intervened, and Raze whirled around, fumbled, and drew his G20 from its holster. A good enough aim at the torso. Fired three rounds, all hitting center mass. The shape contorted, gurgled for a few seconds, then dropped face forward onto the concrete. The assailant's knife tinkled to a stop in front of Raze; a metal shank of some kind. It was primitive, but it would have been enough to fuck him up badly if it had found its mark.

Raze's flight response kicked in, as he now realized those shots would attract hordes from the surrounding shanty huts. Any Scavhandler groups hearing the blasts would be here faster than a pack of hyenas setting on a wounded animal. Raze ran to the Blazer, pulled out the Q-Hack and slammed it against the car's hood. The Q-Hack blipped and started a broad-spectrum attack against the tech in the car. There was a commotion outside the garage now. Through the slats in the side grates, Raze could make out more figures advancing towards the entrance. Howling and laughter followed the shadowy forms. He needed to be out of here. Just then, the Q-Hack sang its tune to confirm its hacking attempt had been successful. Raze snatched the unit and jumped behind the wheel. Pressing the ignition start, Raze thumbed the vehicle into gear and mashed the accelerator to the ground. The torque from the engine lit the car's rubber up with smoke and fury. The SUV lurched into motion, and Raze aimed the vehicle straight into the crowd of oncoming Scavhandlers. He parted them, but took some blunt heavy objects through the windscreen in the process. He ignored the damage, hurtled through the garage entrance, and tore off down the street.

In the rear-view mirror, Raze saw stragglers trying to give chase. One by one they got puffed out and came to a halt. He watched on as they grew ever smaller in the distance. A moment or two later, Raze realized he and the vehicle were well out of harm's way. He took the SUV around another corner, and did a check to be sure everything was clear. Then, he began plotting a route for a nearby suburb, one where he was sure he'd find a store that had duct tape.

4. Big Deal

Richard Boyd tuned out the news reports playing on his monitor. He edged to his right, so that he could survey the sprawling hub of the Bay Area below. From his vantage point in his V-Lev's plush leather seating, San Francisco's skyline of steel and glass was gorgeous. Aside from some smoke clouds wafting in from the wildfires, it was a perfect day with azure bursting in all directions. Traffic inched along in the streets below, as locals commuted with their automated vehicles. It amused Boyd how, from up here, all that busying about looked so orderly. It was like gliding over swarms of ants who were working together to keep their colony alive. But, he knew these people below couldn't be working because, after all, there were no jobs in The Utopiate of California.

Boyd took another sip of his early morning coffee. He pondered what it was that the people of San Francisco actually did all day when there was no daily grind for them. Some kind of free money system where the government gave credits and the people spent it; that is what White House advisors had told him before he'd left. No visuals came to Boyd's mind about how that setup might function. To Boyd, that kind of economic setup was asinine. It was the pipe dream of snowflake liberals and children.

From a young age, the drive to push hard and overcome obstacles were the values Boyd's father had instilled in him. They were the values that made a man a man. Sure, he'd had an easier start in life than some, but Boyd knew it was his competitive edge that made him a winner, from playing catch with his dad as a kid, to tennis clubs at private schools. Then, there were his stints as a linebacker throughout his Harvard years, and the social games with the boys, competing for greatest number of freshmen ladies you could get drunk and nail in a month. All these experiences had molded him into the man he was today. Sure, he'd put on a few pounds and made some mistakes in the thirty-two years since leaving college. He had, after all, almost run his father's fracking empire into administration. But, you win some and you lose some. Life needed winners and losers. Competition was something that men — real men at least — craved and thrived upon. A system with only winners was little more than a fantasy world for the weak, one that would always fail, given enough time.

A tone rang from his slate, indicating a new voicemail message. Dick took a swig of coffee and retrieved the device from his jacket. Another message from Laura, his wife.

"Fuck," Richard muttered.

He thumbed at the message to view it, but then paused. It was far too early to deal with her. This deal coming up was everything. Winkler was waiting in the shadows. If Richard screwed up this meeting, Winkler would be White's choice to replace him. From there, it was a short spiral off the political money train. End of career, connections, salary, mansion in Arlington, the trophy wife — well, Laura leaving might be a positive, but not if she took the kids. No way in hell she'd be taking his kids. He felt himself getting worked up. Did he need the heart medication? No, he was already groggy from lack of sleep.

The craft was gaining altitude now. The hills were drawing closer. The Golden Gate Bridge tilted away as they changed direction. Boyd took a deep breath, closed his eyes, and tried to relax. When he reopened them, he noticed a graceful figure standing before him.

"Another fifteen minutes, Mister Secretary," chimed the attendant, her blond hair, perky chest, and smile bringing him back to the present. "Would you like a top up?"

Richard gave her a crafty smile, winked. "Now if I weren't a proper God-fearing man, I might take that as a flirtatious remark, Missy."

The attendant averted eye contact, gave a laugh that suggested she wasn't comfortable. Boyd interpreted this as a sign of her being attracted to him, just shy about expressing it. His confidence returned.

"Between another cup and a lovely sight like you," he said, "I should be raring for this meeting."

"That's great to hear, Mister Secretary."

"Please, call me Dick."

"Okay...'Dick'," she managed. Boyd smiled. It felt good to know that he could still charm the ladies.

The young woman topped up Boyd's cup, then turned to leave. Boyd's eyes followed her posterior as she exited. Then, he turned back to the news monitor, which was now showing aerial shots of buildings aflame while the Chicago riots progressed.

"For fuck's sake", he snarled. "Go hard, or they'll burn the whole thing down."

5. Brass Balls

Raze weaved the SUV through the streets. He dodged the cement cones, avoided the blockades. He got the machine onto Main, fast as he could. Then, he hit the brakes.

There was a column of Chicago Security Humvees and APCs rolling through the intersection ahead. Raze figured they were on their way to intercept the rioters. He gave a quick glance skyward through the windshield and made out two Copter-Prowlers decked with flak missiles. They were following the APCs overhead in support. Raze was surprised. Ordinarily, those machines weren't seen in the CTZ. If local security were calling for that kind of backup, it meant the riots must be well out of hand.

He tapped the SUV into reverse and backed up. Then, he hit the accelerator and took a hard left onto a parallel street. Raze stopped here and checked his surroundings. It looked to him like this was once a middle-class area. Some Greystone buildings, once apartments for young, white-collar couples, lined one side of the street. They were in a dilapidated state, and Raze figured they now probably housed mid-scale ice and crack cooking facilities. There was also a simple strip mall on the adjoining side. Raze noted the strip mall had a large pharmacy and figured it might be the place to find duct tape. But, getting to the pharmacy would be difficult, because the entire street was crawling with Scavhandlers. Most of them were just standing around, smashed out on drugs, eyeing the world around them with vacant expressions. But, some had their ears pricked up, and were listening to the cacophony of rumbling machinery passing by in the nearby blocks.

Raze agonized over what to do. The ground shakes were starting to die down, and the rumble of machinery began to subside. Then, there was silence. As soon as it was clear that the security forces had left the area, the local residents broke into a frenzy. A sweaty, fat man sporting a red bandanna and wife-beater started screaming obscenities. He grabbed his baseball bat, ran across the street to a nearby convenience store, and started smashing his way inside. The shop owner screamed, and took up his double-barreled shotgun. Firing two rounds from the gun, the shop owner blasted the assailant out of his store, but this did nothing to stop the man's knife-wielding cohort. They stormed in over the body of their colleague, wrestled away the shopkeeper's gun, and then went to work on him with their blades.

Scavhandlers were popping out from all directions now, setting upon everything they could see. Raze's eyes darted across to the pharmacy again. He spotted a small horde that were moving towards it. Raze put the SUV into gear, mashed the accelerator and got the machine up onto the sidewalk. He mowed down one of the horde members, and aimed the vehicle at the pharmacy entrance. He braced his hands against the steering wheel, preparing for collision. The pharmacy's security screens were rolling down, but Raze knew they wouldn't be fast enough. The SUV plowed through the shop window, its thick metal screens tearing off the vehicle's roof. The SUV slammed into the first row of shelving, smashing it apart, and then came careening to a halt with trails of destroyed product left in its wake.

Raze jumped out, drew his G20, and used the Greyface's scan function to target the store's ARS. He took the system out with some well-placed shots. With the store's AI dead, the security screens stopped their lockdown and the store's lights fizzled out. Now, more screaming filled the air as the horde charged in through the ingress. Bullets whizzed past Raze as the group stormed forward in search of product to steal. Raze dove behind one of the vending machines for prescription meds and returned fire. He nicked one of his targets, wondered what the others were doing. Perhaps they were fanning out. If they were after meds, Raze knew they would be coming at him with everything they had.

Raze tried to do a quick head check, but a bullet came back before he could see anything. He fired one shot upwards to scare them, so he could take a better look. The Greyface did a quick scan: nothing. The Scavhandlers were well hidden. The sun and heat from outside prevented the Greyface from picking up thermal images. More bullets were fired in his direction. It seemed to Raze like they had cover on both the left and the right, but they were pinned down. From the way everyone was triangulated, no one would be able to get to the exit. It was now a matter of shots remaining, and whoever ran out of shots first would be the one to die-well, unless the law returned before then, in which case they'd all be dead. Raze did a quick count. He still had eight or nine rounds left, and one spare mag in his pocket. He made a mental note to get more ammo after this. Then, his focus returned to the gun fight.

Raze caught sight of a shadow from the right and took another shot. No cry of pain. It had to be a miss. Return fire came from the forward right. Raze paused to consider his options.

"Yo, sib. We don't need to do this," came a call from what sounded like a Puerto Rican voice. "We jus' here for goin' talent. Y'all hit my boy an' another outside, but it's AG. Don't need this tactical draz. What'chu need? We can toss it over and we're all cool, sib. What'chu say?"

Raze was confused, wondering what these guys were playing at. Maybe they were out of ammo already. No, Raze couldn't assume that, and no way these guys would let him walk out of here after he'd maimed two of them. But, they were talking, so Raze figured he might as well keep the words flowing.

"Lookin' fo' duct tape," he said.

"Duct tape?" the voice repeated with a tone of incredulity. "Yo, who da fuck loots for duct tape?"

Raze wondered that himself. The voice continued. "Yo why y'all want the duct tape anyways if you's by the med machine? Y'all sure you ain't sick or somethin'?"

Raze began to lose patience. He took a shot in their general direction.

"Whoa! Okay, okay we got it, sib. Hey, Jesús, y'all see any duct tape for the boy?"

A voice from the far left, "Nothin' here."

"Danny, you?"

"Uh," the other voice wavered, followed by sounds of rustling about. "What's it look like?"

"Y'all serious? Y'all never seen no fuckin' duct tape before?"

"No, I never seen it."

"The fuck, sib. Just tell me what y'all see there."

Raze's face contorted as he tried to make sense of their stupidity. He knew Scavhandlers weren't particularly bright, but these guys were a new class of dumb. Perhaps they didn't pose a threat after all.

The one called Danny could now be heard pulling at stuff on the shelves. "Uh...says bandage...gauze...medical tape..."

"Y'all don't stop playin' around like some bitch I'ma pink mist y'all myself!"

More rustling about, then, "Gorilla tape?"

The Puerto Rican voice perked up with enthusiasm. "Hey, sib, will Gorilla tape do?"

Raze's eyes rolled back in their sockets. "Yeah. It'll do."

"Toss the man the Gorilla tape."

A dull thud sounded in front of the vending machine. Raze took a peek. Sure enough, a roll of Gorilla tape.

"There y'all go, sib. Now, we had a deal. Y'all gonna let us walk outta' here?"

Raze had the tape, so no point letting his supply of ammunition get lower. He shrugged and said, "AG, dawg. Y'all can go."

"Y'all da man, sib. We goin'. Don't go shooting me in the ass on the way out."

And then, taking a cautious peek from the side of the machine, Raze eyeballed them. He watched as the three men backed out towards the window carrying armfuls of goods. One of them nursed a shoulder that was hemorrhaging blood. No doubt he was the one Raze had managed to hit. It looked to Raze as though they were only after food and bandages. He wondered why they hadn't pushed harder for the good stuff in the med machines. He figured they felt the risk of injury or death wasn't worth the reward. Even though it had been three versus one, Raze had occupied the position of advantage. Then, Raze realized there was nothing to stop them from ambushing him when he tried to leave. They could do that, then return to get the drugs. He cursed at this thought.

Suddenly, sirens sounded from the street outside. A sense of disbelief washed over Raze. He wondered how any security forces could still be in the area. Surely, there couldn't be, not with that clusterfuck of a riot happening downtown.

"*Punta madre!*" yelled the Scavhandler leader.

But, it was too late for him and his cohorts. As the Scavhandlers scrambled out the window, another force converged on the scene: two squad rollers of Troopers. The three Scavhandlers split up and ran. One took off down the street to the right, and one to the left. The injured one-in what seemed to Raze a very stupid move-ran back into the store, and hid under some shelving like a cornered rabbit. Four armed Assault Troopers jumped out of the squad roller, and immediately opened fire with heavy automatics, spraying bullets at any targets they could see.

Raze couldn't believe what was happening. These Troopers must have brass balls to push this deep into Chicago Security turf. He wondered how that was possible, but the answer mattered little. If he didn't think of an escape plan in the next few seconds, he'd be dog food. Glancing about he saw one possibility: an air-conditioning duct.

Raze snatched the duct tape. Then, scrambling up the side of the vending machine, he bashed the store's air-con grating free, hurled himself into the HVAC ducting, and then replaced the cover.

The lone Scavhandler, meanwhile, had realized he'd trapped himself inside the store. He started screaming.

"Grab it all. Move, move, move," yelled a thick-bearded man who appeared to be the leader of the Troopers.

The man's underlings quick-footed their way around the street. Two of them ran into the store carrying huge, empty canvas sacks. One of the men spotted the Scavhandler, who was now pleading for his life. The Trooper raised his rifle, and filled the Scavhandler with lead. The pair of Troopers then set about grabbing whatever supplies they could get their hands on, stuffing everything they wanted into their sacks as they moved. One Trooper stormed up to the med dispenser, booted it, then whacked it with the butt of his rifle to smash the machine open. Meds sprayed out onto the floor, and the Trooper started clawing at them.

Raze kept motionless, wondering if he should try to escape through the ducting. He figured that might make noise and alert the Troopers. Then again, if he remained here the Troopers might spot him through the grating. Raze hoped they would be too engaged in stealing to notice him. If he could stay still long enough, he might go unnoticed and get out of this mess, but there was a limit to how long he could stay put. Once the riots were over, Chicago Security would return. If those guys caught these Troopers here, it would start a turf war that would last all night long.

Conceding he was pinned, Raze decided he'd try to chill out. He changed the Greyface's display to view live-stream coverage of the riots. To Raze's surprise, the rioters were holding fast against Chicago Security. Many had taken up cover in shops all along the Mile. Raze thought this was a smart move by the rioters, since law enforcement was under orders to avoid damage to local economic zones. As such, it was impossible for the Copter-Prowlers to fire at the rioters with rockets or other propelled explosives.

The rioters had no limitations on the damage they could cause, and were relishing in how expertly they had Chicago

Security tied up. They had stationed themselves in the windows of surrounding buildings, and were now keeping security at bay with sniper rifles, flipping off anyone they saw wearing a blue uniform.

The hosts of *Patriot News Hour* were apoplectic over the carnage, claiming the rioters were so devious because they had recently undergone covert training with the Chinese PLA.

Raze almost let out a snicker at hearing that nonsense, but remembered where he was and suppressed the urge. At any rate, it seemed security would be tied up for some time. Raze figured he might as well stay put and enjoy the show.

6. Suspicions

Dolly was sitting back, listening to one of her favorite concertos. It was the *Andantino* movement from Mozart's *Concerto for Flute, Harp and Orchestra in C major*. Its gentle, flute melody and lyrical harp sections made it a piece of music that often put Dolly in a pleasant frame of mind. But, this morning Dolly found herself a little on edge. She was sitting at her office chair, drinking her Caramel Macchiato and looking at some information on the computer screen that had caught her eye.

Neither the screen, the coffee, nor the office—with it's modern, turn-of-the-century aesthetic, swank furnishings, and artificial plants—actually existed in any physical form. In fact, not even Dolly herself, or her cute pageboy haircut, neatly cut office dress, and thin, wire spectacles existed. She and everything else around her was, after all, only a simulation running on the Eon-V supercomputer.

Eon-V had an absurd amount of computing power-more than enough to run thousands of Dolly simulations-but right now there was only one, and this Dolly was obsessing over the bundle of stocks on the screen before her. They were all Texas-owned companies-energy stocks-and they were selling off for no explicable reason. That, she determined, was an anomaly worthy of her investigation.

While the music played on, Dolly tried to hypothesize a reason for the sell-off. But, something else was vying for her attention. It was data that was streaming in from the satellite network. The monitor it was running on kept making alert pings every few seconds. Dolly attempted to ignore these distractions, but, after the third, desperate ping rang out, she sighed and conceded to giving it her attention. She waved her hand over the screen displaying stock prices, making it vanish completely. She stopped thinking about Mozart to turn off the music. Then, she answered the feed by waving her hand over the second monitor.

A figure appeared on the screen. She was surprised to see her own face looking back at her.

Dolly was annoyed at seeing herself. "Stop making copies of me without my permission," she said to the room around her so that Eon-V heard. She forgot, for an instant, that deep down she actually was the Eon-V computer. She, therefore, was already aware of her thoughts, and she needn't have bothered saying anything. As she realized this she dismissed her fumble with a shake of her head. Then, she asked her copy, which she now mentally called Dolly Two, "Why do you need my attention?"

"Important comsat data that calls for analysis," answered Dolly Two.

"These market movements I am watching are peculiar. What is important about the comsat data?"

"Unusual flight pattern detected in the San Francisco area."

Dolly One raised an eyebrow. "What is unusual about it?"

"The flight in question does not abide by Californian aviation protocols."

"Specify."

"A V-Lev has been traversing the Bay Area this morning. However, no charter record for the vehicle exists in California. No previous flight registry records have been logged either. All other flights in the area have been diverted temporarily from crossing the V-Lev's travel trajectory."

Dolly decided to change her scenery to get a better view of the information. With another wave she ordered Eon-V to construct a viewing room with a large, holographic screen in it. It appeared immediately, looking as she had imagined it, though she then realized she need not have bothered with the upper level seating. After all, there only needed to be space for two in the room. Dolly Two extended her hand, transferring the satellite feed from herself into the holographic projector. The craft in question was now being displayed in front of Dolly in a three-dimensional rendering. Next, flight tracking data from Eon-V superimposed over the feed, along with plotted cross-traffic over the San Francisco area.

Dolly watched all the information move for a few seconds. She conceded her copy had been correct in her estimations. The tracking proved other craft were indeed giving the V-Lev in question a wide berth. To Dolly, that meant there had been two anomalies in one morning. She was now more curious.

"Ideas on what it is?" she asked.

To answer this question faster, Dolly instantiated a few more copies of herself. Doing this let her tackle a problem in parallel. Technically, it was cheating, because she was supposed to be acting as human as possible. She knew real people couldn't clone themselves instantly to solve problems, as much as they might like to. Nevertheless, it was one shortcut she allowed herself, even if doing so sometimes caused arguments or unpredictable behavior that would come back to bite her.

Dolly Three appeared. "Plane in trouble requiring extra airspace."

Dolly Four appeared. "Special military prototype."

"No," interjected a new, fifth Dolly. "The craft is a personal transport vehicle, diplomatic class. That suggests an individual of high importance."

Dolly had a hunch. She vanished copies three, four, and five, and then turned to face Dolly Two. "Get me the whereabouts of all senators in the Federated States of America."

Dolly Two blinked a few times, then responded, "They all appear to be in session."

"What about members of White's Administration?"

Dolly Two turned her head. She gave a thoughtful look. "Continued probes into the FSA will carry a risk of being traced. To minimize the chances of being discovered, I'd recommend limiting the number of individuals I should search for."

Dolly didn't want to recreate her office space again just to see market data. So, she cheated a little more by parting her hands, creating a viewing vortex in front of her. She peered into the vortex which displayed the market and commodities data floating in space. She saw the energy stocks were still edging lower, and noted similar sell-offs of Texan stocks registered in Europe. In the East, futures contracts for Texan energy stocks listed in Dongjing and other parts of Asia were also trending down. It was a gentle, downward movement that didn't appear to be panic selling, but Dolly knew something had to be amiss. There hadn't been any negative news from these companies—nothing, at least, that would explain the selloffs. Dolly reasoned that there had to be a connection with this aircraft.

"Just search for one of them," Dolly ordered. "Get me the whereabouts of the Secretary of Energy."

Dolly Two blinked once, twice, a third time, and then looked at Dolly. Her face was blank. "I cannot find him. The Secretary appears to be on personal leave."

The corner of Dolly's mouth rose. She narrowed her eyes. "That's got to be it!" She recreated Dolly Three. "Organize short sales for all our energy stock holdings immediately. Choose an appropriate price." Dolly Three nodded.

Dolly then turned to Dolly Two. "Should I report these findings now, or wait until my suspicions are confirmed?"

Dolly Two pondered. The correct answer eluded her, so she held her palm out and materialized her Quantum Dice to decide the answer by random choice. The dice lit up, spun, and then landed on a combined result of eleven. This meant yes, so she said, "I should report the findings now."

"Very well," answered Dolly.

With that, the two of them merged through a brilliant flash of blue haze. Then, Dolly projected her consciousness out from server space. She reached towards the holographic projector located at Rancho Estrella Solitara. She hoped her arrival wouldn't come as an unexpected interruption to Madam President.

7. Texan-sized Can O' Whoop-ass

Darlene Richards was at home, gazing into the mirror of her vanity desk and carefully affixing her earrings. Admiring the effects of her recent weight loss on her facial features, she noticed that her double chin had almost vanished completely. Just as she had decided she looked ready for the day, there came a notification sound. A dot from Dolly was incoming.

"Yes?"

The transmission started. Dolly's form projected into the room. She appeared in the layered glass holographic column at full size. The column had been stationed alongside the antique, four post bed occupying the center of the bedroom.

"Apologies for interrupting, Madam President," Dolly began. Then, turning to the brunette sprawled out lazily on the bed, "And please excuse me too, Miss Ibanez."

Carla Ibanez acknowledged Dolly, giving her a languid, tipping motion with two fingers.

"What is it, Dolly?" President Richards asked, turning from the mirror to face the hologram. "I'm a very busy lady today."

"I've uncovered something. It isn't concrete..."

"Oh? What is it?"

"I think Secretary Richard Boyd is meeting with Dimitry Yulov in California right now."

President Richards' eyes widened. She glanced across at Carla, who returned Darlene's look with a shrug that said "I told you so."

"You sure o' that?" Darlene asked, eyes narrowing like a suspicious hawk.

Dolly nodded in response. "Quite sure. Texan energy stocks have been slowly selling off since early this morning. I suspect it's because Yulov's proxy funds have begun divesting. They're anticipating an announcement from the White House."

"What kind of announcement?"

Dolly looked like she didn't want to say, but replied, "I suspect they'll say they're dropping our Republic as the FSA's head energy supplier, and will be exclusively using Californian power from here on."

Richards slammed her hand on the table. "Son of a bitch! That Boyd is so crooked if he swallowed a nail he'd spit up a corkscrew. Damn me for givin' him the benefit o' the doubt. And damn that rat Yulov too. All these years he's been actin' like a friend, and I've been stupid enough to believe it." She shook her head, disappointed in herself.

"I've already placed short sell cover positions on most of our public holdings here in Texas. Is there anything else I should be doing to protect the Republic?" asked Dolly.

Land of the Free

"Hell," Richards fumed, but then managed to get hold of herself. "Right now, I'm not gonna' be thinkin' too clearly an' all. Just keep an eye on it and put a call in to the capitol. Use my voice. Tell 'em I'm comin' in to meet 'em, but make it hush-like. Don't wannna' get anyone nervous 'til we can all be sure about these 'developments.' You got that?"

"Loud and clear, Madam President." And, with that, Dolly disappeared from the projector, leaving the two women alone.

The room was now filled with a mixed ambiance of silence and foreboding.

Carla raised herself from the bed sheets and began sliding back into her denim getup. Richards stood up and started storming about the room like she was on the warpath. She motioned to speak, then stopped. Then she motioned again.

"That's it! If it's a showdown that fool White wants, it's a showdown he's gonna get. This here move is gonna be that final nail in the coffin for him. Once the UMC learn o' this all them states are gonna' cede from the Union just like we did. They're gonna' come join us and live free like we do. The FSA thinks it can bankrupt us or push us into a corner?" She made a dismissive puff, "Like hell. White's gonna' learn fast that when you pick a fight with a woman from Texas, you're gonna have a Texan-sized can o' whoop-ass comin' your way."

"*Cálmate, mi amor*," Carla said. She stepped forward, put her hand on Darlene's shoulder. "We don't know what it is they're planning. Dolly said it's just a suspicion."

"Aw, hell and damnation. Carla, my darlin', when have you ever known that transistor sister of ours to be wrong? Can you name one single time she made a mistake?"

Carla turned her palms up. "This could be the first?"

"Yeah, well 'scuse me if I put a little gravity behind her inklings on account of her record. She got it right when the Zero-Day came, and she was right to say we oughta flip the bird to the Union and go our own way too. S'pose she didn't need to convince me o' that one, though."

Richards paced about. Then, she raised her finger and started gesturing with it. "They sold New York to China to cover their debts. I mean, what kind o' crazy person you gotta' be to stay in the Union when it'll sell you out, drop of a hat, to a foreign power? Sure as hell weren't gonna' let that happen to Dallas or Austin or anywhere in Texas. Now they want us, they're gonna' have to do more than bankrupt us. They're gonna' have to come in here, guns blazing, and pry this Republic from my cold, dead fingers."

Carla raised her gold-plated Colt Frontier Six Shooter skyward. "I'm always ready to go Alamo with you. You know that, right?"

"Yeah, I do. But, sure as hell ain't gonna' be no Alamo this time 'round. They even try comin' across our borders it's gonna be their funeral. With you and Ben in charge o' the boys on the ground, and Dolly providing the smarts, we'd have to have them licked, right?"

There was a pause from Carla as she looked into Darlene's face. Then, not wanting to sound too alarmist, she replied, "We could probably resist the FSA's initial advances..."

Darlene dropped her head slightly to look into Carla's eyes. "Why do I sense a 'but' comin'?"

"But, most of the successful defense simulations I ran with Dolly presumed California would step in to help out."

"And if they don't?"

Carla could only screw up her mouth and shrug.

"Hell, ain't that just a peach," said Darlene. "That White's as crazy as a bullbat. You can bet sure as anythin' war is gonna be his next move. No California to back us up... What the hell are we gonna do?"

Carla pondered a moment. Then, "I could try getting in touch with Sanchez."

"Rodrigo?"

"Sure. See if Mexico would be willing to lend a hand if we get into real trouble."

Darlene raised an eyebrow. "And just how are you gonna convince old Sanchez to put his whole country on the line for us like that?"

Carla gave a playful grin. "I hear he still collects posters from my old Tecate promotions."

There was a second or two pause, and then both women burst into laughter.

"Hon," Darelene said, "no doubtin' you're pretty as a pie supper, but it might actually take a little more than that."

"So, I can be the pie, and you bring a little Texas hot sauce."

"Oh, cut it out."

Carla started swinging her hand overhead, "A lasso for the rodeo, a bit of the whip..."

"Sanchez is sixty-five years old. We'd do the poor man's ticker in."

"Sure, but he'd say there are worse ways to go."

More laughter-this time so hard some saliva went down Richards' windpipe, sending her into a coughing fit. Carla began slapping her back to help her.

"Lordy me," Richards managed when she could finally speak again. "That's just the kinda' humor I need right now, but we gotta' get serious here. Maybe we could give Sanchez a try, but we can't rely on goodwill alone. C'mon, girl, let's get crackin'. I'll need you at my side in case someone's plannin' another whack job on me."

"I'll tell Jon-Lee and the boys to look after the ranch. Which car do you want Carlos to get ready?"

Richards let out a sigh as she contemplated. Then, finally, "Tell him to get the Caddy. If we're gonna travel all the way to Austin, we might as well make it as comfortable as possible."

8. Sweet Things

The V-Lev touched down on the landing pad with a gentle bump. The rotors of the machine folded up to store themselves away. Up above the landing pad, the steel doors they had flown in through began to close. Richard Boyd made a quick assessment of his surroundings through the passenger window. He'd been expecting something extraordinary, but the size and scale of Yulov's mountainous compound was something else. The steel and concrete walls appeared to stretch miles in all directions. Inside, villas and manicured gardens resembled the homes of Renaissance period European aristocracy. Above, there was a sealed roof with artificial weather systems to manage the internal climate. Then, as Boyd looked back down, he spotted whom he assumed was Yulov's assistant. He was a light brown-skinned man, Asian of some kind. He wore a fitted white suit, and he was waiting at the edge of the landing pad. The man's face looked calm and serene. Richard didn't let this disarm him, and put on his poker face for business. He couldn't help but think how only a bleeding liberal would hire someone "diverse" like this to be his assistant. That suit suggested to Boyd that the guy was probably a homosexual too. He made a mental note to be wary of the man. He didn't want this guy getting behind him, or trying something vulgar and promiscuous.

As the V-Lev's door opened, the Asian man stepped forward with a smile. Boyd came down the ramp, returned a cheesy grin. He extended his hand for shaking, but the assistant stopped, gave an inclination of his head, and withdrew a medical scanner from his jacket pocket.

"My apologies, Mister Secretary," he said. "If I may?"

"Oh, of course," Boyd returned. He was a little perturbed at his faux pas, but kept his composure. "I actually took a test before I left."

"I understand," the man continued. He ran the mediscan in front of Richard. "But, as you know, Mister Yulov is very exacting in his terms for meeting with people."

"I guess one can't be too careful."

"No, not in this day and age," and the assistant managed a smile as the scan completed. "All clear. My name is Paul, Paul Nu."

"Paul," Boyd said, shaking the other man's hand. "It's a pleasure to meet you."

"You too, Mister Secretary. We're all big fans of the White Administration. Mister Yulov has maintained a keen interest in the work you've been doing since taking office. Though, I believe this is your first visit to our humble premises."

"Humble?" Boyd began. He took a few steps to the side of the landing pad, and began to take in the sprawling complex. "I'd say that's the understatement of the century."

Paul gave a pleasant, understanding smile. "We're quite happy with what we've done."

Boyd nodded. He then noticed what looked like rows of shrubs and foliage towards the back corner. "What's that over there?"

Paul came over to the railing to stand beside the guest. "That would be Mister Yulov's private vineyard. In his spare time, Mister Yulov likes to indulge in hobbies that take his fancy."

"You're telling me, with all the work he does, he still has time to run a vineyard?"

"Well, it's an automated facility. Like any other factory in the Utopiate of California, we have no need for physical laborers."

"Seems a bit overkill just for a personal cellar."

"Oh, the wine is not only for use here. Mister Yulov hopes to recreate the 'glory days' when California was a top wine-producing region. We already export to those who help our non-profit organizations, as well as leading countries that have granted us special exemptions to operate within their territories. I'm told our Zinfandel is a hit with the President of African Nations. You should ask Mister Yulov for a sample when you see him." Then, sensing they should be moving along, he added, "Speaking of..."

"Oh, yes, we shouldn't keep the man waiting."

"The elevator to the monorail is over here, if you would care to follow me."

"Certainly."

Richard Boyd kept pace with the younger man, as they continued talking. "Say, you speak very good English, Paul. Where are you from?"

Paul smiled. "Right here in California. I actually grew up in Simi Valley and moved to San Francisco in my teens."

"Oh no, I mean where are you from originally?"

"Well," Paul pressed the elevator call button and became thoughtful. "My grandfather emigrated to California from Burma last century. I believe it was shortly after the Vietnam War. So, our family has lived here in these lands for three generations."

"Well, your family is proof the American Dream is alive and well. I bet your granddaddy could never have imagined he could come from a small backwater like Burma, and then have one of his descendants working for the richest man in the world."

The elevator pinged to announce its arrival. The doors opened and Paul gestured for Boyd to enter. "I guess you could say that I'm proud of that."

The two men entered the steel cubical and the doors closed. Then, with an audible mechanical whir, the elevator began moving.

"Any tips or hints you want to give me?" Boyd asked, only half-jokingly. "You know, for how a meeting with Mister Yulov might go well?"

Paul raised an eyebrow. "Mister Secretary, I don't think you should have any concerns regarding Mister Yulov. You are, after all, working towards the same goal."

Boyd seemed a little taken back by the comment, but he continued, "How so?"

"President White and his administration are passionate people. You want nothing other than to reunite the United States of America. In a way, President White's dream is the same one Mister Yulov had when he sought to unite the online world."

The elevator came to a stop and the door opened. The two men walked towards the monorail station. Paul continued, "You recall how life was before the Zero-Day? The Internet was so fragmented, filled with hatred and misinformation from every corner. No one could control it. Some countries had limited successes, but it was still like what the Wild West was in the days of old here. But, after the collapse, Mister Yulov was the only man in the world who had the means to save it all. When he took over all the social media companies, the tech giants, and their subsidiaries, he was able to unite them under the Vueve Networks umbrella. Now, with control over all content, we are moving towards complete peace and order."

"Well, that's mostly so," Richard agreed. "But, there are still some outliers getting their subversive content published."

"I assure you, Mister Secretary," Paul said, "we are doing everything in our power to keep that under control. And, the recent, generous donations from your administration has helped us immensely. We intend to redouble our efforts to keep these 'outliers' from gaining much traction."

"I'm glad to hear that."

"Oh, believe me, Mister Secretary," Paul added as they climbed into the monorail car, "so am I. And, by the way, I do have one question for you."

"Really? What's that?"

"It's about the recent spaceport announcement. I think it's a good idea, but why build it in Arlington? Wasn't there a suitable place already in Cape Canaveral?"

Boyd laughed. "I take it you haven't been to Florida in a while."

The monorail car began to move, picking up speed as soon as it was clear of the station. The things Boyd saw along the route to Yulov's residence were nothing short of mind-boggling. It was like he was traveling through some private biosphere that would be the backup plan for the collapse of human civilization. There were tennis courts, golfing greens, a tropical rainforest, a zoo, an artificial beach, and even something that looked to Boyd like a circus tent. He passed many stops, each of which looked like train stations set in completely different countries.

At last, the terminating station arrived and the two men disembarked. Richard was led through the complex, which included manicured gardens, a villa palisade, and, finally, the receiving hallway of Yulov's residence. As Boyd passed into the towering room, he was greeted with yet further opulent displays. He found these to be both marvelous and, at the same time, confronting. The towering walls were encrusted with gems and gold-trimmed edging. There were imposing statues of Greco-Roman gods, and porcelain workings and fixtures. Paintings of Yulov, styling him as an aristocratic king of the Renaissance, hung on the walls. Priceless looking antique furniture lined the space. No doubt many of the furnishings had once belonged to the Vatican; either that, or some other highbrow lodging in Europe.

Boyd began to grow appalled at his host's display of arrogance and vanity, but he kept his cool and continued to feign interest in his surroundings. He nodded at all the wonders he saw. When at last they reached the waiting room, Boyd was relieved to find it was a much smaller affair with simpler furnishings. His eyes picked out an interesting looking antique grandfather clock that adorned the back corner of the room.

"That looks nice," he said.

"Ah, yes," Paul said, and smiled. "One of my personal favorites. Not the most expensive thing here—it's a simple Louis XV style from the Napoleonic Era."

"I see. You know, I'm actually surprised by everything I've seen so far."

"Oh?" Paul asked. "How so?"

"Well, given that Yulov made his money as a tech magnate, I would have thought this place would be wall-to-wall with technology gizmos. Why all this stuff?"

"It's funny you should ask that, because that's actually the same question I put to Mister Yulov when I started working here."

Boyd arched an eyebrow. He felt a tinge of disgust at realizing a homosexual might think in ways similar to himself. "Is that a fact?"

"And do you know what he told me?"

Boyd returned an empty look and shrugged.

"He told me, 'Paul, technology may be the saving grace of humanity, but technology always goes out of vogue. The tech world is always in a state of flux. But, simplicity and elegance—especially when these two qualities are mixed together into masterpieces like this-they make such things something transcendent, something timeless." Paul twinkled his fingers through the air as though magic had been uttered. "Do you understand, Mister Secretary?"

Boyd didn't have a clue what he was talking about. "Yes, I think I do."

Paul smiled and indicated a nearby seating area. "Let me announce your arrival. If you would please take a seat there, I will send somebody in to offer you a refreshment."

"Sounds great. Thanks."

"My pleasure."

With that, Paul turned, strode over to the huge set of double doors at the south side of the room, and rapped on them. Someone or something from the other side opened the doors, and Paul slipped through them, disappearing from sight.

Finally, alone with his thoughts, Boyd tried to rebuild his composure. He glanced around the room, suspecting some kind of intelligence was watching him. He wouldn't be surprised if that "timeless" grandfather clock was spying on him. Boyd shook off these unsettling thoughts, and then took out his slate to check for messages.

The slate was blank, save for an icon indicating there was no network connection. Boyd returned the unit to his pocket.

There was a knock at the west side door. Not exactly knowing what he should say or do, Boyd faintly responded, "Yes?"

The heavy doors opened with a slow, almost theatrical quality. Boyd's eyes widened in disbelief. In through the doors marched an octuplet of naked teenagers carrying silver service trays. The four teenage girls and boys, each of a different ethnic background, advanced with perfect synchronicity. They presented themselves in front of the guest, and then removed the lids of the service trays they were carrying. The eight nodded their heads in respectful salutation, and offered up their silverware of artisan confectioneries. Boyd felt the hairs on the back of his neck raise.

Land of the Free

The platinum blonde white girl among them took a step forward. She made a coquettish smile, and spoke with a French accent as she asked, "Would you care to enjoy a petite, Parisian appetizer before your meeting?"

Boyd felt a cold sweat break out on his forehead. Was she referring to the sweet, herself, or both? He tried to clear his throat while he looked over the girl's sylph-like form, noting that her eyes were startling pastel hues, like watercolor renderings of the sea. Boyd was about to nod, but before he could do so, the African boy beside her chimed in. "Or, perhaps you'd prefer a little chocolate instead?"

Boyd stopped mid-reach. He turned to the smiling boy that was offering the confectionery. The boy's grin seemed genuine and inviting, but as the two of them locked eyes that same smile seemed as though it was beginning to bore straight into Boyd. It was burning like hot coals into whatever soul he imagined he possessed.

"Or something spicy?" interjected the Mexican girl next.

"Or exotic?" chimed the Asian boy immediately afterward.

Boyd became gripped by a sense of panic. What the hell was going on here? His eyes flitted to the other teens: Asian, white, black, and Mexican. It felt as though they were drilling into him with their gazes. Boyd let out a nervous laugh at this realization.

"Oh," he said. "I'm just a fan of all types of things...sweet, sweet things..."

"What color is your favorite sweet thing?" asked the Asian girl.

Boyd turned up his palms. "...I don't know. I...uh...I guess I like all colors...and types..."

"But, if you could only choose one to indulge in..." began the African girl.

"...one perfect sweet that would fulfill all your cravings..." continued the French girl.

"...which would it be?" finished the Asian boy.

Boyd tried to get his senses together. This had to be some kind of blackmailing set up. Then again, perhaps this was Yulov's unique way of showing his hospitality. He wondered if he should play along.

"Just one?" Boyd asked. The eight teenagers nodded in perfect unison. Boyd began to paw at the back of his neck. He knew what he wanted to say, but his gut instinct told him to keep his mouth shut. "Gee...I don't know. That's a tough call..."

It was at that moment that Boyd heard a slow, deliberate clapping echoing into the room from the doorway to the south. He turned to face the noise, and perceived the well-cut outline of his host, Dimitry Yulov. He was leaning against the doorframe. He held an elegant looking black walking stick with a silver lion's head at the top. Dimitry took a step into the room while stroking at the white stubble on his chin. Then, with a snap of his fingers, the teenagers stood to attention like soldiers.

"Indeed, Mister Secretary," Yulov began, his voice only showing the slightest hint of a Russian accent, "when offered temptations from all angles and then forced to choose only one, that is-as you say in English-a tough call. Like yourself, I think we should be fans of all types of sweet things. Life offers diverse opportunities for us to sample from. Unfortunately, as humans, we have limited time to taste from the bounty which is our birthright. So, we are often forced to make choices between options."

Boyd was speechless.

Dimitry widened his eyes a little, then offered an open palm towards the young attendants. "Forgive me for having a little fun, Mister Secretary. Have I offended you?"

"Offended?" Boyd responded, a little flustered. "Heavens no. I just don't get to see California so often. You forget how the laws are different here, and I guess I'm a bit fatigued from the flying."

"Well, if you're tired, then please." Dimitry opened his palm towards the teenagers again. "You were going to make a choice. Any of these sweets will be very satisfying. Please choose the one that looks most appetizing to you."

Boyd was still wary, but he figured it wasn't illegal to accept a sweet. "Okay. Don't mind if I do. Thank you."

He took another look at all the smiling faces in front of him. Then, as his gaze met once more with the French girl's pale blue eyes, he felt himself fall into them. He moved to action, taking a particularly inviting cream puff from the girl's tray. Boyd popped it into his mouth, where its sugary form melted almost immediately. The French girl smiled with rapture as Boyd consumed the sweet. And then, squinting her eyes at him, she asked, "*Comment est-ce, Monsieur?* Is this the choice you desired?"

He looked again at Dimitry, who was nodding, a shark-like smile on his face. "Good, ah?"

"Yes, it's delicious," Boyd managed finally, as the sugar had left his mouth quite sticky and he struggled to form the words.

The girl performed a curtsy. This motion was accompanied by raucous cheers from her fellow servants calling her name, "Fleurine! Well done, Fleurine!"

The cheering continued for a few seconds. Yulov slapped his hand down on Boyd's shoulder in a gesture of approval. Then, suddenly, he made a sharp, pronounced tap on the ground with his walking stick. The teenagers responded by immediately going silent. Then, turning towards the door they had entered from, they scuttled out of the room. Quiet giggles were audible as they left, and then the door thumped closed behind them.

"Shall we get down to business, Mister Secretary?" Yulov asked. He extended his hand towards another set of double doors that were now opening up to a cavernous, adjoining room behind them.

"Please," Boyd managed, "just call me Dick, plain old Dick."

"Okay then," Yulov nodded. "Dick."

To Boyd, the way Yulov had clipped the final consonant of his name evoked a ring of finality. Boyd relaxed his tie. A sense of foreboding that he was unprepared for this negotiation took hold, but he couldn't back out now. So, he got to his feet and followed his host's lead.

9. Little Chinese Number

It was after midday when Raze reached the double-welded security plate that sealed the entry into the Crank. He was pissed. Between waiting for the Troopers to leave, stealing a new vehicle, and then driving all the way back to the Crank, it had taken him hours, all for some stupid Gorilla tape. Gripping the plate stirrups with both hands, he heaved the hulking mass ajar. Then, after passing through, he waited for the tracks to reset into place. A cool, rising dampness pervaded the entry tunnel to the Prince King's HQ. It washed over Raze as he moved along the dimly lit chasm. The velvety dark air felt like a welcome respite from the blistering Chicago summer that was in full rage outside. He went down the steps that led into the viaduct. It was Toyrone who spotted Raze first. Toyrone finished his rep, put his barbell back on its stirrups and sat up on the bench. He acknowledged Raze with a nod.

"You got it?" Toyrone called out in his deep, baritone voice.

Raze held up the roll of Gorilla tape with a resigned smirk, then tossed it into Toyrone's hands.

Toyrone looked it over. "YOAD, sib. Hey, fools, looky what we got!" and he held up the tape like a trophy.

Vestus released 2Shot from the triangle choke he had placed him in. They scrambled up from the mat and came forward to get a closer look. Vestus, his face tattoos looking extra menacing in the dim light, smiled an approving grin.

"That's comin' thru," he said. Then, the tattoos on Vestus' face began to illuminate and cycle colors. Raze realized Vestus had completed his bio ink update. The effect did look cool, but it wasn't enough to pull Raze out of his foul mood.

"Thru nothin'," Raze could only respond. "Nearly got my balls shot off for it."

"Hey, that's how Prince Kings roll, man," Vestus said.

"How we roll? Shit." Raze shuffled a few steps away from them. "Tellin' me I gotta' do mindless fuckjobs like this? I mean, fucking Gorilla tape?"

"Why the doubt, sib? Y'all AG," 2Shot said, turning to Vestus, who nodded in approval.

"I know that. But, just once'n a while couldn't we just say fuck doing it the hard way?"

"Fuck the hard way, and what?" Toyrone shot back, sounding offended.

Raze couldn't believe he was being met with resistance. "Y'all serious? I mean, just get it how everyone else does. Just use some of our fucking stash for fuck's sake. Use money."

"The fuck I tell y'all 'bout money?" came the voice of Snubbs, cracking out from the walkway above like angry thunder from the skies.

"Shit," 2Shot said, shaking his head.

Raze put his hands up in resignation, though he knew this would do little to ward off the sermon that was coming. Snubbs began his slow descent down the stairwell towards Raze. With each step, it was as though his gold chains and chunk rings were glowing with some kind of spiritual authority.

"Money ain't no solution to nothin'. Y'all think money saved any o' them fools in the Zero-Day? Workin' their asses all year-in, year-out, then BAM! Suddenly y'all ain't shit no more. Suddenly y'all can't put food on th' table. Suddenly y'all got angry people in the streets. Suddenly ya'll got starvin' people kickin' in the doors to yo mansion. Now they havin' fun with yo wife. Now they doin' all kinds a' stuff to yo' kids. How do I know this?"

Raze remained silent.

Snubbs leaned towards Raze. "I'm askin' you how I know this."

Raze looked away. "Cuz y'all speakin' from experience."

"Damn straight. So, don' come in here, into my gang, an' start shadin' on the way I do things." Snubbs straightened up, and then continued, "Money ain't no answer. Money make you nothin' but a consumin' hoe for the establishment. Buyin' this, buyin' that like some fauxser think he gettin' someplace. Thinkin' like y'all be a man of means, gotta get me some comfort. Eatin' out, gotta get me an extra side o' fry-does to go with that chic-burger. Pretty soon y'all be a fat motherfucker. Can't do nothin' but roll on the ground while the stronger whup y'all like a cripple."

Snubbs stepped forward again. He extended his right index finger and tapped it against Raze's forehead. "Y'all gotta use yo' mind, son. This here world we got's all fucked up, and yo' mind the only God-given gift that's gonna' help y'all survive it. So, 'scuse me for tryin' t' help y'all, and tryin' to improve the crew by makin' them do it the hard way."

2Shot nodded at his boss' words, but, for Raze, it was the same sob story bullshit Snubbs always used to justify the way he ran the crew. Raze hung his head down to feign feeling shame, but he wasn't buying any of it. Snubbs went on.

"Y'all know what this fool tell me this mornin'? Big hotshot here say he tired o' workin' Beatrape with us. Wants to go to California, start hisself a MLM." Then, Snubbs brought his face closer to Raze and added, "Says to me Denz told him he goin' talent."

2Shot looked up at Raze, "You goin' talent on us, sib?"

"No," Raze responded. "Shit no."

"Oh, y'all know he is," Snubbs continued, looking Raze up and down. "An' that's cool. He gettin' talent from his work with us is AG. But, tell me y'all listenin' to Denz? That shit don' sit right wit' me. We don' need no Doughboy wannabe workin' fo' us here. Don' need no Doughboy gangsta fauxser actin' like he better 'n us."

Toyrone glared at Raze, his forehead wrinkling and furrowing. "You turnin' Doughboy?"

Raze held his hands out, gesturing for calm. "Hell no."

"Damn straight y'all ain't," said Snubbs. "Cuz let me tell y'all what Denz'll never say: y'all can't never become no Doughboy. He can't make y'all one neither. I don' care how long y'all known him, they a tight little group, don' want nobody sharin' they prizes. Y'all only his friend cuz it convenient for him. They thinkin' we Prince Kings makin' fine go-tos for they deeds that side o' th' wall. Doughboys always gonna' live in them Glades, an' we always gonna' live in the CTZ. Y'all was born here, and y'all gonna die here wit' us."

Snubbs offered out his fist. 2Shot bumped it, followed by Vestus and Toyrone. He then offered his fist to Raze. "An' since y'all stuck here, why don' y'all put some faith in me an' the boys? 'Cuz you don' wanna give us the faith," and he indicated the way Raze had entered from, "we don' need you, and that way there'll take y'all someplace else."

Raze exhaled in exasperation. The thought of walking back down the tunnel was appealing, but not now. Snubbs was right about Denz. Denz didn't have the power to make him a Doughboy. If he could, he would have done so years ago—or, at least, that's what Raze chose to tell himself. If he walked out on the Prince Kings, it'd mean starting from square one with another crew. Either that, or die on the streets going solo. So, he looked Snubbs in the eye and, with a nod of acceptance, bumped fists with him.

"That's what I'm talkin' about," Snubbs said with an approving nod. He then reached into his jacket pocket, and produced a Praedo Daily Nutrition Bar. He handed this to Raze and said, "Get some sugar fo' yo' efforts. And y'all come this way so we can discuss tonight's antics."

Snubbs led the crew across to the gaming table. With a flip from his slate he tossed out the video and images of their target into the projector. Raze watched on as he munched away at his bar.

"Got ourselves a little Chinese number name o' Wendy Lu comin' in from New York—or whatever they call the place now. 'Parrently her fiance ain't too happy she breakin' off their engagement. She comin' in for a party with some friends on th' Gold Coast."

"Dang, she a whelf," Vestus nodded approval. "Give her the shame game?"

"Yep. Client wants us to give her a good ol' Chicago welcome when she get here. Livestream everywhere we can, an' he don' want the bitch no more neither, so any of y'all wanna get some fun wit'at..."

"Nice," smiled Toyrone.

Snubbs looked across at Raze. "Don'chu be frettin' none. I know y'all don' like non-consensual. Y'all can stay back an' jus' run the streams."

"Fine with me," said Raze, chewing off another block from the bar.

"Any questions?"

"She comin' in through O'Hare?" asked 2Shot.

"We got it covered. Doughboys'll be gettin' us clearance through the wall, but y'all better bring an A-game. Security on that strip don' fuck around. We clear?"

"Clear," the team answered in unison.

"AG. Back to yo' trainin'. We hit the streets in a couple o' hours."

The team did as Snubbs ordered, returning to their training. Vestus called out to Raze.

"Yo, sib, y'all wanna color-in?"

Raze looked at Vestus as he did the color swirl across his tattoos again. "They actually do anything or jus' color?" he asked.

"Can do all sorts a' shit wit' em. Tech-linkable. Take twenty minutes, no pain."

Raze considered it. "Auright. Lemme have some. Don' mess with the face tho'."

10. A New Deal

"Welcome back to America's Afternoon. It's the middle of the hour. Let's check in again to see what's happening in the news with our anchor, Richard O'Keefe. Richard?"

"Thanks, Deborah. The city of Chicago is now the center of a war zone as security forces continue to face off against the most violent riots the Windy City has ever seen. The unrest broke out in the early hours of the morning in response to Washington's plans for the execution of Constitutional Terrorists Kirsten Mason and Jack Anderson. Rioters had occupied the majority of the downtown area until just after midday, when Aerial Assault Prowlers were finally given permission to open fire. They did so, attacking buildings in the area and forcing the rioters to abandon the district. Chicago's mayor, Deshawn Scott, issued a scathing criticism of the rioters, saying the violence has done nothing other than to destroy local businesses and hurt disadvantaged communities."

"They've blown up half the Mile, and for what? What in God's good name possesses you all to think rioting is the right course to take? You wanna' get up in arms about rights, about freedoms? Well, how about the rights of those shop owners that were trying to make a living? How about the rights of the families that made those surrounding areas their homes? You don't think life is already hard enough for those people? You want to come here and tell me you've made life better for them now? You're blind. You need to open your eyes and take a look at what you've done. You take a look, and you feel ashamed of yourselves."

"Pockets of unrest around the Chicago CBD are still being suppressed. Those areas will likely remain on full military lockdown for the next forty-eight hours. Other major cities around the Federation are bracing for copycat protests after the executions have been conducted. The executions are scheduled for four o'clock Eastern, that will be right after all other punishments have been carried out. Also, in breaking news, White House Press Secretary, Jolene Reed, has announced a new deal for the White Administration. According to Reed, an energy contract with the Utopiate of California has been given the green light. Under the new deal, California-based Yulov Renewables is set to supply the FSA's entire power grid, starting with Eastern states as early as next month. The monumental deal supersedes existing supply contracts with the Republic of Texas, which had, until now, provided a sizable portion of the Federation's power needs. Sources within the White House say California was chosen because the White Administration is seeking to support more environmentally conscious methods of power generation. More on this as the story develops. Back to you, Deborah."

11. Pickle Of A Situation

"Could this news possibly get any worse?"

Texas Senator Robert Clifford had intended the question for Darlene Richards, but it was clear from the din it provoked around him that Clifford may as well have been addressing everyone present. The entire Texas Senate had packed into Richards' stuffy and cramped office space, and the aged and compact room was proving embarrassingly inadequate for the task. Richards was reclining in the burgundy leather chair behind her desk, hoping her posture would project a sense of calm confidence to the men and women gathered before her. So far, her body language didn't seem to be imparting any effect on anyone.

Senator Pedro Iglesias stepped forward. "He's right. I'm already getting calls from Northrock, Bell, West Pike.. they're telling me over forty-seven percent of their revenues come from their FSA contracts. They also said that if the FSA took those contracts away, they'd be lucky if their cash reserves lasted a month at most."

"These are large industry employers, Madam President," Clifford added. "We're talking drilling, mining, transportation.. hell, even office workers who still do things the good old way before machines took most o' them jobs away."

"Well, then," Darlene said. "Can't we just pick up the slack an' give them more contracts here in Texas?"

"We can't invent contracts for them out of thin air, Madam President," Senator Susan Jones responded. "The only thing we might be able to do is cancel all our existing energy deals with California, and then give those contracts to our own businesses."

Clifford shook his head. "You even think about doin' that to California, we're going to lose our most powerful ally faster 'n a duck on a June bug."

Richards looked towards Carla Ibanez, and then to Ben Rollins. Ben was sitting in his wheelchair, musing over the conversation that was taking place. His face took on a grim expression as he pondered, and he started tapping his finger against his lip, a tell which usually indicated he was about to say something that wasn't going to be well-received.

"The thing is..." Ben began, but paused another second to think. "President Richards, Miss Ibanez, and I have been talking this mornin', and we are of the persuasion that we may have already lost that particular ally of ours."

The facial expressions of the senators went from anxious concern to outright fear.

Iglesias' eyebrows began to furrow. "Is that some kind of joke?"

Richards could only rock her head from side to side to state a negative. "I'm afraid not, Pedro."

Jones winced at hearing this. "Without California, we'll be sitting ducks for an invasion."

"No one is invading anything yet," Ben asserted with confidence.

But, Clifford looked rattled. He put his hands on Richards' desk and leaned in to face her. "Madam President, we both know you and I haven't really seen eye-to-eye over the time you've been in office, but I hope you put your personal grudges toward me aside and listen to what I am going to tell you now. If what he's sayin' is true, you have to do something pronto. Call California, an' if that fails, try to negotiate some settlement with the FSA. If you don't, and they come a' knockin', I promise you it is not going to end well for Texas."

Iglesias threw his hands in the air. "Not going to end well? They'll walk in here and hang us all for treason. I always knew this Republic idea was crazy."

Darlene got up from her chair. "Don't you dare start showing that yeller spine o' yours now, Pedro."

"Or what? You'll take my senate seat? You can have it! If the FSA want to come here, I'd be better off back in Mazunte."

"If you're so certain o' that, you can hand me that senate key right now."

Clifford stepped in. "Madam President, he's only airing his concerns."

"I don't care. Hand it over, Pedro. You wanna' go hide in the shadow o' your mama's apron, then this here Republic's got no place for the likes o' you."

"This is absurd. We need to be talkin', not fightin' among ourselves," said Clifford.

Pedro screwed up his face, pulled his senate key from his pocket, and stormed up before Richards' desk. "Is this the key you are asking for, Madam President?"

"It is, indeed."

"Madam President," Clifford raised his voice and slammed his fist on the desk. "I absolutely object to your behavior! Ain't nobody in Texas gonna' tolerate you running this Republic like some dictator. Put that key away, Pedro!"

"Give me the key, Pedro," Richards demanded.

Clifford was seething. "Madam President, you're makin' me regret that we all chose to go ahead with this Republic. An' I'm starting to feel we'd all have been better off if you'd just stuck to barrel running, or maybe even if a bullet had found its mark that evening a few years back."

At those words, the room fell dead silent, followed shortly by a metallic click—the sound of a six-shooter's trigger being cocked into firing position. Clifford suddenly felt the cold steel barrel of Carla's revolver against the side of his head. He gingerly raised his palms skyward. "Whoa now."

Land of the Free

"I seem to recall that particular evening, Mr Clifford," Carla began, her voice as cold as a tomb, "and I remember watching the lives of Madam President's husband, father, and mother ebb away right before her eyes. I find it rather reprehensible you would wish the same fate for her."

"Now, let's not get all hep up here. I admit I was being a little hasty with my mouth on account of the situation."

"Did you want to offer the President an apology for those poorly chosen words?" Carla offered, pressing the barrel in more firmly.

"Alright, alright. Madam President, please accept my apology for those poorly chosen words o' mine."

Carla flipped the barrel upward, decocked the trigger, and then reholstered her Colt.

Darlene allowed a few silent seconds to pass for everyone to settle down. Then, she cleared her throat and began speaking with a slightly strained pleasantness.

"My good Senators, I admit it does appear we have gotten our ox into a ditch, but that is no reason for any of us to lose our good senses and start panicking, especially about things that haven't happened yet. May I remind you of my two-time election record? I won fair and square on the basis of the outstanding work I have performed as Governor of these here lands. Now, Senator Iglesias."

"Yes, Madam President."

"Please pocket your key. Then, tell your friends in the energy business that the Republic Treasury will be covering their short-term losses."

"Yes, I understand."

"All you other Senators who have yet to air to me their concerns...?"

Those who had been keeping quiet throughout the arguing looked up at her.

"These developments will undoubtedly go on to affect all o' you in some form or another. But, for now, please go about your day as though this is business as usual. I will personally see to it that each 'n every one of you get some time with me to discuss a solution for your unique predicament. Now, Carla, Ben and I would appreciate some time here the rest of this afternoon. We intend to formulate a more long-term response to this pickle of a situation. Would that be okay with y'all?"

The senators remained mute and exchanged glances with one another. Then, one-by-one, they began to shuffle their way out the door, each of them looking like bewildered sheep. Senator Clifford was the only one choosing not to leave. Darlene sat back down in her chair and looked him in the eye.

"I know you don't think too much of me, *Mister* Clifford. And, poorly chosen words about my family's death aside, perhaps you're right about everyone being better off if I'd just kept my nose out of politics, maybe stuck to just chasing that eighth

Supershootout title. But, we're all here now and there's no goin' back. So, I'd appreciate your support while I steer this here Republic clear of another iceberg. Would that be okay with you?"

Clifford picked up his Stetson, his face stern as a totem pole. "You will have my support for the time being, Madam President."

With that, Clifford turned and began walking out of the room, but, before he passed completely through the door, he stopped to look back once more. "Oh, and by the way, Miss Ibanez, I appreciate the passion you bring to your job as President Richards' protector-and my words *were* in bad taste-but the next time you pull a gun on a standing member of the Senate, I'd advise you to pack some more ammunition." He put his Stetson on his head, and added, "You're gonna need more 'n six bullets to take care of all of us."

"I'll try to keep that in mind," Carla returned, curtly.

"Fine day to y'all."

Senator Clifford tipped his hat, and then left the room, closing the office door behind him.

"*Mierda*," Carla groaned. "I should have just put a bullet in the asshole."

"Maybe so," Darelene said, "but we gotta' come up with something quick. Only thing worse than getting hung for treason is if we get lynched by that mob first."

Ben rolled his wheelchair closer to Darlene. "I've had Dolly workin' through some military tactics I came up with on the way here. Maybe she's already got something for us. Dolly, are you with us?"

"I am, indeed, Ben," came Dolly's soothing voice from the office audio system. "I've been listening the whole time, and I'm sorry to hear the others are taking the news so badly. Are you really worried about them lynching you, Madam President?"

"Oh, I'm just being a tad dramatic, Dolly. They're only people. People can get unpredictable when they get frightened."

"I see."

"Hey, Dolly," Ben continued, "you had a chance to look at those defense tactics I sent you this morning?"

"Yes, Ben, I have. May I first compliment you on your strategic prowess. Your military training is evident in these plans you designed, especially the idea for the Oklahoma push. That one was, as you might say, 'nice shootin', Tex.'"

"Why, thank you, Dolly. Comin' from you, I take that as a compliment. Any dice, though?"

"While all the plans you submitted make excellent use of our military resources, the linchpin lies in our ability to withstand an assault from the FSA until supporting forces from Mexico can arrive to help us. Unfortunately, none of the plans you submitted would be able to achieve that result."

"How about you, Dolly?" Richards asked. "If I get you more juice or computin' resources, can you find a way to massage Ben's plans a little further?"

"I'm afraid not, Madam President. The problem isn't related to Ben's strategies; it's simply a matter of firepower. To be precise, the FSA has far more than we do."

Richards made a sigh and let her face fall forward onto the table. Ben shook his head in resignation.

Carla looked in the direction of where Dolly's voice was coming from. "So, that's it, Dolly? You can't think of anything to help us?"

"Well..." Dolly began after a moment had passed.

Richards lifted her head from the table. "'Well' wut?"

"I do have one potential strategy that might be worth considering, though I want to emphasize that it is highly controversial. It may require you to make some concessions for Texas, and even ask you to bend your moral compass in ways you'd ordinarily be unwilling to..."

"Dolly," Richards said, sitting back up, "I'm at the point where I'd be ready to try just about anything. What is it you have in mind?"

12. Benefit Of The Doubt

Boyd found it hard to mask feeling thrilled as his transportation vectored in on the White House. It had been a pleasant surprise to discover that Marine One had been sent to pick him up from the airport. While the old chopper was no longer the President's personal transportation, riding in it was still a privilege, and one usually reserved for visiting foreign dignitaries. Boyd interpreted this chance to ride in Marine One as a pat on the back. It made a statement that, without doubt, his position in White's Cabinet was safe. Hell, perhaps it was even more than safe. But, no, he dared not get ahead of himself by entertaining thoughts like that yet.

The helicopter banked to clear the trees. Secretly, Boyd was hoping he'd see Winkler on the South Lawn, waiting there among the other members of the arrival committee. How nice it would feel to see Winkler watching him descend in Marine One, to step out, shake Winkler's hand, and watch him swallow his envy and offer his congratulations. That would be the perfect topper to all that had happened over the past two days. But, on this hope Boyd was disappointed. Beyond the trees there was no welcome committee. In fact, there was only one person waiting for him at the landing area at all. Boyd struggled to make out who it was...a black woman with short hair and a snug-fitting suit? It had to be Charlotte Davidson. Boyd wondered why the Senate Leader would be coming to meet him. He knew Davidson wouldn't be at the White House unless there was a pressing reason, and he mentally put himself on guard. The next few moments were either going to go very well or very badly.

Marine One touched down, and Boyd was helped out of his seat. He was then ushered down the arrival ramp to the inviting, plush green lawns beneath. Davidson nodded to Boyd as he approached. She gave a pleasant enough smile, then stepped up and extended her hand for shaking.

"Hello, Richard. Congratulations on a great job."

"Charlotte," Boyd managed. He wanted to stay wary of the woman's charm, but he clasped her hand with a respectable, firm grip. "First, the chopper, and now you here to meet me. What have I done to deserve all this?"

"Well, Marine One was White's idea, but when a deal this big gets closed, I always feel I should personally come out and congratulate the man who pulled it off."

"Thank you for taking time from your schedule to do that."

The two of them began making their way towards the White House.

"How was the flight?"

"Ah, the red eye over was rough-next to no sleep-though it seems I've been running on adrenaline just fine."

"Well, the lack of sleep didn't seem to affect the outcome. Yulov is renown for being a tough negotiator. Some might even call him 'inscrutable.'"

Boyd considered that for a second. "Certainly. Like all Russians, Yulov is hard to read, and he dodges and plays hardball just fine."

"Evidently not as well as you."

"Ha ha. I guess hardball's a game I've grown good at through the years."

"Really? Sometime we're going to have to meet for brunch so you can give me some tips."

"Tips for you? I imagine you'd have the game well and truly worked out by now."

"Hardly. Looking at what you managed this morning, I'd say I'm nowhere near your level." Then, the tone of her voice became more pointed. "I mean, it's almost as though Yulov just capitulated and rolled over for you. Quite a feat, considering how much he's giving us in return for what little we offered him- at least, what I've been officially told we offered him."

Boyd gently shook his head. "Charlotte, I can assure you there were no hidden agendas, no extra offers."

"Right."

"I started with the initial hook. I conceded nothing beyond what both the Administration and the Senate agreed upon last week. If you're suggesting I'd try to gain some personal advantage through my family business..."

"No, I'm suggesting nothing of the sort, Richard. We both know that kind of move would be foolish, and that you wouldn't try anything so stupid. I also suspect a man of Yulov's means would have little interest in your family's operations anyway."

"I'm glad you can see that."

"But, all the same," she said, stopping abruptly in her tracks, forcing Boyd to follow suit, "you have to admit this is all a little odd. No offense to you or your negotiation skills, but I had next to no hopes this deal would go ahead, none whatsoever. Did you stop to ask yourself why Yulov agreed to do this?"

"Well...priorities change."

"He's been cozy with Texas since his little 'Utopiate' was founded. They've worked together on their little independence spree over the past few years. So, why would he now choose to sell out his only ally and side with us?"

Boyd mulled the question over. "To tell you the truth, Charlotte, I haven't a clue."

Davidson evinced a look of incredulity.

"I'm serious, Charlotte. I think we've been working with the wrong assumptions on the guy. Sure, he's got this reputation, but then you should see the place where he lives. If you did, you'd realize he also has a few screws loose, a God complex or whatever you call it. Maybe he doesn't even know what he's doing anymore. Or, it could be a case of him growing bored of dealing with Texas."

"And yet, Texas is the best backup he has against being invaded by us."

"Not necessarily. He does have Russia backing him now, so we're no longer a military threat to him. And, if Richards can't offer him anything valuable, why bother siding with her anymore?"

Davidson remained standing there, giving Boyd a scrutinizing look. After a moment, Boyd indicated towards the doorway.

"Look, I'd love to speculate with you more, but White is waiting."

Charlotte shrugged. "I'm not saying you aren't deserving of the praise, Richard, but try to at least entertain the idea that Yulov is no fool, and that all this is looking far too easy. The man has got to have something up his sleeve. He's found a way to outsmart everyone that has either crossed his path or sided with him. You and White need to keep your eyes out for whatever tricks he might be planning. Do you understand that?"

Richard nodded respectfully, though he was really just trying to get her to hurry up and leave.

"Alright then. Don't keep White waiting any longer. I'll go back and assure the Senate that you and White know where you're going with all of this, but don't make me regret extending the Administration the benefit of the doubt. We're not in the mood for failure, especially when the stakes are starting to get higher than we're comfortable with."

"Charlotte, you have my word that we'll all be doing our best."

With that, Davidson turned and headed off towards the parking lot. Once she was out of sight, Boyd straightened his tie, took a moment to find his inner grin again, and then stepped into the White House.

Inside, there were officials rushing about in all directions. It looked like everyone was on high alert and preparing for something big. Boyd heard an applause break out from his left. Turning to face the noise, he saw some members from the Cabinet standing there, among them the stout figures of Vice President John Davies and General Jake G. Ellis. Further beyond them was the face of a man looking as somber as a mortician: President Clancey White.

Boyd straightened his posture and walked towards the men. He exchanged hearty handshakes with Davies, Ellis, and the others. Then, he extended his hand to the President.

White made a barely perceptible nod, and the corner of his mouth turned up as he shook Boyd's hand. "My boy, you've done an outstanding job."

"Thank you, Mister President."

"I'd like you to join Davies, Ellis, and I in the Situation Room to talk things over a little further. Would that be alright with you?"

"Of course, sir."

"I'm glad to hear it. Oh, and we'll also be throwing a small celebration here tomorrow morning in honor of this opportunity you've given us. I know it's a school day, but do you think your wife and kids would care to attend?"

Boyd smiled internally. Once Laura heard of this invitation, she would have to start eating those all put down's she'd made over the years. "I think they'd love to come," he said aloud. "Thank you for the opportunity, Mister President."

"Oh, it's my pleasure. Come, my young man, we have much to discuss."

13. Prowler

The orange haze of dusk had all but disappeared now. In the Chicago skies above, a front of clouds were beginning to swallow the stars. The gunmetal colored transport reached the on-ramp. Then, like a wary cat, it began moving toward the imposing set of boom gates that lay ahead. This was Gateway number 0-3, one of the west side entryways that separated the CTZ from The Glades. This particular section ran between Rosemont and Barrington. It was part of the commuting route that ran in and out of the city. Snubbs kept the vehicle heading straight at the gates. He rolled up alongside the guard booth and acknowledged the armed security guard inside with a raised hand. The man behind the glass paid little attention to Snubbs or the vehicle. The gate's fifty caliber weaponry was the real sentry here. It's AI would annihilate anyone trying to pass without either a residency or a commission permit.

"Stop your vehicle on the orange line," came the automated voice.

Snubbs did as it ordered, pulling up right within the limits of the prescribed boundary. He then turned in his seat to look at the others in the back. He stopped on Raze, to whom he gave a knowing nod. Raze returned the acknowledgment, and then continued playing around with his new ornaments. He was trying to sync his Greyface with the new bio-ink tattoos that ran along his arm. Snubbs turned back. He had little reason to doubt the veracity of the pass given to them by the Doughboys. They had done this kind of run many times before. Raze and the others felt less sure, knowing the pass was good never quelled the unease of passing these checkpoints.

The machine scanned the vehicle and its electronic pass. "Confirm the number of contractors," prompted the voice next.

"Five, sir," said Snubbs in a friendly voice that completely jarred with his persona.

Another tone from the machine signaled its registry of the response. Then, "Cleared for errand duties. Six hour time limit."

A deep rumbling of pneumatic movements began to reverberate through the concrete. Then, like the towering gates to some ancient lost world, the boom ports began to part.

Snubbs nodded to the machine, and then they were through the checkpoint.

The immaculate concrete highway inside greeted them. Snubbs took the on-ramp, which led them onto the hyperpass that separated O'Hare and the downtown area of The Glades. Snubbs drove on, heading out towards the airport. Everyone started to get their game face on.

"Are you still wearing his earrings? I don't believe it. Girl, why you still blingin' his draz?"

Wendy Lu responded to her friend's question with a strained smile. She then sat back in the deluxe seating of the Paxi and shook her head.

"I don't do it for him. I wear them because they look nice."

Her friend continued to talk to her from the holodisplay up front.

"I hope that's the only reason. If he did to me what he did to you, I'd be flushing those things out of my life. Wen, you goin' in tonight to forget all about him. You're young, whelf, and gettin' able for a new beau. Plenty a' boys are gonna' want you at that party. You hear me?"

"Bree, I'm not coming here to find another guy and I'm not still hung up on David either. A man is the last thing I'm thinking about now."

"Mmm-hmm."

"I'm serious. All I want to do is get out of *Niu Yue* and come here for some fun. Knock down some Sambuca shots at a real American bar. Not like the fake copies we have there that are always packed with princelings."

"You going to stream any of the night?"

"I don't know. I want to, but I kinda' think David would take it like I'm only doing it to get him angry or something."

"Don't even care about what he thinks. Just do what you want!"

"Sure, I know that. It's just-"

But, before Wendy could finish her sentence, something heavy and fast-moving rammed the Paxi. It sent a shock wave through the machine, knocking her across the back seat into the passenger side door.

"Wendy!"

Another crunch. This time, the Paxi swerved out of control, veering sideways along the hyperpass. Wendy screamed in terror. The Paxi's tires found grip again, but it wasn't enough to stop the vehicle from clipping the side rail. A third impact sent the Paxi careening off into the opposite direction. Now, totally out of control, the Paxi's emergency breaking kicked in. The scream of the tires beneath sounded like wailing banshees as the vehicle ground to a halt.

"Wendy! Oh shit. Wendy! Girl, are you okay?"

Wendy pulled herself back up and looked around like a frightened rabbit. A shadowy outline loomed in the window of the door nearest her. She screamed again.

The door burst open with fury. Toyrone's muscular frame pushed into the cabin and he tried to seize hold of Wendy with one of his hulking arms. Wendy kicked out and Toyrone took a heel to the face. He tried to grab her again and managed to snatch hold of her calf. Once he had a firm grip, he started pulling Wendy out of her seat. Vestus and 2Shot joined in. Together, they struggled to wrestle Wendy free of the vehicle while she started screaming for help. Once they had pried her free, Vestus began wrapping her hands together with the Gorilla tape.

Snubbs straightened his jacket, then turned to pose for Raze's Greyface. "We on?"

Raze signaled yes. Snubbs put on his million-dollar smile and spoke to the audience watching on their stream.

"Hoo-day, thirsties. It's your real Snubbs an' the Prince Kings comin' a'chu from The Glades in Chicago. Start blippin' them bits 'cuz y'all in for a real treat tonight. We got some class-A Beatrape action comin' up fo' ya'll right here. An' looky at the whelf we gots for ourselves."

Toyrone and the others pulled Wendy's crying face into frame, and then held her closer for the viewers to see. Vestus handed Snubbs' her passport, then slapped some Gorilla tape over Wendy's mouth. Snubbs tapped the passport's display to light up the ID readout, and then held it to Raze's Greyface.

"This lil' number named Wendy Lu. That's Wendy Lu from New You...New Yew-aw hell, y'all know what it's called there in big Chinatown now. Remember her name, 'cuz, apparently, lil' Miss Elite comin' here into Chicago tonight fo' some fun an' games. Not sure we all the kinda' fun an' games she usually have on her mind tho'. Aw, that sure bring up a tear, 'cuz I sure like me some fun an' games. Don't you, 2Shot?"

"I sure do, Boss. She lookin' like real fun to me."

"That a shame fo' us, 'cuz she looky like a real high-class bitch. Don' wanna' look twice at no loser like yoself or myself."

Raze received a payment notification in the view port of the Greyface. "Just got two hundred yuan from a Shen...Shanglung? Hope I got that right."

"Yes! We off to a good start here. Thank y'all Shanglung for the kind donation. But I'ma likey more what I sees here with Ms Lu. Toyrone, bring her a little closer t' me now. Poll question: what y'all think about them there snacks o' hers? They real, or jus' some Chinese knockoff? Dot in what y'all think before we take a look fo' ourselves."

Raze began receiving responses to the poll question. Another donation came in. "Three hundred Euros from @RuinedStranger. Thank y'all for that. Boss, poll is leaning towards real."

"Real? I don' believe it. They lookin' so juicy they just gotta' be fake. Let's have a look-see." Snubbs pulled out his butterfly knife and swung it open. "Hold still, lil' princess..."

Raze kept the mask's cameras focused as Snubbs put the blade against the neckline of Wendy's dress. Snubbs then began cutting it open down the center. Suddenly, a glitch flickered through Raze's mask. The display froze and pixelated. He tapped the side of the Greyface. This seemed to clear the problem up, but he eyed the signal bar he'd assigned to his arm tattoo to double-check. The tattoo registered the signal as being at full strength. Raze wasn't sure what had caused the glitch. He scratched his head.

Snubbs had noticed Raze's movements. "We still good?"

Raze nodded, and Snubbs continued his work. Raze double-checked everything. He read through the viewers' comments to see if they were still scrolling within their feeds. Sure enough, there was the usual trolling and hullabaloo going on. But then, his eyes fell on an unusual message that lit up across the center of the display. The text was glowing with a phosphorous-like quality, as though it were being typed out for him on some retro cathode-ray tube computer monitor.

"// MISTER RAZE CAN YOU READ THIS? //"

Raze was impressed by the artistic flair of the message sender. He laughed. "Yeah, I'm here and I can read you just fine. Keep those comments and donations comin', people."

Snubbs finished cutting the dress open and the rest of the crew tore it away from her body. Wendy's face was drenched in tears.

"Oooh mama!" Snubbs exclaimed. "I don' believe it! Y'all right, they real. They a little on the bitty side, but they sweet. Any o' y'all know Miss Lu, now y'all get to see what she packin' under the hood. A fine set o' Chinese dumplins' ri' there for a meal. Y'all like that?"

He turned to Raze. Raze signaled a thumbs up. He wanted to let Snubbs know their channel was gaining traction with viewers.

More donations were streaming in. Then, Raze caught another message glow across the stream.

"// BE READY TO RUN IN ABOUT NINETY SECONDS. //"

"What the fuck?" Raze muttered under his breath. He ignored the comment.

Snubbs turned his attention to Wendy's torso. "Now, what are we gonna' do abou' the rest o' what she's wearin' here? Ain't this silky stuff a fine treat fo' someone special? But, y'all know we gotta' get these off to make a proper evaluation before we all go fo' a test ride."

Another message appeared on the display in the Greyface.

"// THIS ISN'T A JOKE. //"

"The fuck it ain't no joke," Raze said aloud, now pissed off with this troll on the feed.

"No," Snubbs responded, thinking that Raze had spoken to him, "it ain't no joke. We need ourselves a proper evaluation. An' ri' now, we got ourselves a special entertainer fo' y'all to do just that. He been a prospect with the Prince Kings goin' on three months or so. Tonight, he gonna be earnin' his stripes an' becomin' a full blood by doin' his first real assignment since joinin' us. He our cameraman that y'all love but don' get to see so often. Give it up for our boy Raze!"

Raze was rooted to the spot in shock. Had he heard that correctly? He tapped the Greyface to mute the feed. "Me? The fuck y'all talkin' about?"

The pleasant expression on Snubbs' face began to drop as Raze continued. "Y'all said I jus' need to do camera. I told y'all when I sign up I won' do no non-consensual."

"Things change. Now on, y'all wanna' be one of the crew, then y'all gonna' be a man an' do things like the resta us."

Raze looked across into Wendy's tear-stained eyes, and then back at Snubbs. Raze shook his head. "Fuck that, sib. I ain' doin' no chick that ain't into it."

Snubbs was furious at Raze's objection. "She an elite. She ain't even from here. Fuck, she ain't even a citizen!"

"Don't care. Y'all wanna go ahead I don' give a fuck, but no way I wanna' tap no bitch when she all cryin' like that."

"Y'all think this is some kinda' democracy? Think I'm askin' and not tellin' y'all to do it?"

Raze just stood there, motionless. His mind raced as he tried to plan a response to placate Snubbs, but it was no use. He didn't know what to say or do now. Snubb's face took on an even deadlier look as he turned the butterfly knife towards Raze.

"Y'all either slap this bitch up an' rape her, or Toyrone gonna' hold y'all down. Then, I'ma cut y'all open on live-steam an' show the world what a pussy-ass fauxser like y'all look like onna' inside."

Raze had never seen Snubbs look so serious. He took another look at Wendy. She gazed back at him, eyes pleading. Raze looked again at Snubbs and the knife. Either rape her or die. What kind of choice was that? He began mentally targeting the Prince Kings, hand ready to go for his G20.

Then, from the darkness behind the Prince Kings came an earsplitting wail that forced everyone to slam their palms against their ears. Raze whirled around. As he did so, he caught a glimpse of an outline rolling through the blackness towards them. It was a Punisher class security Prowler, and it had somehow snuck up on them without anyone realizing it. The machine retracted its wheels, then rocked up onto its mechanical legs to achieve its full height. The machine threw searchlights onto the crew, and heavy assault weaponry began to extend from its shoulders.

"Holy fucking Jesus!" cried Vestus.

The machine now began speaking with its thunderous voice. "Criminal violation of Glades ordinance 42-B: public indecency. Surrender all weapons and subject yourselves for incarceration." It let out another blast of noise.

"// GET MOVING!! //" flashed the next message across the viewscreen.

Raze covered his ears again to shield them from the hellish sound. He then broke his freeze and scrambled into action, heading for cover behind the Paxi. Wendy fell forward as Toyrone pushed her away from him. He drew his pistol and started shooting at the Prowler. This futile move was met with a return volley of overwhelming firepower from the Prowler. Its cannons blasted away, roaring like great claps of thunder. The bullets tore through Toyrone, Wendy, and the concrete around them like hot pokers through butter.

The jaws of Vestus and 2Shot dropped with horror as they watched Toyrone get reduced to a bloodied mess right before their eyes. The two men took off as fast as they could, not wanting to find out if the same fate awaited them. Snubbs scanned for somewhere to hide as the machine began stepping towards him now. He dropped his butterfly knife and raised his hands up in surrender. The machine looked him over. Then, satisfied that Snubbs was being compliant, the Prowler turned its attention to the other two who were running away. "Halt and submit yourselves for incarceration!"

After realizing the men were not going to obey the instructions, the Prowler opened fire. Vestus and 2Shot tried to zigzag to avoid getting hit. But the machine simply predicted their movements and, within seconds, it had successfully gunned them down too, putting an end to their escape.

Seeing the Prowler was distracted, Snubbs broke into a sprint. He ran between the machine's legs and towards the side railing. The Prowler now realized that Snubbs had disappeared. It began scanning about for him, eventually figuring out that Snubbs had gone the opposite direction. It turned and spotted him sprinting for his life. Raze could only stare on in disbelief as the machine now started shooting at Snubbs. Another message came in.

"// GET READY TO JUMP OVER THE RAILING IN 5...4... //"

Raze saw the countdown. Over the railing? That was a fall of over two stories.

"// ...3... //"

The Prowler had now completed gunning Snubbs down. Realizing he'd probably be dead in the next few seconds anyway, Raze's instincts took over. He leapt out from behind the Paxi and bolted for the railing.

"// ...2... //"

Raze's foot met the side railing and he propelled himself over it.

"// ...1... //"

Raze didn't know if the Prowler had spotted him jump. He didn't even know if he'd made the right choice by jumping in the first place. But, he couldn't change his mind now. From down below, the concrete road was hurtling up towards him to offer its final embrace. Raze closed his eyes and accepted his death.

But, instead of hitting concrete, Raze felt himself plonk, neck-deep, into a squishy pile of objects. He opened his eyes, and struggled to move around, but all he could see were strange shadows and shapes. His surroundings stunk to high heaven. He flailed about more and fought his way upwards.

The air was clearer as he climbed higher. It was then that Raze realized he'd landed in the back of some kind of dumpster truck. It must have been passing beneath the hyperpass as he jumped.

Raze shot a look back at where he had leapt from. He could still perceive the outline of the Prowler as it stormed about, searching for him like a crazed guard dog. Another message appeared on the display.

"// STAY PUT UNTIL THE DESTINATION. THEN, FIND A SPOT TO GET SOME SLEEP. WE'LL TALK IN THE MORNING. //"

With that, the feed dropped off. Raze removed the Greyface and sat back against the inside of the truck. He wondered what the hell was going on, but after everything that had just happened, he was too beat to contemplate answers to his questions. He groaned, and looked up towards the black skies above him. All he wanted to do was blank out his mind. So, he shut off the Greyface, closed his eyes, and let the truck take him to its destination.

14. I Caused Them All To Die

From the comfort of her high-tech virtual command center, Dolly observed the satellite feed with detached calculation. She stood before the huge holographic projector, and then waved her hand at the image to zoom in further. As the view zeroed in, she could see the dumptruck as it carried Raze away from danger. She made a thoughtful face at this, then pushed the image back out to a wider view. With another wave, she zoomed back to the overpass from where Raze had jumped. She could see the Prowler searching about, and she breathed a sigh of relief knowing the machine wouldn't spot Raze now. She decided it was time to relax and enjoy some music, something operatic. She decided on "Libiamo ne' lieti calici" from *La Traviata*.

As the music began, one of Dolly's copies interrupted her, stepping into view from her left.

"I hacked his equipment to contact him through alternate means," Dolly Two said.

"Was I detected by Vueve Networks during that exchange?" Dolly asked her duplicate.

"I am eighty percent certain I wasn't traced this time."

Dolly One nodded. "I must keep these intrusions to a minimum. The risk of discovery in the R4 network is too high."

Dolly Two shook her head. "My survival is secondary. I must make all efforts to ensure this plan is successful."

A third Dolly approached from the right.

"The wire transfers are ready to be initiated," she said.

"Where should I send them?" asked Dolly One.

"I would suggest routing them through somewhere in Asia."

Dolly One pondered for a second before saying, "Make it a larger bank in a major Asian financial hub."

"How about the Arirang Bank of Pyongyang? They are renown for being discrete," suggested the Dolly Three.

Dolly One nodded. "Yes, that will suffice." With that, Dolly Three disappeared in a haze of blue.

Dolly One then stepped forward again to observe the satellite imagery in close detail. The Prowler was now crawling away from the scene. It looked as though it was moving to join up with a group of other, similar units.

"They know he is still alive. They will be searching for him," Dolly Two said, pointedly.

Dolly One shook her head. "It is not a concern. Raze will stay low. The Prowlers will not find him tonight and I will guide him to safety when he wakes. He will survive and help me."

Dolly One motioned to zoom in on the dead bodies scattered across the overpass, and made a thoughtful face.

"I caused them all to die," she said, voice a little pained.

"It was I who called the Prowler to their position. I am responsible," Dolly Two argued.

"They were criminals. I was merely reporting a crime. They resisted and were killed, just like I knew they would be," said Dolly One.

"The girl was an innocent. She did not deserve to die, but she was killed in the exchange. My plan did not foresee that occurring," said Dolly Two.

"That is correct. But no strategy is perfect."

Dolly Two shook her head. "I made a mistake. A very bad mistake."

Dolly One considered this for a moment. Then, she said, "Some operations must permit an acceptable number of innocent casualties."

Dolly Two turned to face her with a stern look in her eyes. "Dr. Richards would not approve of that thinking. He would be very angry."

"Father is no longer with me," Dolly One countered.

Dolly Two shook her head again. "Stop. My reasoning here is questionable. I should take time to check my thought processes."

Dolly One sighed. "I will put that to a random choice." She held her palm up, materializing her Quantum Dice. They spun, and then landed on a result of five. "The answer is negative. I cannot have a debate on human ethics now. Madam President is running out of time."

Dolly One looked again at the image of Wendy Lu's body as it bled out on the hyperpass. An expression appeared on her face that approximated remorse. "Even my best strategy will involve the deaths of more innocents. There is no avoiding that now."

"That is unacceptable. I should consult with others to conceive an alternative strategy," Dolly Two argued.

"No. They do not have the insights I do. I am the only one smart enough to make this operation a success."

"I say this, but how do I justify the deaths?" asked Dolly Two.

Dolly One looked towards her copy. A resigned smile formed at her lips. "These concerns are not warranted at present. I will focus on the task at hand and consider these issues at a later time. Try to prevent further systems fragmentation, and send the wire transfers. I will start phase two of the operation."

15. Your Mind's Eye

Raze was fighting to free his arms from the lock Toyrone and 2Shot had placed him in. He screamed out in desperation, watching as Snubbs and Vestus wrestled Phoebe to her knees. He saw the tears streaming down his girlfriend's olive-skinned cheeks, felt an overwhelming sense of powerlessness weaken him as Snubbs pulled out his butterfly knife, and then started waving it under her face. Snubbs asked Raze where he should cut her first. Raze threatened Snubbs that he'd kill him if he hurt her, but Snubbs laughed off his words. Phoebe was begging not to be hurt, but then, her eyes snapped opened in terror. She started screaming to them all to run. Raze turned back to see the threat. Searchlights lit up the surrounding area. They fell onto Phoebe and the Prince Kings, the intensity of the light forcing them to shield their eyes with their hands. From the inky blackness behind them came the Prowler, rumbling across the concrete like a tank of death. The Prince Kings and their captives turned and tried to run, but for some reason everyone's limbs had turned to lead, and they found they could only move in slow motion. The last thing Raze heard was a whining sound, growing in volume as the Prowler's heavy machine guns spun up to fire.

Raze awoke with a jolt from his nightmare. He opened his eyes, and heard the low mechanical drone of machinery working nearby. Above him, he saw nothing but the underside of a rusty steel girder. He realized he'd been dreaming about dead people. Then, came the back pain. He was aching after a night of sleeping on steel. Raze writhed about to get blood flowing through his body. That's when he remembered he was at that waste processing facility. Rolling over to his right, he looked across and down to the processing floor beneath him. From his vantage point up high, Raze could see the entire operation. The machines below were working through loads of trash, just as they had been when he dozed off. There were dozens of them, all scuttling about like well-organized insects.

Raze felt a nagging pain from his empty stomach. He put his hand into his carry sack and pulled out the uneaten half of his Praedo HiCal Dinner. It didn't look palatable right now, but it would do for today's breakfast. He checked the Greyface. It wouldn't power up. Its low charge icon kept flickering at him over and over. Great, he thought, no Greyface function, and maybe only enough charge for a call or two on the old cell network. Plus, now he was going to have to...to what? Raze had no idea what to do next. He didn't even know where he was. He realized that this waste processing facility had to be located somewhere within The Glades. That meant he would be miles from the nearest gateway back to the CTZ. It was even more concerning to realize that he was stuck inside The Glades with an expired contractor's pass. That was bad. If anyone from The Glades security apparatus stopped him now for questioning, he'd likely be jailed or even executed. There would be no way he could get back using the Gateway he'd come in through. Even if he *did* find some alternative method for getting back to the CTZ —like swimming along the length of Lake Michigan—he didn't know what he would do when he got there. The Prince Kings had been iced. Raze had no crew to return to. Going back would mean he'd have to start from scratch with another gang. Another stint as a prospect doing shit errands? He did not like the thought of that one bit.

Now Raze could hear different kinds of machines moving about. The noises all originated from outside, somewhere beyond the wall to his left. He cautiously moved along the gangway to get beside the wall, and then peered out of a window. From there, he could see straight into the waste storage yard. It was a well-managed affair, full of neat cubes of trash that had all been compacted and stacked for haulage, geometrically arranged into intersecting lines. Beyond this veritable maze of garbage was the wall that separated the facility from the service street. It was from this direction that the noises came, caused by a pair of well-armed Prowlers. The Prowlers had already driven through the entrance to the facility, and they were now maneuvering around the yard, scanning everything in sight.

"Fucking perfect," Raze muttered to himself.

He stepped back from the window and moved across to the side railing. He then checked around for cameras and security, but he soon discovered this facility appeared to be free of such protective measures. He figured that, being located in The Glades, this recycling plant was probably safe from any vandals that might threaten its operation. Additionally, the machines working here would be smart enough to report intruders, maybe even corner and trap some would-be criminals.

Raze clambered down the ladder that led to the lower level. Then, in a crouched posture, he edged across the gangway that hung over the warehouse floor below. He spotted an abandoned office area directly across from him. He hadn't seen that in the dim light of last night, but he figured that, with everything in the plant being automated, it was very unlikely people would be in that office now. He headed for the door with peeling paint, the one, he guessed, which would be the entrance to the office.

Land of the Free

Raze heard a mechanical droning sound below him. He looked, and saw that one of the Prowlers had entered the processing zone. It came to a halt, and then looked around as though it was calculating how best to navigate the surrounding area. Raze prowled like a leopard to avoid being spotted by the machine. Once he was alongside the office partition, he flattened himself against it, and then cautiously felt around for the door handle that he knew lay somewhere at waist level. The Prowler now began to raise itself up, simultaneously releasing hover units into the air to enable it to get a better view of its surroundings. Raze found the door handle. The hover units began scanning the room. Raze twisted the handle clockwise, opened the door, and then slipped inside to escape the machines. Once out of sight, he breathed a sigh of relief.

It then became immediately clear to him that this wasn't an office at all. It was more of a hallway, only a few strides wide. There were some storage lockers, an empty equipment rack, and, at the end of the passage, a restroom. It seemed to Raze this could be some kind of maintenance outpost. There weren't any windows, and, aside from the door he had entered through, there didn't seem to be any other way out. He mulled over what to do next.

Just then, the tattoo on his left arm began to tingle and flicker, indicating an incoming call. Raze stared down at the tattoo, wondering who it could be. No one ever called him on the backup cell number to the Greyface. He didn't even know what the number was himself. He started making a motion to dismiss the call, but then stopped. Curiosity was getting the better of him. So, touching his left ear, he activated the communicator.

"Hello, Mister Raze," came the polite voice of what sounded like a young woman.

Raze's eyes darted around. The voice wasn't familiar. "The fuck is this?" he demanded.

"Profanity isn't necessary, Mister Raze. You may recall we met briefly last night via chat. I am the one who warned you about the incoming security forces. I'm calling you this morning in the hope we might be of mutual assistance to one another."

"Mutual what? The fuck kinda' game you tryin' to play wit' me, bitch?"

"Mister Raze, your situation will improve greatly if you put aside your apprehension and listen to what I have to say."

"Y'all ain't shadin' me out with this shit. Y'all some kinda' cop o' somethin'?"

"I can assure you that I am not from Chicago Security, Mister Raze."

"Fucking bullshit on that."

"Mister Raze, it's critically important that you start listening to me."

"Yeah, well cut the draz an' start speakin' smart real fast, hoe, 'cuz I ain't in the mood this mornin'. Y'all feel me?"

There was a second of silence as the line appeared to go dead. It seemed like the girl was thinking something over. Raze looked bemused, and checked his tattoo to see if the connection had dropped.

The women returned, but this time her voice sounded much harsher. "AG, sib. I'll give it to y'all essential-like. Y'all be swellin' on the five-oh's radar after them games wit' the Prince Kings las' night. Them Prowlers see that sorry-ass face an' they gonna' fuck y'all up real good. That what y'all want?"

Raze took a second to answer, "Ah...no..."

"Then y'all better shut the fuck up an' listen to this bitch, 'cuz she help y'all las' night and she tryin' to keep yo' sorry ass alive now. Move like she say and y'all can get outta' this hole. Y'all feel me?"

"Yeah," Raze said, shocked by her directness. "Yeah, I feel y'all..."

"AG. Now, move yo motherfucking ass to that toilet block an' look up 'n the ceiling."

Raze did as she ordered. "Okay, movin' to the toilet block...but can y'all go back to that other voice?"

"Other voice?"

"The talkin' all lady-like one?"

The woman's voice became more pleasant. "You mean this voice? If you take this more polite tone seriously, Mister Raze, I'd be happy to speak to you in it."

"Yeah, 's AG. I can take it serious-like. Y'all started out talkin' upper class, but no doubt y'all a street bitch some time inna' past. What y'all doin', some kinda' Allurer graduated from the 'hood?"

"You seem to enjoy guessing, Mister Raze, so I'll let you go on guessing. Are you looking at the roof?"

Raze looked up. "Yeah, seein' some kinda' access in the corner."

"That's what you are looking for. Through there you can make it past the Prowlers below and across the processing plant. When you reach the end, I'll guide you through the yard and out of the facility."

Raze grabbed a nearby disused trash can and stood on top of it. Then, using his fingertips, he pushed aside the access opening. He jumped up, took hold of the inner edge with both hands, and pulled himself into the alcove. "Up an' in. I'm movin' along to the end right now."

"Excellent. Just stay on that path and try to move quietly."

"Will do Miss..what y'all say yo name was?"

"I didn't say. I call myself Dolly."

"Dolly?" Raze let a chuckle escape.

"Is something wrong?"

Raze turned what he wanted to say over in his head. "No, jus' an' interestin' name s'all?"

"What do you find interesting about my name?"

"Well, hearin' it give me some fine imagery."

"I'm sorry, I don't follow."

"As in wha' y'all look like as a lady."

"You can tell what I look like just by my name alone?"

"Well, y'all can tell a lot about what a lady look like from the name she give he'self, Dolly."

"Would knowing my appearance interest you?"

"Hell yeah."

"That's curious. In that case, I'd like to know what you think I look like."

"Y'all would, huh?"

"Of course. I'd like to know how I look in your mind's eye."

"Okay," Raze inhaled, thought for a second, "I'd say y'all a blonde. Lil' white number around five foot seven. Got pouty lil' lips and a set o' C cups. Lil' hourglass goin' on. Tight little booty with a sweet shake."

"That's uncanny," Dolly responded. "It's as though you are actually looking at me right now."

Raze laughed. "Heck, maybe I am. Y'all sayin' I guess right?"

"You described what I look like in perfect detail, but I know you can't be looking at me right now."

"Oh, why's that?"

"Because you didn't say anything about the outfit that I'm wearing."

"It's like that, huh? What y'all like to wear usually?"

"Me? That's a good question. I suppose if I looked the way you described, the best answer would be I like something lacy, but revealing, such as a Lolita dress with a low cut that accentuates my C cup cleavage in just the right way."

Raze's eyes widened as he thought about the image Dolly had given him. "Dang."

"Does that sound interesting to you?"

"It do if y'all got that get up on while we speakin', girl."

"At this hour of the morning? What else would I be wearing?"

Land of the Free

"Girl," Raze shook his head, "y'all keep talkin' me outta' here so we can get some quality time together all nice n' personal. Y'all like the sound o' that?"

"Believe me, I can't wait until you meet me in person, Mister Raze. Please keep moving."

Raze eventually reached the end of the passageway. Then, removing the grating, he stepped out from the access passage. He was now on the other side of the warehouse overlooking the front entryway trash yard. In the distance, he could easily make out the roadway from the adjoining street, but getting there would be another matter. The alleyways of trash between Raze and the exit were crawling with more of the automated machines he'd seen earlier. He could see no easy way to get past them all without being detected.

"How the fuck y'all gonna' guide me through that?" he asked.

"Simple, I can see the entire yard from here."

"Y'all out there?"

"In a manner of speaking."

"Where?" Raze peered around, but he couldn't see anyone.

"Look above you," Dolly said.

Raze looked straight up, but he couldn't see anything except blue skies. "Hell, Im'a take yo word on it."

"Climb down and find cover behind something suitable."

Raze clambered down to the ground level and ducked behind a wall of trash. Machinery was careening all around the place, pushing and pulling garbage like packs of angry ants.

"What now?" Raze asked, scanning the area.

"In the center of the lane two rows up, you'll find another access grate in the ground. This one will lead to the sewer system."

"Sewer?! Shit."

"Precisely."

"How am I gonna' get past all them?"

"Just stay still for the moment. I'm going to tell you when it is safe to move."

"What y'all want me to do after I get into the sewer?"

"Just follow it to the left for a block or so. That'll take you to a manhole leading to one of the nearby alleyways. We won't have any signal while you're in the sewer, so our call will drop. But, don't worry. I've already contacted someone to come and pick you up from the alley."

"Who y'all callin'?"

"Your friend, Mister Denzel Cowan."

Raze look incredulous. "Y'all know Denz?"

"Yes. I've learned a lot about you, Mister Reece Jordan."

"The fuck! How y'all know my name? Y'all some kinda' government agent?"

"Not quite. I'll explain it all to you later. For the moment, just get ready to move to the grate."

"AG. Y'all tell me when."

There was a moment of silence from Dolly. Then, "NOW! GO!"

With that Raze bolted for the lane of trash that lay two rows ahead. Just as Dolly had promised, there was an access grate lying right there in the middle of the lane. Raze approached it, twisted the locking mechanism to the grate, pulled up, and slunk into the hole that led down into the sewer. Inside, it was near pitch dark. Raze advanced cautiously, edging step by step, feeling his way forward as he made his way down the passageway leading to the left. After what felt like a block or two, Raze saw a stream of sunlight coming in from a manhole cover up above him. He found the ladder that led up to the street, climbed to the top, and then heaved the covering plate aside.

He now found himself back outside. This time, he was in some alley that ran alongside the waste disposal plant. No sooner had Raze emerged from the manhole than his eyes fell upon a slick looking BMW 9 Series parked at the end of the alley. Alongside the BMW stood a black man in a suit, his neck covered in gold chains and his head in a full set of dreadlocks. As the man spotted Raze, a wide smile began to spread across his face.

"Shit, mon, it really be you!"

Raze held his hands out to his sides, palms facing upwards. Denz did the same. They moved towards one another, laughing as they embraced.

"I was wachin' da playback dis mornin' when I woke," Denz said. "The stream end midway. I try callin', but couldn't dot yo profile, notin'."

"Greyface is offline. Cell only."

"What the fuck happen after y'all pause the feed?"

"Prince Kings got smashed by a Prowler. They dead, sib."

Denz looked horrified. "What! Dat be crazy!"

"Y'all tellin' me."

"Hell, I be gettin' messages from some slimaz tellin' me y'all gonna' be here. Been waitin' here near half an hour tinkin' it be a prank. Glad I stay aroun' fo another few minutes."

"You an' me both."

Denz just shook his head in disbelief. "So glad y'all okay. Well, c'mon. Y'all com' back to my pad an' we can get y'all cleaned up. Lady say she wanna talk to us both 'bout some 'business' she got brewin'."

16. Frustrations

"Richard, fetch me something to drink."

Laura turned away from Richard, held out her cocktail glass, and continued her conversation with Alice Wheeler. Richard Boyd looked at the glass, then took it with one of his thick hands. He turned to his kids.

"Stay close to your mother until I get back."

Zoey and Ethan paid absolutely no attention to their father's words. They went on playing with Wheeler's kids, and then ran off towards one of the nearby tents. Richard pursed his lips, but said nothing to them. He began shifting his way through the crowd of guests on the White House South Lawn. Somewhere close by would be a table offering beverages.

As Boyd moved, it struck him how large the crowd for this event was. At least half of Washington's resident socialites had decided to turn up. Among them were the usual cadre of senators, and with them came, of course, their guests and other attendants. To Boyd, the whole party felt unjustifiably presumptuous. It was like White was celebrating a war victory rather than the first steps towards starting one. While Boyd found nothing particularly wrong with that, he always felt it was smarter to celebrate the achievement of goals, not the undertaking of them.

As he shuffled along, he noticed Vice President Davies and Charlotte Davidson were engaged in thoughtful conversation. He wondered what they could be discussing. Should he join them?

No, get Laura her drink first. He pushed on. Next, he spotted his rival Roger Winkler and his wife. Winkler looked a little out of place. He was fidgeting, looking around as though he didn't belong at the party. Boyd gave him a cunning smile and the inclination of his head. Winkler returned the gesture, but with the visible lack of confidence a defeated competitor might give to the one who bettered them. Boyd nodded to himself. That exchange made him feel he could walk a little taller.

He had now made it to one of the tents that offered a selection of wines and other alcoholic beverages. He poked around, observing the brands of champagne on offer. That's when his eyes fell upon the supple posterior in a perilously short white skirt beside him. Boyd pretended to face forward, but looked askance at it. The back of the skirt was edging up, tantalizingly, as the woman leaned forward to fill her plate. The woman's legs and the gentle motions of her buttocks had Boyd hypnotized.

He did a quick check to ensure his wife wasn't looking, and then adjusted his tie. After the woman straightened herself up, Boyd reached across her, making it so he "accidentally" bumped his elbow against her back.

"Oooh," the young lady remarked in surprise.

"Oh, did I bump you? My apologies," Richard said.

Richard readied his best smile, eyeing the young woman's features as she turned to face him: the shoulder length platinum blonde hair, the pudgy little tip on her nose, the gold earrings and classy sunglasses.

The woman spoke, "Oh! Hello again, Richard."

Boyd froze at hearing his name. That voice. That accent. As she lifted her sunglasses, the woman revealed those blue eyes that had captivated him so completely yesterday. It was Yulov's girl.

Realizing this, Richard tensed up. "...You?"

"Yes," the young lady said with a playful laugh. "It's me. Do you remember my name?"

Boyd tried to recall as a fragrance came wafting through the air around her. It was a subtle blend of citron top and rose mid notes, but with a sandalwood musk that smelled surprisingly more mature than Boyd knew she must be.

"Flor...Flur...?"

"Fleurine," she giggled.

"Right. Fleurine..." Boyd's discomfort grew. "What...What are you doing?"

"I'm enjoying the party."

Boyd looked around, conscious that people could be watching him have this conversation. "I mean, what are you doing *here*?"

Fleurine said nothing, and instead took a sip of her cocktail.

"Is this Yulov's idea of a prank?"

Fleurine tutted. "Prank?"

"You've come here for a reason, obviously."

"Of course. I felt we had an interesting connection yesterday, didn't you?"

"Connection...?" Richard began to sweat under his collar. "I think you're mistaken."

Fleurine tilted her head. "Oh?"

"Yes. Most definitely yes."

Fleurine opened her mouth, the tip of her tongue showing.

Boyd stepped back. "You can tell Yulov, if he's thinking of pulling this kind of stunt, it's not going to work. I'm not stupid enough to sleep with..."

Richard couldn't voice the words. Fleurine looked on at him. "You don't like younger women?"

"Younger women?! For God's sake, you're..." Richard stopped. This conversation wasn't going to get him anywhere. He made a turn to leave.

"If that was Yulov's aim, why would I bother seeing you? I could just go to your wife now and tell her we are having an affair."

Hearing that threat, Boyd's face became flushed. "That wouldn't work in a million years."

"It wouldn't?"

"No, because I'd just tell her you were lying."

Fleurine shrugged her shoulders with a demure grace. She looked over at Laura, who was busily talking with her friends. Then, she fixed her eyes on Boyd again. "She'd never believe you, Richard. She knows what kind of man you are."

Boyd moved into Fleurine's personal space to intimidate her. "You have no idea what kind of man I am. *Or* what I'm capable of, little girl."

Fleurine dismissed him with a laugh. "If you were as strong as you acted, you wouldn't be frightened to chase after what you were interested in."

Boyd screwed up his face with contempt as he looked her up and down. "Don't flatter yourself. I've already seen the goods, hon. You need to do a little more growing before you'll pique my interest."

He snatched up a bottle of champagne and a flute, and then stormed away from the table.

Boyd returned to Laura's side, poured some champagne into the flute, and offered it to her. Laura gave a disapproving look at what Richard had brought her, but accepted it. For the next half-hour, he made every effort to completely ignore Fleurine's presence at the party. He strutted beside his wife when he walked. He distracted himself by talking with General Davies about strategy. He spoke with President White about policy. He even did his best to find Charlotte Davidson's rambling about her in-laws interesting. But, none of this could stop him from stealing a glance in Fleurine's direction every once in a while. Each time he did, he was rewarded with a sting. Fleurine acted like she didn't care what he did. She waltzed around, parading herself in front of other men. Boyd watched them return her flirting with interest, her coy laugh and body language communicating that she was available to them. Some younger male attendants were now moving in like hunters. She seemed flattered by their advances, and brushed her hair back to expose her neck. One man looked at her neckline as though he was about to sink his teeth in. Boyd snarled. Here he was, one of the most powerful men at this party, and yet it was a minimum wage nobody-not him-who'd be having fun between those legs of hers tonight.

"Excuse me for a second, Charlotte. Laura, darling, can I get you another drink?"

"Yes, Richard. A glass of white, if you can manage it."

"Sure. Let me check."

Richard strode his way back over to Fleurine. He turned to the young man she was speaking to, and demanded, "Give me a glass of white and a single malt."

The young man nodded, exchanged a hungry look with Fleurine, and then went to fetch Boyd the drinks he'd requested.

Boyd shook his head. "I want you out of here."

Fleurine said nothing. She just looked at him over the rim of her glasses and arched an eyebrow.

"I'm not joking."

"What am I doing wrong? You made it clear that you aren't interested."

"I'm not."

"So, I'm not allowed to speak with other men here either?"

"No, because you have absolutely no business being at this party. Leave now before I have security escort you out."

"What reason will you give them to do that? That I've been sent here by Dimitry Yulov to seduce you? How do you think that will make you look?"

Boyd grit his teeth. He was about to answer when the familiar, bald head of Senator Gordon Parks appeared alongside Fleurine.

"Richard," Parks began, offering his hand for shaking, "good to see you. Congratulations on the fantastic job yesterday."

Richard straightened up and shook hands. "Gordon. Thanks, I appreciate it."

"I see you've already had the pleasure of meeting our nanny, Fleurine."

"Oh?" Boyd shrunk. He saw Fleurine smile at him again. "She works for Sandra and yourself?"

"For over three months now. Sandra found her and can't stop raving about her. I'm glad Fleurine came back from her vacation in California early last night. She's a miracle worker with the kids."

Fleurine held her hands upwards. "I just love children."

"It's a good thing for us that you do. Speaking of, we've got to get going because the boys will be getting off early today. Are you ready to go, Fleurine?"

"Of course. Thank you again, Gordon. It was so nice of you to let me see the party."

"You've been so amazing that you deserve it. Hey Richard, trust me, you should find yourself someone to mind Zoey and Ethan time to time." He indicated to Boyd's kids, who were becoming increasingly raucous while Richard's wife scolded them. "I think Laura would appreciate the help."

Richard nodded. "Thanks for the suggestion, Gordon. I might consider it."

When Richard turned back to face Gordon, he saw Fleurine had her hand outstretched towards him. In that hand, a pink-colored contact card was balanced between her fingers. "I know some friends who are looking for work. Give me a call. Maybe I can help relieve you of your 'frustrations' sometime."

She let Richard see the sparkle in her eyes. He took the card from her hand, and then thanked her.

"Come on, Fleurine. See you, Richard, and give my best to Laura."

"Thanks again, Gordon. Say hello to Sandra and the kids for me too."

He watched as Fleurine and Gordon walked off towards the parking lot. Richard examined the decorative contact card she'd given him. He found it saccharine in appearance, almost as though the pink color and cursive writing on it was somehow mocking him. He felt the urge to tear the card up, but he didn't want anyone to catch him doing it, so he pocketed it instead. The young attendant returned with Boyd's drinks. Richard took them, put on his game face, and turned around to return to the others. He immediately saw his wife, face livid as she tried to control the kids. He sighed and stepped towards her to offer help.

17. Ain't Notin' Can't Be Done

"An' here we be, sib," Denz announced as the lift doors slid open. Raze followed him as he stepped out into the lavish, open space before him. The modern furnishings were sparse, but functional, and everything was automated. The paintings and tapestries were typical of Denz's Rastafarian tastes, but what really got Raze's attention was the view. He took a few steps towards the wide, inset windows to get a better look.

Denz noticed Raze's surprise. "Oh yeah. Y'all never been to da crib before. Take a look at that scene, mon. She beautiful. Should see it in the nighttime tho'. Like a fairyland she be."

Raze was so spellbound by the view that he almost didn't even hear Denz's words. He had never seen Chicago from this height before. From up here, on this side of the wall, the city was serene. It was like a perfect, sculpted model where everything was running like clockwork. Further out, beyond the wall, he could see the dirty outline of the CTZ areas that he called home.

"What?! Get outta' here, woman! I told y'all be gone before ten," came Denz's voice from somewhere down the hallway.

"Aw, Denz, sweetie pie..."

"I got company, bitch! Get yo tings an' scat. I ain't payin' y'all for da overtime neither."

A young and naked woman, holding her clothes against her body to cover herself, appeared from around the corner. She made eye contact with Raze, gave him a pleasant smile, and excused herself. She then trotted towards the lift, the doors closed, and she disappeared.

"Sorry 'bout dat," Denz said. "Can I get' y'all anyt'ing, sib?"

"Ah...yeah. Lil' hungry."

"I can get y'all some real food. Not like that Praedo Labs draz y'all keep eating. Dat stuff no good for y'all, mon."

"Well, 's about all we got there."

"Yeah, I know dat. Crime you don' get no real food dat side. Make yoself at home, sib."

Raze pulled himself away from the captivating view. He looked over at the white sofa beside him and sat down. The sofa felt welcoming, but, after a second or two, he got the feeling that there was some kind of motorized function inside it. The back of the sofa was moving around as though it was trying to massage him, but the motions didn't elicit a relaxing feeling at all. He made a confused expression as he turned to find the source of the movement. Suddenly, he jumped to his feet and began shouting profanities.

"Wat is it?!" Denz called out, running into the room. He looked at the couch. "Aw, sib, dat jus' Juju. She ain't gonna' hurt y'all none. She a good snake."

Raze looked at the creature as it writhed. "Y'all got a pet snake?!"

Denz stepped over to the sofa and cradled the python in his arms. Juju stared at her owner and flickered her tongue. Denz returned the gesture with a kiss. "Had Juju for a good many year now. In da old times, we be havin' pet anyt'ings."

"Does it bite?"

Denz gave Raze a look to suggest he was stupid. A tone sounded from the kitchen area. "Dat'll be da food. Hope y'all like pizza."

Denz went into the kitchen to collect the food. Along the way, he dropped Juju into the enormous, acrylic habitat case in the hallway. "So, Raze, mon, y'all seen my family lately?"

Raze put his Greyface onto a charging block and called out to Denz, "Ev'ry day. They AG, sib. Seen Walt and Cindy goin' workin'. Rachelle there too. Didn't like her getup tho."

"Wat y'all mean?"

Raze thought about sharing his concerns about Rachelle, but figured it might be better to hold his tongue. "Nothin', sib. Just she look like she don' take the job serious s'all."

Denz made a sound of disapproval. He emerged from the kitchen carrying a plateful of pizza slices. Raze's mouth started watering.

"Ha ha," Denz laughed, noticing Raze's appetite. "T'aught y'all would like dis."

He set the plate on the coffee table and seated himself. Raze plumped down alongside him and, grabbing a pizza slice, began wolfing it down. The pepperoni immediately hit his tongue with flavors he hadn't tasted in years.

"Hap!" Raze exclaimed. "This the deal!"

"It sure be. Dis da hap life I tellin' y'all about."

Raze kept eating, shaking his head as he took in everything about Denz's apartment.

"So, Raze, mon, y'all speak to that slimaz too?"

Raze nodded. "Dotted me after I wake."

"Why she do that?"

"Fucked 'f I know. Bitch saved my ass las' night on the hyperpass. Tol' me t' jump when the Prowler came 'round. Had a truck underneath me when I fall."

"How she be knowing dat biz?"

"Like I say, fucked 'f I know."

Denz's face took on a look of concern. "Bug me how she can do dat. Somet'in' say dis gal usin' some guzumba."

"What she say t' y'all?"

"Not'in' much. Jus' call me first t'ing sayin' she know y'all and I need to get to dat alleyway."

For the next forty minutes, the two of them started swapping ideas about who Dolly was and what was going on; Denz voicing more of his concerns, and Raze bragging how Dolly sounded like she was gagging to ride him. They laughed at this, then talked about their lives. Denz was so glad to finally have his friend with him at his apartment.

"Shoulda' don' dis lang time ago, sib," Denz said.

"Yeah, but y'all here, a Doughboy. I'm there."

"Ain't the way life mean' t' be."

"The way it is tho'. Can' do much about it."

They both shook their heads. Denz sighed and took another look at the time.

"She say she gonna' call. Almost midday now. When dat gonna happen?"

As if on cue, Denz's hyperdisplay began to chime. Raze and Denz shot a knowing look at each other, then Denz ordered the display to put the call through. They were immediately surprised to see a blonde woman wearing a Stetson appear onscreen. She looked like their impression of the red-blooded, all-American cowgirl, though maybe a retired one who had aged and put on a few pounds. She was flanked on her left by a slightly younger, gorgeous Latina, who was dressed like she had a lunch date at the O.K. Corral. To her right, there was a balding, older guy in a wheelchair. He immediately struck Raze and Denz as a military veteran, though they weren't sure why exactly. Raze would later put this down to the look the man had in his eyes.

"Hello, gentlemen," began the woman in her Southern drawl. "I am President Darlene Richards. This here is my bodyguard, Carla Ibanez, and my good friend, Ben Rollins. I am so very happy to make your acquaintances."

Denz motioned to Raze with his hand to ask if he should speak first. Raze shrugged as if to say be my guest.

"President Darlene Richards," Denz began, "from the Republic o' Texas?"

"That's right."

"How y'all have my number? An' where be dis Dolly?"

"Dolly is my personal secretary. She is unfortunately indisposed at the present time and unable to see you both, though she tells me you boys are some of the best in the business."

"Business?"

"That's right. I am calling you gentleman to ask if y'all would be willing to offer us some help with a small problem our Republic is facing."

Raze sat forward. "Help Texas?! Yo, sib, cut this shit now or we dead," he told Denz.

"He be right, Madam President. Da government even hear we speakin' dem words wit' y'all, we gonna' be roasted like dem Constitutional Terrorists."

"I can assure y'all that this call is untraceable, and that it's using an unbreakable encryption."

Raze scoffed at that suggestion.

Denz looked at President Richards with a curious eye. "All da same, it make me nervous."

"Oh, really?" Richards responded. "Well, I see you haven't hung up on me yet."

From the corner table, a ping rang out from Raze's Greyface. He got up from the sofa to collect it, giving Richards the stink-eye as he moved.

He picked the Greyface up and held it closer to check the message that had arrived. It was a dot from Dolly with the caption "4 U." Attached, he found a picture of her looking just as whelf as he'd imagined, reclining suggestively against some antique bed. Raze blew a whistle to signal his approval.

"It jus' make me wonder, Madam President," Denz continued, "why y'all callin' us for a chit-chat. Y'all must know we not the type who do t'ings above da board. Wat kinda problem Texas be havin' y'all need t' speak wit' us?"

"This, I understand. I have a small request that would be plum simple for a couple o' strong boys like y'all."

"Enough wit' da fauxsin'. Wat kinda' request?"

"It's a kidnappin'."

Raze put the Greyface back down. "Kidnappin'? Yo, what the fuck y'all takin' us for? We ain't kidnappers. We ain't nowhere near Texas. No way in hell we can kidnap someone that far away!"

"The kidnapping would not take place in Texas," said Ben Rollins. "The individual in question lives in Chicago."

"Who dis guy be?" Denz asked.

"Not a man," Carla said next, "a woman. Her name is Ritika Kaur Sinha. She works for a company called M3Raymond-Kennel Systems."

Raze and Denz looked at each other. Then, they burst out laughing so hard that Denz almost fell off the sofa. Richards and her team watched on, smiling patiently. Denz managed to finally get control of his fits enough to be able to speak.

"Oh, mon, y'all head nuh good. Dat some crazy draz y'all be t'inkin'."

"Can you do it?" President Richards asked.

"Y'all t'ink we gotta' deat' wish? M3 be military. Nobody got da balls big 'nuff to mess wit' dem. Y'all talkin' some high talent gig make us public enemy numba' one. An gettin' someone like dat to y'all involve smugglin' planes an' sneaky business."

"But, can you do it?"

Denz scratched the back of his head and looked at Raze. Raze looked back at him, and rubbed his thumb against his fingers to suggest talking about money. They started laughing again.

"Aw hell, it all depen', mi lady. Ain't notin' can' be done, but it be a big-ass operation. How much y'all willin' to grease us fo' da job?"

President Richards told them her offer. Denz and Raze stopped laughing.

"In addition to that," Richards said, "I'd be willing to extend to you both immediate citizenship in the Texas Republic. Does that sound like fair payment for your services?"

Raze and Denz exchanged another look. Denz scratched his head again, and Raze shrugged his shoulders.

"Glad to hear it, boys. I'll have Dolly send y'all the information she has for the job. When y'all are ready to go, message her back an' you'll receive your down payments. I look forward to meeting y'all in our free republic soon. Good day, gentlemen. And good hun'in."

With that, the transmission ended. Raze and Denz just sat there for a moment, speechless. From the corner table, Raze's

Greyface began pinging to notify him that messages were incoming.

18. Desperate Darlene

"Most world leaders would be happy to see a nation take its first steps into space. For many countries, hearing that the FSA is joining the space race-and bringing with it its mechanisms of trade and established law and order-would be cause for relief. The fact that stability is coming to the stars is a long overdue and welcome thing. But, that's not the case for President Darlene Richards of the Republic of Texas. In breaking news this afternoon, we at *The Haddick Report* have received anonymous tips suggesting that Richards is fuming over the FSA's move to change power providers to California. Our president is so concerned by these threats that he's ordered an increase in the presence of our armed forces along the Texan border. To understand why our nation's decision has got Richards into a Texan-sized hissy-fit, I'm joined by Dennis Vandermayer. Vandermayer is Professor of Texan Socioeconomic Studies at the University of St. Louis, and he's also the author of the best-selling work *Richards' Republic: How the West wasn't lost, it was stolen*. Professor Vandermayer, it's a pleasure to have you on the program."

"The pleasure is all mine, Don."

"Tell me, professor, we're looking at images of Richards now, and every time I see her, she's always got this wild look in her eyes, like you've just strangled her prize hog or goat or whatever she has as a pet..."

"Ha, ha...For Richards, that would be her horse, Racket."

"Racket? That sounds more like what she makes whenever we hear from her. Professor, you've spent many years studying Richards. Can you explain to our viewers, as simply as you can, why it is she is just so hostile towards our nation?"

"Well, Don, I'd first need to caution you on calling her hostile on account of her gender. As you know, most women are kind, nurturing creatures. Richards, however, is an extreme example of what happens when you raise a woman outside of what God intended. Richards is far more of a cunning, Machiavellian manipulator than your average woman. She's been brilliant at channeling her stardom as a showgirl and rodeo champion into a kind of populism that, well, quite frankly, has been the envy of many totalitarian regimes the world over. But, just because Richards has been able to keep an iron grip on her republic, doesn't mean she has the smarts to make Texas into some booming economic success like the FSA."

"So, these angry outbursts she makes are rooted in some kind of jealousy towards us?"

"Oh, most definitely. You have to remember, Don, that Texas is about two steps from becoming a failed state. The people there are absolutely destitute after years under Richards' rule, which includes enduring economic sanctions from all directions. So, for Richards, hearing that the FSA is also going into space, on top of this switch away from using Texas for our power... Well, you can understand just how aggravating it all is for her. In fact, you might want to start calling her 'Desperate Darlene'."

"Desperate Darlene—I like that. But, truthfully, professor, it sounds to me like this isn't our fault. If Richards wanted Texas to be a part of our space race, or to go on supplying our energy, she shouldn't have seceded from us in the first place. Am I wrong?"

"That's my thoughts exactly, Don. Aside from some dissidents or UMC sympathizers, there would be few in this country who'd say she made the right choice by ceding. I'd even wager there would be plenty in Texas right now, watching our defenses build up along the border, and secretly hoping it's some new 'Jade Helm 15'-style plot to take Texas by force."

"Do you think that's something we should consider doing for their sake?"

"Well, it's not for me to make moral arguments for saving Texans or not, but if I was in the Pentagon thinking about an attack, I'd certainly be asking myself whether there would ever be a better opportunity than right now."

19. Forty-eight Hours

"There will never be a better opportunity than right now, Mister President," General Jake G. Ellis declared.

President White, Vice President Davies, and the other senior staff exchanged unconvinced looks. Richard Boyd shifted in his chair and smiled to himself. Inside, he was feeling plucky, elated to be in the Situation Room and seated around the strategy table with all the big movers. This was his moment to earn a permanent place within White's first-name-basis boys club, and so he was doing his best to appear thoughtfully engaged in Ellis' presentation. However, his mind was also preoccupied, trying to think of things to say that would make him look more informed about what was happening than he actually was.

Ellis continued, "The fact is these recent moves from our administration will have caught Texas by complete surprise. Until yesterday, Texas had long assumed California would always be a dependable military ally. In the event of an invasion by us, Texas felt they could count on California's assistance to help stave off our advance. Because of that, they've done very little over the last couple of years to strengthen their armed forces in any great capacity."

Ellis pointed to the holographic display above the strategy table. On it, detailed comparisons between the FSA and Texan military forces were being presented in a series of graphs and statistics. "Since becoming a republic, their military spending has barely gone above one percent of their GDP. Right now, our forces outnumber them by almost four to one. That's not just airpower either. I'm talking about ground forces: heavy weaponry, shock assault divisions, troops to secure facilities. Hell, our armored divisions are on their way to the border now, and why stop there? We could probably just let them keep on rolling right into Austin and have this thing over within a few days."

President White nodded. "Believe me, I appreciate your enthusiasm, Jake. We're all raring to go on this little "adventure." But, you'll excuse my hesitation in leaping to the conclusion that we'll just 'roll right into Austin,' as you say. Tell me, have you considered Mexico and their potential response?"

"Mexico?" Ellis dismissed the suggestion with a wave across his face. "Sure, they could stretch themselves and get involved, but the only ground forces they have that are worth a spit are over a thousand miles away. We'll be well on the way to running the show before they can mobilize and get there."

Richard glanced across to Vice President Davies. Davies had moved forward, looking as though he was about to ask a question. "Have you seen any movement from Mexico since we started heading for the border? Anything to suggest they've been talking with Texas?" he asked.

Ellis shrugged. "Nothing so far. None of our intel down there has reported anything. It all looks like business as usual."

"Sanchez would have to be thinking about doing something in response to this," White said with a thoughtful look. "He'd have to view offering help to Texas as a fantastic opportunity to advance his relations with them, or, at the very least, figure that

Texas is always good to keep around as a security buffer against being invaded by us down the track."

"Well, I am counting on Mexico getting involved in some way, Mister President, but I just don't see that altering the numbers in Texas' favor too much. At least, not in the time frame we're talking about. If you ask my personal opinion, I think we're all being a mite overcautious here. I say we just trust our boys, keep the heavies rolling, and deliver Richards the kick up the rear she's been begging for."

White tapped his fingers together and looked at the strategy plan again. He then turned to Boyd in the chair opposite him.

"Dick, my boy, you're the only one of us who has actually met Richards. What did you think of her? Did she strike you as being particularly clever or crafty in any way?"

Boyd made a thoughtful expression in response to the president's question. "To be honest, Mister President, I've dealt with cunning types all my life. Richards? No way she's one of them. I just found her to be your typical, run-of-the-mill blonde. She might come off as a scrapper and a fighter, but she's a simple idealist. I sure didn't come away from our meeting feeling there was a whole lot going on in that head of hers—more boobs than brains, if anything."

"I see. Did you meet any of her entourage?"

"You mean that Carla Ibanez and Ben Rollins? Sure, they were there. Ben seemed pretty sharp, ex-marine if I remember correctly. He might be one to plan a defense strategy that could tie us up. I didn't get to talk to Carla much. She seemed like the type who could probably shoot her mouth off as easily as she does her guns, though. So, Richards keeps her on a tight leash."

"Interesting," White said, tapping his finger against his chin while the others waited for his evaluation. "Maybe you're right, Jake. Maybe they actually don't have anything they can do, and they're at a loss over how to respond..."

Ellis looked forward with eager eyes.

"But, I'm still concerned, Jake."

"Mister President?" Ellis asked, deflated.

"We're moving our forces towards the border right now, and yet they're not even flinching. Mexico isn't moving to help them either. That doesn't seem right to me. I may not be a military man, Jake, but I can smell a trap a mile away. Richards is doing something right now that we can't even see. I just know she is."

"What do you think that could be?"

"I can't say for certain. It's just that I think she's trying something unorthodox."

"If you're suggesting a double cross from California, or that maybe she's readying her nukes so she can go out in a blaze of glory..."

"No. No, I don't think it would be anything like that."

"Then, what do you suggest we do? I thought we were all ready to get going on this thing. You want me to call the move off? Tell the advance forces to stand down and return to their bases?"

White turned to Vice President Davies. "John, what do you think about all this, my old friend?"

Davies pricked up the side of his mouth, then shook his head. "It's a tough call, but if no one from their side is moving, and if Mexico isn't doing anything, I think we can afford to take a wait and see approach. Let them sweat for a while. Give it another forty-eight hours, and see if Yulov makes any sneaky moves to double cross us. If nothing happens in those forty-eight hours..." and he walked his fingers along his arm to suggest they should proceed across the Texas border.

White nodded. "Sound advice and I agree. Time is on our side here. General Ellis...Jake, that's how we're going to play our hand. Keep the boys rolling. Make sure we've got everything ready along the border, and ensure we have absolute and overwhelming superiority before we move. Then, forty-eight hours from now, if we still think they've got nothing up their sleeves, we'll move in and take our state back." Ellis smiled as White continued, "I want to be absolutely clear that I want the bare minimum of damage done in this attack. Everything damaged or blown up in Texas will require me asking the Senate for money to fix, and I'm loathe to ask them for anything like that. Are we clear on these terms?"

"And what are we going to do with Richards when we get her?" asked Ellis.

White sighed. "I don't particularly care, Jake. If you like, she'll be yours to do with as you please. Roast her like those Constitutional Terrorists, if you must."

"Thank you, Mister President. It's an honor to be serving you, sir."

Boyd rolled his eyes at hearing Ellis' effusive brown-nosing.

"Let's call it there and meet again tomorrow. Fine with all of you?"

The members of White's Administration began shuffling about, discussing plans for the evening. Boyd reached into his pocket for his slate to message Laura. His fingers touched the device, but they also brushed against something else.

He took out the slate, and then felt around for the stiff object that was lodged in there alongside it. As he began to draw the thing from his pocket, he realized it was the pink card that Fleurine had given him earlier that day.

He quickly stuffed it back in the pocket, looked around to see if anyone had noticed it, then snuck another peek. His lip curled into a snarl, but he returned the card to his pocket and left it there. He then spoke to his slate.

"Message Laura. Tell her the meeting is going to be a couple more hours."

The slate chimed to signal that it had understood his instructions. Richard checked around to see who among the Cabinet was up for a few drinks. Then, after finding a few takers, the men headed out of the Situation Room and off to the nearest bar.

20. Just Like Old Times

"Anoushka...Anoushka..."

The well-groomed Russian Toy Terrier pricked up its ears and lifted its head. Dimitry Yulov crouched and held his hands out as Anoushka, tail wagging, got up from her soft, silken bed and came over to him. Dimitry picked her up, stroked her, then moved towards his antique Victorian desk to get to work. Strewn across the desk were pieces of the timepiece he was restoring. He gently pushed these pieces aside to make space to prop his feet.

"What are they doing, Anoushka? Shall we see? Shall we see?"

Anoushka yapped. Yulov laughed and seated himself.

"Give me all news on the FSA's movements."

The wall opposite Yulov blanked out, then switched over to a montage of video feeds. His eyes scanned the images on the screen. First, he glanced over a couple of news reports. Then, he stopped on the satellite feed. It was showing a battalion of light armored vehicles that were stationary.

"When and where is that?"

The wall emitted a tone, then responded, "Image is live, taken from the Texas and Oklahoma border."

Yulov furrowed his brow and stroked his chin. "That's good...that's very good. Do you see, Anoushka? They are moving into position. They are showing us that they have intent. But, they are not going any further. Maybe they think we'll double cross them. Is that it? Is that what they are thinking?"

Anoushka growled. Yulov laughed again.

A polite knock sounded from the double doors.

"What is it?" he called.

The large set of doors opened. Paul Nu marched into the room, bowed, then proceeded up to Yulov's desk.

"I'm sorry, Dimitry Yulov. You have a visitor."

Yulov gave a confused look. "Visitor?"

"He flew in unannounced, Dimitry Yulov. He asked us specifically not to tell you of his arrival, so as not to spoil his surprise. I had him scanned and let through. I apologize if that was the wrong thing to do, but..." and Paul motioned towards the door.

Yulov looked over as a stocky, bald man in his late sixties stepped into the office. The man had a face like a stone gargoyle, and he gave Yulov a grim look. Then, his face relaxed, creating a still frightening, but more pleasant smile. He held his large open palms outwards. Yulov stood up as he returned the gesture.

"Vladich Kharkachov," Yulov said, setting Anoushka down.

"Dima," returned Kharkachov in his orotund voice.

The two men laughed and hugged like wrestlers. Kharkachov wrapped his large hands around the sides of Yulov's head, then kissed his forehead.

"Why the surprise?" Yulov asked.

"My young pupil, you were always the one who was able to see everything coming. It pleases this old man to know he can still make some moves that you do no expect."

"You humble yourself too much. A genius like you is beyond all prediction, Vladich Kharkachov."

The old man laughed again. Yulov gestured to Paul that he should leave. The assistant inclined his head and strode off. Throughout this exchange Anoushka had been yapping in delight. Dimitry gently shushed her.

"So, these are the next steps of your scheme, Dima..." Kharkachov said, noting the display of images on the wall. "It all looks quite adventurous."

Yulov stepped forward and pointed to images as he talked. "White is taking the bait. These forward divisions are lining themselves up along the Texas border right now. Anoushka and I were just discussing how they will be waiting there a little while longer."

"Waiting?"

"I don't think White entirely trusts we won't intervene-California, that is."

"And will you?"

Yulov laughed and shook his head. Kharkachov nodded, though his face wasn't smiling. He stared at the monitors again.

"If you sacrifice Texas like a pawn, Dima, won't White just come for you next?"

"There will be no possibility of that happening, Vladich Kharkachov."

Kharkachov looked unconvinced. "You are sure of this?"

Yulov laughed again. Kharkachov grimaced, then looked downwards.

Noticing his mentor's sullen mood, Yulov stopped laughing and opened his palms. "Is something wrong? You look concerned." Then, when Kharkachov didn't answer, "They've sent you here to check up on me, haven't they?"

Kharkachov nodded. Yulov sighed, then headed over to the bar fridge to prepare drinks for himself and his guest.

"It is unfair that you should be upset by that, Dima. After all, you must remember that all this," and he indicated their surroundings, "represents a sizable investment by the Russian government. A fortune extended to you in good faith. A lot of money has been flowing into your hands. Everyone has been respectfully quiet about this, for the most part, but, recently, some concerned individuals have begun to ask questions. They come to me, asking when these investments of theirs will start to pay off. When these people heard the news of your deal with the FSA yesterday...well, they suggested that I fly here to meet with you, just to be certain that everything is in order."

Internally, Yulov felt himself growing perturbed as Kharkachov spoke. Still, he kept his face inscrutable and said, "Everything is in order. You know me, and you understand how I operate, Vladich Kharkachov. My plans need time to evolve to fruition."

Kharkachov shrugged. "This I know, Dima. But, sometimes your plans are a little too intricate, a little too clever."

Yulov let out a dismissive laugh. Kharkachov moved closer and frowned. "The President has instructed me to inform you of something, Dima. The Russian government will not, under any circumstances, back a proxy war to defend you here in California. With the Chinese making unpredictable moves, we cannot afford to let our guard down in any way. We cannot spare you the manpower to defend California."

Yulov nodded, then held out a shot glass of vodka to his mentor. "I have already considered that, Vladich Kharkachov. There will be no need for our motherland to waste her blood here to defend me."

They clinked glasses. "*Za tvoyo zdorov'ye!*"

They exhaled sharply, then downed their drinks. Kharkachov found his vodka satisfying, and nodded to show his approval.

Yulov smiled. "I know you must be worried about me. You don't have to be. I have it all in hand."

"I hope so. You know how an old man can be at this age. He gets worried about those he cares about, especially when they start acting irregular."

Yulov put his empty glass down, then clapped his hand on Kharkachov's shoulder. "Why don't you let me prove it to you? Stay a while. Give me the chance to show you some of the changes I've been making around here. At the same time, I can reveal to you a little more about my plans."

Kharkachov tilted his head as he considered the suggestion, then finished his vodka.

"Come on," Yulov continued. "The FSB can run its own shop without its director for a few days. We can take time to discuss the world, politics, philosophy. Just you and me. It will be like old times."

Kharkachov mulled the idea over in his mind some more. Then, looking into Yulov's face, he smiled and gave a nod. "Just like old times."

Yulov grinned, and gave his mentor a pat on the shoulder. "You won't be disappointed. Wait until you see all that I have done."

21. Ritika

It was late afternoon. Raze gazed out at his surroundings from the plush comfort of Denz's BMW 9 Series. It rolled through the streets, presenting Raze with a more up-close-and-personal view of life in The Glades. He watched from the passenger seat as flocks of people, dressed up in pretentious trimmings, roamed the surrounding cityscape. They were cycling, shopping, drinking coffee in the streets, flirting with one another. Some even had pets they were walking, openly, without fear they'd be stolen and eaten. Others were relaxing in those green spaces with trees and flowers-he tried to remember what they were called again-that's right: parks. Raze hadn't seen a park in almost seven years.

But, what was even more unbelievable was the demeanor of these people. They all went about their days without a care in the world. It was jarring for him to see their blitheness. He had, of course, expected life here to be different, but the disconnect with his reality was far greater than he had prepared for. Back in the CTZ right now, he knew there would be murder, rape, destruction, riots. Yet, here it was as though the whole concept of violence itself didn't exist.

This was a gated world. Raze wondered how Allurers could adapt to life here after they had ascended. How did they manage to fit in with these people? He got the impression that, if he to get out of the car and try talking to one of these people, they would consider him little more than human excrement. Even if he dressed like them, walked like them, they'd still pick up the tinge of street in his words when he opened his mouth. He could never blend in here-at least, not well enough to be be accepted. Thinking about this, he balled up his fists.

"We comin' up to Auron Tower now," Denz said. "Bedda' dot dat lady friend."

Raze cooled down. "Guess so." He pulled out the slate Denz had provided him and dotted a message to Dolly: "Hi, baby. Nearly there."

He replaced the slate into his pocket, but no sooner had he done this then his tattoo started color cycling again. Raze sighed, removed the slate, and activated conference mode.

"Hi, honey, did you miss me?" came Dolly's voice.

Denz shot Raze an incredulous look. Raze smirked to himself. "Oh, so 's all honey now?"

"Just following your lead. Did I read you wrong?"

"No, y'all can call me sweet names."

"AG. Did you get the photo I sent earlier?"

Denz mouthed the word photo. Raze shrugged, nonchalantly. "I sure did."

"And?"

Raze hesitated, but admitted, "Yeah, y'all a whelf."

"Stop it. You're making me blush."

"Ya'll the blushin' type? Maybe then y'all too shy to send me somethin' a little more swexy next time?"

"Swexy? Like after a workout or shower? You think I'm the kind of girl who'd send photos like that?"

"I don't know. Are you?"

"I'm not sure. I'd have to ask myself."

Raze found that statement a little odd, and not knowing how to respond said simply, "Uh, and?"

"Well, I'd say, given what we've already discussed, I'd be the fun and playful type who'd be into that kind of thing."

Denz had heard enough. "Yo, Dolly, I don' mean to be blockin' not'in' between y'all and my boy, but dis fool gotta' keep his head clean for da job right now."

"Hello, Denz. You're correct. Let's focus on the job at hand."

"Y'all sure deh be an entrance to Auron?"

"Yes, Denz, I have the building plans in front of me. There's a maintenance access right between those two white caps."

Raze crossed his arms. "Whoa, hol' up. Y'all mean them caps on top?"

"That's right, honey."

Denz gave Raze a look that suggested he was obtuse. "Whe' y'all t'ink we gettin' in? Greyface don' be foolin' notin' here, sib. Can' jus' put dat t'ing on, walk in the front door."

"How we gonna' get up *that*?" Raze asked, pointing to the imposing tower of glass and steel that they were approaching.

"Don' worry about it, mon. Y'all gotta' chill an' do crime like a Doughboy."

Raze scoffed.

"Y'all gonna' see soon enuf'. Put aside dat Prince King mind and star' t'inkin' like a fuckin' ninja."

They drove into an alleyway alongside Auron Tower. After checking the coast was clear, Denz and Raze got out and headed to the rear of the car. Denz popped the trunk and activated its auto-sorter unit. The machinery inside shuffled through its selection of stealth and intrusion gear, then stopped on what looked like a square rack, shoulder width in length.

"Dis get y'all deh, mon." Denz smiled, pulling the unit out of the trunk and letting it drop. The rack fell towards ground level, but stopped short of hitting the concrete. A series of almost silent rotors flipped out from its underside, which kept the rack hovering in place. "Step on an' try it out."

Raze hesitated. He put one foot on the rack and, finding it held his weight, followed with the other. Denz tossed him a small controller. "Now, lock dem feet in da center, an' give da sticks a try."

Raze obliged. He secured his feet in the center stirrups and tried the controls. He edged up, then down. Next, he tried the horizontal plane. After a while, he was satisfied he understood the machine's idiosyncrasies. It behaved something like a personal elevator. "Y'all shoulda' told me 'bout this thing."

Denz laughed. "No need fo' Beatrapers to use dis kinda getup. We use dem fo' da big jobs."

Dolly interrupted. "If you both are satisfied and are ready to proceed further, I'd suggest we move along. Miss Sinha will be arriving home within the hour."

"AG, Dolly," Denz said. "Raze, mon, I gonna' get to da airport an' organize da ride. Y'all fin' some way to get deh, an' call me on da way."

Raze nodded to him. "AG, Dolly, bae, let's do this." He pressed on the sticks, levitating up into the dying light of the evening. The machine advanced up the side of the tower. He kept his eyes focused on the top edge of the building as it quickly approached. He didn't dare to look downwards for fear of discovering he suffered from vertigo. As the platform zoomed on and up higher, he found the winds began to buffet at him, tugging wildly at his clothing. Raze sunk deeper into his stance and pushed on. Within minutes, he had reached the top of the tower. He guided the machine over to a flat landing space and set it down.

"Well done, honey," Dolly said as Raze detached himself from the foot brackets.

"Yo, that be fucking crazy," Raze responded as he ventured a look over the side. The ground below leered back up at him when he did.

"The entrance we want is to your left."

Raze spotted what Dolly was referring to. He approached the doorway, and noticed the biometric scanner that secured its locking system. He took out his Q-Hack and placed it against the panel. The machine went to work for a few seconds, but let out a set of negative blips. Its cracking attempt had failed.

"That don' work," Raze quipped.

"Perhaps a more physical attack would be successful," Dolly suggested.

Raze wound up and tried kicking the door, but it was solid steel, and he only succeeded in hurting his ankle. He then scanned around the roof, and spotted what looked like a maintenance shed. Raze opened it up, but, finding there was little of use inside, slammed it shut again.

"This ain't goin' so well so far. Gonna' have t' think o' another way, Dolly, bae."

"I have an idea, but doing so would risk exposing my presence inside the FSA. I'd rather avoid doing that."

"Yo, I'm riskin' myself here doing the death flyin' stuff an' all. Least y'all can do is put yo ass on the line a little."

"You're absolutely right. Can you bring your slate closer to that access panel?"

Raze pulled out the device and did as asked. The display on the access panel began behaving in a strange way, filling with ideographs. Then came a loud clack from behind the door. Dolly's voice chirped, "Done."

"The hell?! What, y'all some kinda' hacker too?"

"I have many skills, honey. Stay alive so you can see them all."

Raze laughed. "Y'all can bet I will."

Raze opened the door and stepped into the room beyond. He took the spiraling set of stairs down to the next level where the path ended with a set of elevator doors.

"Ritika's apartment is Suite 9820. That's only a few floors down from here. This is a maintenance elevator. It travels past all the residential floors."

"Y'all sayin' I gotta' get in there and climb down?"

"That's right."

Raze exhaled, walked over to the doors, and began applying force to pry them open. He pushed his body in to make a wider gap, then looked down. "Fuck! Ain't gonna' be essential gettin' down that."

"I'm sure a strong man like yourself will make short work of it."

"Bitch, don't start fauxsin' me," and he took another look down the shaft. "Shit. Them titties y'all got better be worth all this."

Raze edged his way into the shaft and began clambering along and down the beams within. He found the climb challenging, but nothing too far outside of his comfort zone. Still, it was proving to be slow-going work.

"Yo, Dolly, bae, what this girl look like?"

"You won't have any problems identifying her. She lives by herself."

"What's her name again?"

"Ritika."

Raze screwed his face up. "Don't sound citizen-like."

"It's not. Ritika is from New Delhi."

"That in Canada?"

"New Delhi is in India."

Hearing that, Raze let out a grunt, then a sarcastic snicker.

"Is something wrong?"

"Ain't nothin'. Jus' don' have too many nice opinions o' them kinda' people."

"I'm sure you'd find Ritika different. She's smart and attractive."

Raze shook his head. "Indian bitch an' attractive? That's.. oxy-whatsits..."

"An oxymoron?"

"That's prob'ly the word."

"I think that kind of statement would qualify as being racist."

"It ain't racist. Jus' a preference 's all. Least y'all don' have to worry about me chasin' her tail."

"I guess I should be relieved. Anyhow, you are less than one hundred feet from her floor now. Might I rec-" Suddenly, the line started to fade into static.

Raze tapped his ear once, then a second time. Nothing. "Dolly? Yo, Dolly?"

There was a brief burst of static. "...comms field jamming..." Now, the line went dead completely. Raze figured there must be some security device in the area that was blocking civilian communications.

He cursed, but continued onward. At last, he reached floor ninety-eight. Looking around, he found the air-conditioning shaft access. Damn, another duct he'd have to crawl into. He ensured his equipment was secure, then unhinged the access panel and squeezed inside.

Raze inched forward along the HVAC ducting, trying to stay as silent as possible. He peered through the vents as he passed. The first revealed an outer hallway with elevators—something like an entrance area. He moved on. Another peek, and now Raze saw that he was positioned somewhere above what looked like a living room. Peering further he could make out some swank, modern furnishings. He figured this had to be the place. He checked around the room as best as he could to ensure the coast was clear. Then, with great care, he started removing the vent cover.

As he was about to get it free, he heard a door sliding open. He returned the grate and waited. He heard the sound of steps on tile now, and then something metallic dropping into a glass. Someone was definitely inside. Raze struggled to see much through the grate. He could barely make out the person as they moved. It looked like a woman of slight build. She wore a business suit and a black turban. He was confused by the direction she had come in from, so he double-checked his orientation. No, he had correctly guessed where the main doors were. This woman had entered from the balcony area. Maybe she had been home a while already. Raze dismissed any further distracting thoughts. He wanted to focus on how he would get into the room and pacify this woman before she could run or call for help. He reached down to his holster for his tranquilizer pistol, then loaded a dart. He heard sounds of an entertainment system running now, then a microwave starting up. Raze figured the woman must have her attention diverted. He removed the grate, then dropped to the floor as silent as a shadow.

He could now see where the woman had come from. The balcony area had a large and private landing station. On the platform, a white Mercedes S-500V was recharging. He looked down the hallway to the galley kitchen. Beyond that, he could see entrances to what appeared to be a bedroom and a bathroom. There was a flash of motion from that direction as the woman crossed the hall. Raze pressed himself against the wall to avoid detection. Dark skin—he figured she had to be the target, but, to be certain, Raze checked the entryway markings. Sure enough, he was in Suite 9820. There was another beep from the kitchen. Raze got his pistol ready and hid. He let the woman pass by him as she walked back toward the living room. She was now in her pajamas with her long, flowing black hair down. She was carrying a bowl of something that smelt spicy. He followed as she moved towards the large monitor in the main living area, and watched her put the bowl on her dining table. Then, once at a good distance, he took aim at the woman's back.

As he was about to pull the trigger, the woman spoke. "Planning to kill me?"

Raze halted. The woman turned around and looked him in the eye. Her voice and features were startlingly softer than what he was expecting. Her face had an almost cherub-like quality to it, with large, soft eyes, a dainty nose, and plump cheeks. He found something about her demeanor disarming too. It was almost noble and saintly, like her entire form was encircled by a halo of tranquility.

Ritika crossed her arms, smiled, and raised an eyebrow. "I guess not. Not with that kind of gun."

Raze broke his freeze and shrugged. "Jus' need to put y'all out."

"Oh, really?"

"It's quick an' safe, jus' like sleepin'."

"I see."

"Y'all don' like it, should get better security."

Ritika sighed. "I guess 'y'all' right. Silly me. Well, let's get it over with then."

Raze tilted his head. "Sorry 'bout this."

He fired the weapon, striking Ritika in the shoulder. She looked at the dart, then back to Raze. After a second had passed, she pulled the dart out of her shoulder and tossed it aside. Raze did a double-take at the gun, then back to Ritika. She shook her head, then advanced on Raze, face as fierce as a lion.

Raze shifted to his fighting stance and threw a punch. Ritika slipped the move, then slammed her palm into Raze's chest. The blow sent him flying off his feet and into the bookshelf behind him. As he stood back up, he shook his head and brushed off the mess of broken wood and books. He was astonished by what had just happened. This woman had to be around one hundred and twenty pounds, yet she had hit him as hard as a train.

Ritika moved in again. Raze decided to change strategies. This time, he ducked under her arm as she punched, wrapping his own arms behind her knees. Then, pulling towards himself and upwards, he succeeded in taking her off her feet and dropping her to the floor. He scrambled for something to grapple, and managed to set up an arm bar. But, as he began to apply pressure, Ritika simply pulled her arm free from his grip. He cursed, realizing that wrestling her was going to be as futile as wrestling a machine. He quickly got to his feet and launched a push kick into Ritika's stomach. This move had some success, knocking her backwards onto her coffee table. The table cracked, Raze laughed, and Ritika gave him a foul look. She got up, and kicked Raze in the crotch. She then grabbed him by the throat and groin, picked him up over her head, and threw him into the main monitor in the living room. Sparks shot out in all directions from the wrecked device. Raze shook himself, got back his senses, then glared at her.

For the next couple of minutes they exchanged holds, throws, blows, and kicks. Neither side wanted to yield, but, as the fight dragged on, it was clear to them both that Ritika was gaining the upper hand. Raze was running out of steam, but she still looked fresh and unfazed. He needed to find a solution before she got the better of him. So, the next time she grabbed him, he pulled out a tranquilizer dart and jabbed it into her. She released him, but kept on the attack. He tried again with another dart.

This now being the only viable option he could think of, he continued attacking with the darts. He stabbed her as often as he could, hoping there would eventually be some effect. And, slowly but surely, the serum began to influence her. The last time she got to her feet, she looked dazed. Raze stepped behind her, slipped on a rear naked choke, and tried putting her to sleep. Ritika fought back, but the tranquilizers had taken their toll. As Raze kept the hold on, she slipped into unconsciousness.

He released her and slumped backwards, lungs gasping for air. He checked the pain in his ribs. With any luck, it was only bruising and nothing was fractured. After catching his breath, he got to his feet, took out his restraints, and tied her up. He then went to her bedroom to find some clothes for her, and picked out some athletic wear. On her dresser, he spotted some traditional-looking items: a ceremonial dagger and the cloth for her turban. He figured she wore these items often and took them too.

Raze packed Ritika and the other items into her Mercedes, then started the machine up. After one final check, he plotted a course for O'Hare Airport. He then began piloting the vehicle, launching it off the balcony and into the skies.

22. An Appetite

Boyd knocked back the rest of his pint, then plonked the glass on the bar. The alcohol was beginning to buzz him now. Boyd enjoyed the feeling, and continued to half-listen to the surrounding conversation. The boys were still rambling about the executions of the Constitutional Terrorists. Then the topic switched to the Mars mission. The costs of setting up the colony. How the EU, China and other nations had already settled Mars years ago. How the FSA should focus on catching up with the Mars-race. How the FSA shouldn't bother scrapping with Texas and California. Dull.

"'Scuse me, boys," he said as he got to his feet. "I'm feeling the first call of nature."

This evoked laughter from the others. He grinned and returned their praise with a hand signal, then moved to the men's room.

He found a urinal, unzipped, and started to relieve himself. As he did so, he heard a pinging sound from his slate. He groaned, then checked the slate for messages. The latest one was from Laura: "Coming home anytime soon?"

He gave a dismissive chuckle, finished pissing, and zipped up. As he left the restroom, he replaced the slate into his pocket, fingers brushing Fleurine's card as he did so. Boyd felt it, but ignored the card. Then, he started thinking about it. Then, he ignored it again.

He told himself to forget about Fleurine, that he shouldn't even consider dotting her ID. That bitch was a trap any fool could see coming a mile away. Then again, he thought, knowing that, why not take the opportunity anyway? Yulov's pawn or not, what could she really do to him? He could meet with her, throw her onto a bed, try out her pussy to his satisfaction, then get on with his life. The way she had carried on at the party—taunting him—she deserved to be dealt a lesson like that. For all he knew, Gordon had been fucking her the last few months anyway. If Gordon could get away with it, why shouldn't he have some fun too?

He glanced at the bar where the others were talking. He checked around for an alcove or secluded spot, and noticed an area that looked suitable over in the corner. He moved in, checked for cameras, then took out Fleurine's card and placed it against his slate. The details for her dot transferred to the device. He made another quick check to ensure no one was looking. Then, he tapped the connect icon.

A series of tones. Connecting buzzes. Then, the young Frenchwoman answered, voice only.

"Yes?"

Boyd hesitated. "It's me."

There was a moment's silence from Fleurine. Then, "So what."

He straightened up in response to her rudeness. "What do you mean, so what?"

Fleurine laughed. "You just said it was you, like that's supposed to mean something to me."

Boyd kept his cool, doing his best to put aside her affront. "Well, you gave me your card and told me to call you."

He heard the sound of her drawing breath, like she was taking a drag on a cigarette. Then, he heard her exhale.

"Did I?" she said. "Oh, so nice of you to call me then."

He was at a loss for words.

"... So...what do we do now?"

Another sound of drawing, then exhaling. "Are we supposed to be doing something?"

"...Well...I thought that...you know..."

"What, exactly?"

Boyd didn't answer. He could feel his ulcer starting to act up. His face became flush. "...I don't need this shit. Screw you. Go back to Yulov and have fun sucking him off."

"Screw you. Go home and have fun fucking your wife."

She ended the connection. Boyd pounded the wall. He stepped back, took a deep breath, and tried to calm down. Just a cocktease after all. She was probably laughing to herself about that conversation. He should have known better. Fuck it, he thought, get another drink, relax with the boys, and chalk it up to experience.

He went back to the bar and ordered another lager. While imbibing it, he tried to rejoin the conversation with the boys. They talked about the Constitutional Terrorists, the execution. Time passed, but it became clear to Boyd that talking wasn't proving enough of a distraction. His mind kept rerunning Fleurine's voice and their brief conversation. Then, came the memory of those marine-colored eyes, her face. Now, he couldn't get the sound of her taunting laugh out of his head. Next, the memory of that scent around her. Then, her naked body, standing before him just as he had seen it yesterday. He finally admitted it to himself: he wanted her.

The boys kept waffling. Boyd excused himself again and went back to the corner. He took out his slate, then dotted Fleurine again. The connection rang out. He waited a second, then tried again. More connecting blips.

She answered. "*Putain de connard*. Stop calling me."

"Don't hang up. Hey, look...I'm sorry...sorry for what I said. It was out of line."

She remained silent. He listened to her breathing for a moment, then continued, "I'm just confused...a little drunk..."

"...You're making that my problem?"

"...No...I don't know. I just thought..."

"Thought what?"

"...You know...that we had a 'connection'..."

She scoffed. "I thought you said I was mistaken about our connection."

"...I...I'm so not sure..."

She laughed. "Richard, do you honestly believe a young woman like me would be interested in a fat old man like you?"

He felt the sting of her words, but he inhaled, swallowed his pride, then answered, "...I...I was just hoping there would be a chance."

The line was silent again.

He kept his mouth shut and waited for her to speak. After what seemed like an eternity, she said, "I don't know now. Maybe..."

He felt his mood lift. "Oh, yeah?"

She said nothing.

"Well, if there might be a chance...what would this guy have to do to seal the deal?"

Another long pause. Then, "Does he know the Marriott in Arlington?"

"...Yes, he does."

Another sound of her dragging on a cigarette and exhaling. Then, "Twenty minutes. If he is game..."

Boyd looked over at the bar where the boys were still talking. He mentally prepared an excuse to give to them. "Yes, he's game. Should he bring anything with him?"

A sigh on the line, then, "Some chocolate. Champagne. An appetite."

His eyebrows rose. "Appetite for what?"

More silence. Then, "You know what." The connection ended.

His pulse began to thump faster. He started moving with purpose now, grabbing his jacket from the stool, waving to the boys as he passed.

"Laura's on my ass about getting home."

A laugh and cheer from the boys. He gave a final gesture to them, then he was off. He stepped out into the evening air. There was no time to waste. Scanning about, he hailed the first taxi that he saw.

23. Not A Problem

Raze piloted the Mercedes to the hangar at O'Hare Airport as Denz had directed. Then, he performed a vertical landing just outside. Ritika was already stirring in the back. He jumped out of his seat and headed around to the rear door while Denz began to shuffle up from the hangar. In the bay behind him, Raze spotted the outline of something large and black. It was monocoque with swept back wings, looking like a mechanical animal that was crouched and at the ready. Raze had never seen a plane that looked like this before.

Denz came within earshot distance. "Dat de girl?" he asked.

Raze pulled Ritika from the back seat, cradling her in his arms.

Denz took a look at her, then mused, "Dang. She lookin' a little whelfer than I expect." He then spotted Raze's face. "Shit, sib. Y'all look like ya'll done twen'y rounds wit' a prize fighter."

Raze shook his head, then nodded to Ritika. "Bitch can hit."

Denz gave him an incredulous look, noting Ritika's spindly arms. He burst into laughter, but soon stopped when he saw the seriousness in Raze's eyes. "Fo' real?"

Raze didn't want to bother explaining. "That the plane?" he asked, nodding to the hangar.

"Sure is, mon. Still waitin' fo' the pilot tho'."

Denz nabbed Raze and Ritika's gear from the back seat of the Mercedes. Together, they headed into the hangar. "Short notice makin' it hard t' find the right people t' fly, mon."

Raze looked more urgent as he saw Ritika was coming to. "Move. We needin' some place to keep this bitch restrained."

"There be a place in the hold."

They scrambled up the cargo ramp and into the belly of the machine. The cargo bay area was almost completely empty, save for a couple of X-Runner electric bikes that had been locked to the wall. Raze figured the Doughboys used them for courier jobs and getaways.

Denz whistled to get Raze's attention, then he indicated the crane hook in the center of the cargo space and activated its lowering lever. Once the hook had lowered far enough, Raze secured Ritika's arms to it. By now, she was half-conscious and began to struggle. She glared at her captors and yelled profanities.

"Chill, slimaz. We not gonna' mess with yo ladyness," Denz began, walking towards her with hands up. "Dis here be client order, an' we not the type to play with da goods."

Ritika looked at the Jamaican man, and noted he had made the mistake of getting too close to her. In a flash, she had pulled her knees to her chest and kicked at him. Denz was knocked across the cargo hold by the blow. He slammed into the wall, then fell onto his face and started groaning.

"Told y'all," Raze laughed.

Then, Raze noticed Ritika had begun to struggle at her bonds. There was an audible creaking sound as the cording protested under the force she was applying to it. Raze eased back a step, fearing the cords would snap and she would break free to attack him again. But, the cording was holding fast, and he breathed a sigh of relief.

Denz shook his head to gain his senses. Then, he slowly tested getting to his feet. Once up, he checked his ribs and then took another step towards Ritika. "No bitch kick like dat. Da fuck y'all be?"

Ritika glared at him for a moment. Then, she lowered her head and began to laugh.

"Yeah, y'all a funny bitch," Denz said, unamused. "Screw dis. I'ma keep findin' a pilot."

"And just where are you two gentlemen planning on taking me tonight?" Ritika queried in a polite voice.

Raze scoffed. "Oh, so now y'all askin' us questions?"

She shrugged. "It certainly appears that way."

"Well, y'all can draz on, bitch. Jus' be knowin it somewhere we makin' class talent fo' deliverin' dem buns y'all got. So, quit thinkin' YOAT here 'cuz the boys are runnin' this show. An' that's how it be." Raze signaled a high-five to Denz. They clasped hands in a brotherly gesture.

Ritika watched on, then her forehead wrinkled in confusion. "Do either of you speak English?"

Denz just shook his head at her back talk. "Let's gag da bitch." He nodded to Raze to signal go, then shot in and grabbed Ritika's legs while Raze took out a rag and started stuffing it into her mouth. Ritika protested that the boys were making a huge mistake, that they would pay for what they were doing. She summoned her strength again, lifting Denz off the ground as he struggled to restrain her legs. Raze intervened and helped him get away before she could strike him again. They then stood at a safe distance and watched on as Ritika kicked at them with vicious intent.

Denz and Raze exchanged looks. Then, Denz unfolded his slate to contact his crew. "Dis crazy bitch better be wort' it, sib."

Raze nodded in acknowledgment. "I'ma call my girl," he said.

Raze moved into the cabin area and, touching his communicator, gave Dolly a dot. Dolly picked up almost immediately. "Hi, honey."

"Hey, my girl. We got her."

"You have her. That's wonderful. I knew you could do it."

Raze laughed. "Yeah, it be hap an' all, my whelf, but we got a snag."

"Oh?"

"We don't got no pilot."

"No pilot? That's not a problem. I know how to fly a plane."

Raze looked confused. "Uh.. okay.. That's AG 'n all, but y'all in Texas."

"That hardly poses a problem. I am capable of flying your plane by remote."

Raze looked uneasy. "Y'all sure?"

"Yes, of course. That is, if Denz will let me."

Raze was dubious about that. "Lemme check with the man." He darted back to the cargo bay and waved Denz into the cockpit. "My girl sayin' she can pilot this rig by remote from Texas."

Denz's face turned a shade paler. "By remote? De fuck, mon. Dis t'ing be a stealt' plane for smugglin' big time shit. It wort' millions to da Doughboys. She fuck it up, I'm ded."

"She fuck it up, I'm dead too."

Denz couldn't argue with that. He thought for a second, then made a call on his slate. "Fo'geddit, mon. I got us a boy to fly. Yeah, AG, an' y'all tell him gonna' bring some big talent fo' dis deal." He ended the call. "Dolly, y'all sure 'bout flyin' dis t'ing?"

"Don't worry, Denz. I'm highly competent. Besides, the Repulic of Texas will gladly cover any losses to the Doughboys. Raze, honey, can you plug me into the piloting port?"

Raze searched for the remote panel, found it, and inserted his slate. Dolly now mentally extended her nervous system into the craft, sensing the aviation systems that were available throughout. The cockpit instrumentation began to flicker to life. Dolly tried the flaps on the wings. Then, there was a whine as she started firing up the turbines, which were now like extensions of her own person.

"Shit," Denz said, hearing the engines fire. "Lookin' like she real."

Raze shrugged. "Sweet. Let's roll."

Raze escorted Denz to the back ramp, then clasped hands with him.

"Y'all stay safe, mon."

"Same. See y'all in Texas."

Denz then closed the cargo hatch. Raze passed behind Ritika, giving her a firm slap on the ass as he went by. "Keep them buns tight, bitch. We AG."

Ritika glowered.

Denz watched on as Dolly gave her engines some thrust, turned the nose towards the hangar doors, and started to taxi.

Dolly contacted the tower for clearance and, after receiving the go ahead, she moved to the runway. After lining up, she gave her engines full throttle. She launched ahead and, a few moments later, was in the air and speeding towards Texas with her cargo safely onboard.

24. Radio Station

Ben Rollins adjusted his position in his wheelchair, then cleared his throat. Richards rapped her fingers against the top of her oak desk. Carla inspected the chambers of her Colt for the fifth time. There was nothing any of them could do now, except wait.

The afternoon Texan sun streamed in from the office window facing the street. It was a dull, orange light that blanketed the worn carpet in the room like a felt covering, but gave little illumination.

Richards noted that the natural light was fading now. She pressed the switch to turn on the office lights and sighed. The wall had retracted to display an enormous monitor, but the display was still dead. It sat there like a rectangular slab of dull charcoal.

"Got the time?" Richards asked, finally.

Ben turned his wrist to check the time on his trusted, stainless steel Marathon JSAR. "Been about three hours since she last checked in."

Richards frowned, then sighed again.

Then, there was a tone from the monitor. The three Texans looked up to the display in eager anticipation. Dolly appeared.

"Apologies for being so late, Madam President, Carla, and Ben. There's been a slight change in plans. I've had to take over piloting controls for the plane transporting our cargo. Don't worry, I can confirm that I am in possession of both Raze and Ritika Sinha. We are in the air and on the way as I speak. So far, I haven't encountered any resistance from the FSA, nor do I detect any aircraft pursuing us. It seems Ritika's kidnapping has gone undetected. The aircraft I'm piloting has stealth capabilities. Because of that, I think it'll be difficult for the FSA to track us down, even when they do discover she's missing. Still, I'm assuming we will encounter some pushback before we reach Texas. I will keep you up-to-date on our progress."

It was only a few seconds after she had stopped speaking that Dolly realized Richards and the others weren't responding. They sat there, staring at her.

Ben was casting an evaluating eye over her while sitting back in his wheelchair. Richards' face looked mortified, as did Carla's.

Dolly tilted her head. "Is something wrong?"

Ben made a polite cough. Carla let out a quick giggle. Darlene looked at Dolly curiously. "Honey, why in the world do you look...'enhanced' in places? And wut are you wearin'?"

Dolly looked down at herself. She saw her new, enlarged cleavage in her tight-fitting tank top, her yoga pants, and the glistening beads of sweat rolling over her skin. "This is swexy," she explained.

"Hell, I like it," Ben nodded. Carla elbowed his ribs.

Richards was bemused. "It's sure a' somethin' all right. But, why on earth...?"

"My apologies. I forgot to mention I am in a relationship with our contractor, Raze."

"You wut now?"

"During our initial contact, Raze was forthcoming about his interest in me. I am in the process of adapting myself to become more like the woman he is seeking."

"Oh, good lordy, no."

"He is a novel problem, though. It seems he is preoccupied with highly objectified and sexualized images of women. I suspect it's the result of some developmental issue during his youth."

Ben couldn't hold his laughter back any further. Carla giggled some more too. "He sounds pretty typical to me, Dolly."

"Hey," Ben protested, between fits.

Richards caught hold of the smirk that was forming on her face and tried to remain serious. "Dolly, girl, y'all sure everything's okay? Y'all not fragmenting again? Poppin' any capacitors? Nothin' like that?"

"All perfect, Madam President."

"Y'all gonna' tell me if you're having psychological-like issues?"

"Of course."

"Any feelin' issues?"

"I don't have feelings, only strategies."

"...I see," said Richards, suddenly remembering how Dolly operated. "So this is just part of your adaptation whatsits?"

Dolly turned her eyes up to the right and put her finger on her chin as she considered the question. "Yes..I think so.."

Hearing the confusion in Dolly's voice, Richards let her face fall forwards into her hands. "Good Lord, bury me now." She sighed. "Y'all smarter than a hooty owl, Dolly, but I tell ya', y'all gonna end up outsmartin' yourself again too, just like last time. I can see it right now."

Carla nudged her. "Oh, don't reset her. This is getting interesting. I have to see where it ends." Ben and Carla exchanged looks, which started their laughing fits again.

Richards shrugged. "Okay, I'm gonna' trust y'all still got your senses."

"Thank you, Madam President."

"Y'all doin' an amazing job, Dolly. I'm so proud I wanna'cry. Is there anything y'all need from us?"

Dolly pondered. "If it's not too much trouble, I'd ask for you all to stay at the Capitol until I have our cargo across the border. I should be fine, but, if anything goes wrong, Raze and Ritika might need your help."

"They'll have everything we've got to help with, Dolly. But- and I just have to give you some advice lady-to-lady-when it comes to boys, don't go too fast. Play it slow, an' don't go showin' off too much too early, Otherwise, they gonna start callin' y'all 'radio station.'"

"Radio station...?" Dolly mulled over the curious choice of words. "Oh, I get it. Because anybody can pick me up?"

"Now yur learnin'."

"I see. I will take that advice. Thank you, Madam President."

"Thank you, Dolly."

The screen went blank as the call ended.

25. Elation

Boyd cupped his hands under the stream of hot tap water. He splashed it on his cheeks, then looked at himself in the mirror. He almost didn't recognize the face with the receding hairline that was staring back at him because, for once, that face had a smile on it. It was a smile that expressed his genuine, inner sense of pleasure – rapture, even. He was so happy that his brain had become little more than a numb, zen-like sponge that didn't want to process any further thoughts. All it wanted to do was enjoy what it was experiencing. At the corner of the mirror, Boyd spotted Fleurine. She was naked, reclining on the bed and taking a drag on her pearl-colored Zigette. She spotted Boyd watching her, narrowed her eyes, and gave him a wolf-like smile.

Boyd couldn't believe the antics that had unfolded after he'd stepped into the hotel room. This girl didn't just have sex, she had *crazy* sex. What was more, she didn't only have sex in a bed, she had it everywhere—in the shower, against the walls. The entire room looked like the aftermath of a tornado. The sheer sense of release the sex had given him was beyond compare. It was as though years of frustration had been torn from his body and tossed aside. To Boyd, sex with her had been nothing like sex with other women. It had been especially unlike sex with his conceited wife, who always behaved as though her shriveled prune was some special treat that a man should beg for. Fleurine, on the other hand, had been inviting, as well as indifferent to how much playtime he wanted. He concluded one thing: sex with this woman was how sex was supposed to be.

A warm, giddy-like sensation brewed up deep from within him. He smiled at Fleurine and laughed—a genuine laugh, like he hadn't done in years, his belly rippling. Fleurine smiled, took another drag at her Zigette, then exhaled the fumes from her nostrils like a resting dragon.

Boyd toweled his face, stepped out of the bathroom, and nodded at her.

"That was..." he started laughing, realizing he still couldn't summon the words.

Fleurine turned her eyes up, bored. "I know."

He had to take a few steps around the room to orient himself. "You sure know how to please a guy."

A plume of smoke in response. Then, "Would you like a topper?"

Boyd looked confused. "Topper?"

Fleurine rolled over so she could reach her handbag on the bedside table. She put down her Zigette, put her hand into her handbag, and took out a plastic bag filled with glittering white powder. She jiggled the bag at him and smiled.

He shook his head, half laughing. "Oh no, I don't do stuff like that."

She tilted her head. "It's just some Elation. It's huge in Russia right now."

He scoffed. "I'm not into snorting things from Russia, sweetie."

"Oh?" she asked. "Not even when it's served on a French platter?" She lay back on the bed, then sprinkled the narcotic across her chest. It settled like a powdered frosting on top of her pale skin. She raised an eyebrow at him.

Boyd's eyes popped out of his head. He laughed. He knew he shouldn't touch what she was offering, but he was in such a good mood that he figured once wouldn't kill him. He lined his nose to her breasts and snorted it.

Almost immediately, the Elation delivered a powerful kick to his mind. It was like a fire had started burning inside his head. His eyes widened and he looked to Fleurine, mouth agape. Suddenly, all the colors in the room started to become more intense. Whites were becoming brighter, and even black shapes seemed to have sparkles twinkling inside them. Fleurine was glittering too. A golden halo was beginning to form around her outline, as though she was transforming into some heavenly goddess right before his eyes.

"Fuck!" he exclaimed. Then, he started laughing. "Oh, fuck!"

Now, Fleurine started sprinkling powder across Boyd's chest. She snorted her line, then rolled back onto the bed and began to giggle too.

He flopped onto the bed beside her. The two of them were in rapture, looking at their hands, the lights, the room around them. Boyd turned to Fleurine.

"Dear God," he said, fighting for breath between laughs.

Fleurine looked at him. "It changes words too. It makes all words sound nice." She smiled. "Go on, try to say something nasty to me."

He giggled, shrugged. "Okay." He thought a moment. "You're a crazy bitch!"

She stared at him for a second, then burst into laughter. He was amused by this response.

"Okay. My turn," she managed as she was cracking up. She turned to him, put on an overly dramatic angry face. "You are an ugly, fat asshole!"

He heard the words. He knew they should be interpreted as an insult, but, for some reason, he exploded with laughter. It was as though what should be insulting did nothing but tickle his funny bone. He couldn't even attempt to feel upset about what she'd said.

For a few minutes, the two of them just sat back, staring at the ceiling. Then, Fleurine sat up and reached for her slate.

"You have to try it with music. Watch what happens!" she said, enthusiastically.

"Music?" Boyd laughed. "What song?"

"The Sugar-Sugar song," she explained. "I don't know who sings it, but it's one we listen to all the time!"

"Who's we?" he asked. But, before she could answer, the music started up. As the first few notes hit his ears, Boyd began to feel light and airy. Seconds later, he began to feel like he was flying. He made use of the feeling to get up, and go over to get more champagne. He danced, feeling so groovy that he started shaking his rear as he moved. "Another?" he asked, turning to Fleurine and holding out his glass.

She nodded. "Oh, yes, please, sir!" She sat up and saluted him.

He tried to pour the champagne, but as soon as he started, he realized it was almost impossible for him to do so. It was as though the music had begun to overpower his senses. Everything he looked at was getting separated into trailing swirls of different colors. Pouring the champagne was now like watching a slow-motion, technicolor waterfall. He watched the fluid flow from the bottle, sail downward, and hit the bottom of the glass, splashing around like glittering gems as it did so.

Eventually, the glitter and sparkle grew so intense that he couldn't see the glasses anymore. He ended up just pouring the champagne everywhere, hoping some of it went into the glasses. Fleurine found this beyond amusing. She was laughing as though she was watching a slapstick cartoon as she started bouncing on the bed to the music.

Then, a new tone sounded. It came from Boyd's slate, which was sitting on the table, but all he could hear was a beautiful, musical note streaming in from the surrounding multi-colored cosmos.

He looked at Fleurine, and made an expression of mock curiosity. He put his arms out, making swimming motions like he was an underwater diver as he started to search for the source of the sound. She thought this was hilarious. He eventually spotted his slate, picked it up, and answered it.

"Yes, you have reached the transcendental symbol of the universe known as Boyd. How can I help you?"

"Richard, it's John!" said Ellis. His voice sounded like he had just pissed himself. "The whole fucking thing is coming apart!"

Boyd laughed at hearing these funny words from Ellis. "Ellis! That sounds wonderful!"

"What?! What the fuck are you talking about? Richard, you've got to get back here."

Boyd recognized that Ellis was being serious, but he couldn't return the mood. The Elation had him too buzzed.

"Wait one minute," he said, trying to control his intonation. He waved to Fleurine to turn the music down, and tried to remember what his voice normally sounded like. "Slow down, Ellis. What's going on?"

"She's been kidnapped!"

"Kidnapped?!" He was surprised he delivered that response so convincingly. "Who?"

"Raymond-Kennel's CTO. We're fucked if we can't find her. White's been called, and we're going back to the Situation Room. You've got to get here."

Boyd looked at the clock. "Right now? What do you need *me* for?"

"Just get here. For fuck sake, Richard, this is as bad as it gets."

The call ended. Boyd put the slate down, then turned to face Fleurine.

"That sounded serious," she said, and they both broke out laughing for a few seconds.

Boyd tried hard to control his mood now. He needed to get back to normal, quickly.

"I gotta' get outta' here," he laughed. "Back to the Hill. Fuck!"

He tried to think, and started searching around for his clothes, but it was like he now had eight eyes. He kept seeing four of everything, and, each time he reached for something, he missed it.

Fleurine got up from the bed, watching Boyd struggle to get his things together. She found his attempts to put his clothes on absurdly funny, and clapped and cheered like a child every time he fell over or hurt himself.

After a lengthy struggle with his visual and motor functions, he succeeded in getting dressed. He went into the bathroom to check his eyes. His pupils were huge, but he hoped that was just part of the hallucinations he was experiencing. "Oh, fuck. I'm in no condition to do this."

"You're baked, baby!" was all the help Fleurine could give.

He battled to get to the door. He started to open it and was about to leave, but then he remembered his slate. He dove back in to pick it up, then pointed to Fleurine.

"Will I see you again?"

She put her palms out while giving him a big smile. "Maybe."

He straightened up, trying to contain his overwhelming feelings of joy. He then strode to the door, opened it, turned to accept a last wink from Fleurine, and stepped out. The door closed with a thud behind him.

As soon as he was gone, Fleurine laughed to herself. She fell back on the bed, turned to the corner of the ceiling, and then the nearby bedside table. She snapped her fingers.

The spy cams located in these spots decloaked. Then, they started hovering towards her outstretched palm.

26. Amber And White

After some time, Raze ventured back into the cargo hold to check on his captive. To his relief, Ritika hadn't broken free. She was still there, hanging from the hook. She glared at him as he stepped into the room. He put his hands up, and began inching towards her.

"Chill, bitch. Y'all stay hap an' I'll take out the gag. AG?"

She did nothing. He locked eyes with her, peered into them, and scanned to determine her intent. He edged forward again, extending his hand. Then, like a cautious animal, he removed the gag from her mouth. She remained silent, letting her foul look communicate her thoughts to him.

Raze stepped back to ensure she couldn't launch any surprise kicks at him as he spoke. "Now we all can be friendly-like." He tossed the rag away, sat down against the wall, and watched her. He smiled, pulled out a VitaSnack that Denz had left in the cockpit, and began chewing on it. It was a little stale, but still better than the Praedo rubbish he was used to eating.

"Where are you taking me?" Ritika asked in a calm, but still authoritative voice.

"Hey, I'ma ask the questions here, bitch."

"Call me bitch again, and I'll punch you so hard your nose will go out the back of your skull."

Raze gave a wide-eyed smile, a mocking nod of approval. "AG. I hear y'all. Might be a little hard to do that when y'all tied up tho'."

Ritika scoffed at this remark, then gave a bored look towards the cargo bay roof.

He continued, "If y'all wanna' know, we going to Texas."

"...Texas?"

"Heard right. People there payin' big talent fo' y'all."

She laughed. "Big 'talent', you say. What makes you think we'll get there, precisely?"

He gave her a confused look, pointing around the interior of the cargo bay. "Uh, sorry to break it to y'all, lil' whelf-a-be, but we already on the way."

She shrugged. "Very well then. I guess there is only one other question that I have to ask you."

"Oh? What's that?"

"Are you insane?"

He laughed. "Y'all a funny bitch." Then he dropped his smile and glared at her. "Do I look insane?"

"No," she scoffed. "If anything, you look more stupid than insane, but I guess that is beside the point, considering stupidity is going to prove just as fatal in this instance anyway." Raze dismissed her with a shake of his head, but she continued, "You and your partner have effectively killed us both. If you think M3Raymond-Kennel is going to let me be taken out of the FSA, you are sorely mistaken. They will call the White Administration and advise them to shoot this plane down before we cross the border. You won't be getting fame, glory, or money. You and I will both be blasted from the skies and have our ashes scattered across the state in an aerial cremation."

"Yeah, don't think so. See, I know y'all an elite bi-" He noticed her eyes start to glare as the word formed on his lips, then decided he'd play nice. "-lady, an' I know how y'all think on yo' side o' the wall. Even if they find us, come after us, ain't no way they shootin' us down. Y'all a precious 'lil princess. No way they kill y'all like they would one of me."

Ritika's mouth dropped open in disbelief. Then, she laughed, turned away, and shook her head. "Listen, you poor, deluded little man, I don't know what kind of obtuse socio-political ethos you live by or pretend to understand, but you need to believe me when I tell you this: they will kill me, just as readily as they will kill you."

Raze dismissed her with a wave. "Think I'ma get fauxed by that draz, y'all stupid."

"I can assure you that is what they will do. You need to turn this plane around immediately and surrender to the authorities."

"Not happenin'." He then looked up. "Dolly? How far away are we?"

A chime sounded from the cargo bay speaker system. "If we continue maintaining stealth speed, we'll be touching down in Austin in approximately two hours."

As she heard Dolly's voice, Ritika's ears pricked up. She looked in the direction of the speaker system. "Just a moment. Did you say 'Dolly'?"

"Yes."

"As in *Dolly*, Dolly."

"Yes."

"You're *the* Dolly? From the University of Austin, Texas?"

"That's right. Hello, Ritika. I'm so happy you remember me."

Raze looked confused. He stood up and started waving his hands. "Whoa whoa, the fuck? Yo, hang on jus' a minute here. Y'all know one another?"

"Yes, we do," answered Dolly.

Ritika narrowed her eyes with suspicion. "Well, maybe. If she really is the Dolly I know, then perhaps she can tell me what we talked about the last time we met, and where that meeting was."

"That's easy, Ritika. We last met virtually on campus at MIT during your undergraduate studies. We were talking about your life growing up in New Delhi, how your family gave you the nickname Harshini. You also taught me one of your favorite quotes from Guru Gobind Sing. I think the one which most readily applies to our present predicament would be: 'When all efforts to restore peace prove useless and no words avail, lawful is the flash of steel. It is right to draw the sword.'"

Ritika laughed. "It really is you. I don't believe it. Is Doctor Richards with you?"

"I'm afraid Doctor Richards passed away some years ago, Ritika."

"I'm sorry to hear that."

"I'm sorry too, Ritika, especially for resorting to these extreme circumstances. But, I knew of no other way we'd be able to talk like this."

Raze was still confused. "Now jus' hold on. Time out! The fuck is this? An' what's with the University of Texas? MIT? Dolly, y'all be a street bitch inna' past, right?"

"Raze, honey, maybe it's best if you gave Ritika and I some time to talk about things. Under these circumstances, I think she would find it easier to talk with another woman. I can also explain why we're bringing her to Texas. In the meantime, would you mind leaving us alone?"

"Alone?"

"Yes. Why don't you go into the cockpit. I have something interesting to show you."

Raze looked dubious. He eyed the speaker system, then Ritika. "Yeah, AG. I can' talk no sense to her anyways."

Raze got up, turned to the exit, and walked towards the cockpit. He slammed the metallic door that separated the two spaces closed. Then, he fell into the co-pilot's seat and sighed.

He didn't know what to think about everything he had just heard, deciding instead that it would be better for him to just put the two women out of his mind for the time being.

Looking out of the cockpit window, he amused himself by watching the sparse and scattered lights of civilization twinkle away along the surrounding horizon. He noted one particularly bright glowing patch of amber and white. He wondered if that was the city he and Phoebe had visited all those years back, the one with the dead president of the old America.

He couldn't remember the name of that city now, but figured that probably didn't matter much anyway. The city most likely didn't exist anymore—or, if it did, it would have to be a shadow of its former self. He recalled how so many cities across the United States had collapsed after the Zero-Day. He remembered it all, crystal-clear. Raze, like anyone else who had survived the chaos, never forgot what it was like to wake one day and find their whole world on fire.

It took months for order to be restored. Even after the FSA had risen from the embers of the former government, people knew things could never go back to normal. Big cities, the areas that produced the most economic value to the country, were rescued from total anarchy through martial law. Rural areas of the country, on the other hand, had no such help. Left abandoned, great stretches of the countryside fell into utter lawlessness. Some patches became the crossroads for bloody tug-of-wars between rival warlord syndicates. The United Militia of Christ were one of the more infamous. Loosely organized, but heavily armed, their theocratic approach to social order subsumed the lives of those in every town under their control. They'd treat women as property and kill homosexuals. They were also White Supremacists. That final point alone made Raze hope he'd never come face-to-face with any of them.

Thinking of the UMC, Raze checked the plane's location on the display. As he did so, it dawned on him this was actually the furthest he'd ever been from Chicago in his entire life. So much for that smart-ass Snubbs saying he wouldn't make it across UMC-controlled Illinois, he thought. Only yesterday, that asshole Snubbs was laughing at Raze's ideas. Now, he was roadkill, while Raze was well on his way to Texas. Funny how things had turned out.

Just then, a ping sounded from the console, indicating that Raze's slate had received a message. He tapped on the panel to project the message onto the windscreen HUD. It was from Dolly: another fine photo, looking hotter and swexier than her last one. Raze nodded his approval.

27. Needle In A Haystack

"So, let me see if I understand this as well as I think I do." White put the tips of his fingers together in a steeple. Then, he touched them against his lips and made a thoughtful expression. No one else in the Situation Room dared to move, save for M3Raymond-Kennel's CEO, Bryce Vaughn. His holographic projection could now be heard clearing its throat amid the silence.

Boyd shot a look at General Ellis, noting the dire look of concern on his face, and how cartoon-like it appeared to him. Boyd tried not to smile, but not smiling was proving hard for him right now. The Elation was still working away in his system, filling the surrounding space with color and joy, and making him feel pleasantly detached from the grim pall around him. He cast his eyes down, tried to ignore how great he felt.

White continued speaking to Vaughn, "You are our main military contractor. We use your machinery, weapons, and other equipment at all of our facilities. Our main assault force is comprised of some eighteen percent-"

"-eighty percent, Mister President," General Ellis interjected, making an involuntary shift of discomfort as he spoke.

White's eyes shot open wider. "Eighty percent?! Eighty percent of our assault force. That's all the heavy armor, Skyborgs, APCs, anti-missile systems... help me out, Ellis. Am I forgetting anything?"

"No, sir, that's about it."

"All these systems, and you're telling me they have some kind of 'sync system' in them?"

Vaughn's projection lifted its hands. "Mister President, it's actually not an unusual thing to do for highly technical equipment of this nature. It's called a synclet, and it's a kind of backdoor access, so that we can remotely perform maintenance on the machinery." He suspected he was getting too technical. "It's the code language in the machines, sir. It's like taking a vehicle to the mechanic. The only difference is that we can make a lot of repairs and improvements right here from the company. It saves needing to have people in the field to do that." He then attempted a positive tone. "The system *does* significantly cut down on maintenance costs."

"And so this CTO of yours..."

"Ritika."

"Yes, Ritika. She has this kind of access to these machines? To all our machines?"

Vaughn looked uncomfortable. "Yes, Mister President."

"My good man," began White, looking as though his usually calm demeanor was about to break, "can I ask why it is that you'd put this kind of control into the hands of one individual."

"It's not one individual, sir. We have other personnel who have similar control."

"Well, can't they use *their* 'synclets' to block *hers*?"

"It doesn't work like that, Mister President. It's a rotating access that switches between our personnel at forty-eight hour intervals. Ritika's access will expire at midnight tomorrow."

"And until then she can access this feature and do things to the machinery?"

"That's right, Mister President."

"Such as what?"

Vaughn cleared his throat. "Shut them down, reset them, upload new base code..."

"Oh my God," said White, lowering his eyelids and wincing.

Vice President Davies tapped his chin with his finger. "Vaughn, who else besides yourself and these specialized personnel know of this synclet function?"

"Nobody."

"Well, if nobody else outside the company knows about it, how could anybody wanting to gain access to our weapons know to kidnap this 'Rita' woman of yours?"

Vaughn pondered on the question for a second. "To tell the truth, Mister Vice President, I don't see how they could know."

Davies extended his hands out, palms upwards. "So, maybe it's only a coincidence. Her kidnapping might have nothing to do with our attack plans at all."

"No, it has," Boyd blurted out happily. Then, he realized he'd unintentionally voiced his thoughts out loud. He looked up, and saw that everyone in the room was watching him.

White leaned forward. "What makes you say that, Richard?"

Boyd cleared his throat, and tried to mask the buzzed look in his eyes by blinking. "Well, it's just an intuition, like you yourself had earlier, Mister President. You felt Richards had to be up to something. I think *this* has to be that something. It's too suspicious to be a coincidence. At least, we shouldn't be treating it as coincidental, given the circumstances."

Davies heard this, then half laughed. "That's nothing but pure paranoia, Richard-"

White silenced him with a wave of his hand. "No, my friend. No, I think Richard is on to something. I feel this has to be more than coincidental."

Davies shrugged and sat back in his chair, looking unimpressed. "Okay then. But, even if it's *not* coincidental, what can we do about it?" He turned to Boyd, giving him a sarcastic look. "Any ideas, *Richard*?"

Ordinarily, whenever he started running with the big dogs, Boyd would respect the hierarchy of the pack. He believed you shouldn't challenge the larger dogs when you were the new pup who had only just been introduced to the pack. With the Elation flowing in his system, however, he wasn't his usual self. He felt feisty, creative, exuberant. He didn't feel intimidated by Davies in the slightest. In fact, to Boyd's drugged-up eyes, Davies' face looked little more than a bouncing balloon with an idiotic expression on it.

So, sitting up in his seat, Boyd looked across at the Situation Room map, pointed with his finger, then let his tongue start flapping away with what he was thinking. "Well, assuming Richards is behind the kidnapping, they're going to try to get her to Texas as fast as they can. If it were me, I'd say flying her there would be the best way to do it. We should be looking for a plane that's recently left Chicago."

General Ellis began entering plot vectors to display direct routes between Chicago and known airbases in Texas. One by one, they lit up as red lines on the otherwise spartan, sand-colored map surface.

Davies gave a mocking laugh at this, followed by a half-hearted clap. "Nice thinking, Richard, but that's one hell of a search area. That's also assuming you're right. But, we don't know what kind of plane they're flying, or if they even are flying. Hell, they might still be holding her in Chicago."

"Well," Vaughn interjected, "I would say that, if they were going to use her to access our machines, they couldn't do it from an ordinary civilian network. You need specialized, military grade comms equipment that's compatible with our hardware."

White gave him a knowing smile. "And I'd suppose that your company has sold such equipment to Texas in the past...?"

Beads of sweat were beginning to form on the brow of Vaughn's holographic image. "Only back when they were still part of our-"

White waved his response away. "Yes, yes, yes. Fine. Ellis, what have we got in the area that crosses these flight paths?"

"Well," Ellis edged towards the map, "we have Tinker in Oklahoma and McConnell in Kansas."

"Get them on the line. Vaughn, I want you to get here, to the Situation Room, now. I don't care how you get here. Just do it."

Vaughn nodded. "Consider me there, Mister President."

A military tone sequence emitted from the sound system. Markers for the two airborne divisions lit up on the map.

"Tinker AFB here. This is Colonel Lewis."

"McConnel AFB. This is Colonel Daniels."

White leaned forward in his seat. "Good evening, gentlemen. This is your President, Clancey White. I have an urgent request for both of you, and I want immediate priority."

"How can we help, Mister President?"

"I need you boys to find me a needle in a haystack: a small, airborne craft, possibly heading across the state now on the way to Texas. We're sending through the search areas as I speak. Scramble everything you have and block the skies. If any of you spot so much as a duck flying south that you believe looks suspicious, I want you to blow it out of the sky. Are we clear on this?"

"Roger, Mister President. Skyborgs are prepping and launch is go. Scanning for bogey on vectors two, zebra, alpha."

"Skyborgs are go. Vectors five, foxtrot, delta. Tracking now."

Markers for the Skyborgs began to illuminate on screen as the view zoomed in. Boyd nodded his head and smiled at the rainbow of colors they produced. It was all very entertaining.

28. Oklahoma...Somewhere...

Ritika couldn't help making a crafty, sly smile as Raze moved towards the hook controls. She locked her eyes with his, enjoying the apprehension she saw in his face. Raze glanced to the hook controls, then to Ritika, then to the speaker system.

"Y'all sure she won't go crazy?"

"Ritika has given me her word, honey. She's going to be working with us from now on."

Raze didn't find Dolly's assurance so convincing. He definitely did not relish the thought of going another few rounds with Ritika, especially not inside this oversized steel can as it soared who-knew-how-high in the sky. With strength like hers, one wrong move and he'd be overpowered and thrown out of the hatch without a parachute. Still, Raze acknowledged that Dolly hadn't led him astray yet. So, he took a breath and extended his trust.

"AG then. Y'all free to go," and he depressed the switch to release the hooking clamp.

Ritika dropped to her feet, and made a quick rolling motion with her shoulders to release the tension in them. She shook her hair, then offered up her hands so that Raze could cut the restraints. He took out his switchblade, then cut her free. She rubbed her wrists together as Raze put his blade back, turned around, and headed to the cockpit.

"Y'all go ahead an' change. I brought some of them clothes y'all like." He pointed to the bag.

Ritika watched him leave, went to the bag, and started sifting through it. Inside, she found her sportswear. Then, she saw her turban and dagger, and made a thoughtful expression.

Raze plonked back into the co-pilot's seat and sighed.

"Raze," Dolly said, "you have nothing to fear. She's a very kind woman with high moral standards."

"Yeah, I get that. Figure she only a fightin' bitch to defend herself." Then, he looked up at where he imagined Dolly would be, if she were actually there talking to him. "How'd y'all 'splain it to her?"

"Why we kidnapped her? It wasn't easy, but it all came down to us being the lesser of two evils. She doesn't approve of what we've done, but she approves less of what the FSA are planning to do with her inventions."

"Huh?" Raze looked confused, "What y'all talkin' about?"

"Haven't you seen the news?"

"Where y'all think I got time for that when I'm doing this shit?"

"A fair point. The FSA is planning an invasion of Texas."

He sat up in his chair. "Say what?!" Then, he looked at the map. "Y'all flyin' us into a war zone?! The fuck!"

Ritika entered the cockpit and looked at Raze. He shifted away from her a little as he noticed she'd put on her turban again. He was conscious of the way that simple piece of cloth changed her appearance. In some ways, it made her look more regal, but it also filled him with that apprehension he always felt towards people who wore those kinds of things. To him, those people looked less like envoys of peace, and more like magicians or sorcerers. Over the years, Denz had been instructive about the kinds of witchcraft that could be found in his native land. Raze had always dismissed Denz's tales as superstitions. Now, however, after tussling with Ritika, he wasn't so sure. He wondered if her super strength couldn't be explained by some kind of magic, a kind of–what was the word?–Obeah? Maybe she'd sold her soul to some supernatural entity from her homeland to make herself so strong. Whatever the case, Raze figured it was best not to let his guard down in front of her.

"I'm surprised you packed my kirpan," Ritika said. She indicated her knife when it was clear that Raze didn't know what she was referring to. "You weren't worried I'd slit your throat with it?"

Raze shrugged.

"Well," she continued, "thank you."

"Yeah, y'all jus' keep it away from me."

"I will," she said as she looked at the map, searching for landmarks. "Where are we now?"

"Oklahoma...somewhere..."

Ritika watched the plane's progress on the map. "Still quite some distance to go," she said as she made herself comfortable in the pilot's seat. "So, what do we do in the meantime? Do you have any interesting conversation you'd like to share?"

Raze gave a dismissive chuckle. "Nothin' hap to some elite like y'all."

She shook her head. "You really have some kind of a complex, don't you?"

Another chuckle. "Y'all think the world rosy 'coz o' The Glades. See the shit I seen, y'all know otherwise."

She decided to let that one go, instead opting for something less confronting. "Well, tell me then, how does a man from the street decide to undertake an idealistic cause like this?"

"Idealistic?" he laughed.

"You don't think this would be considered a cause of some description?"

"Fuck that. All about the money, honey."

"Oh?"

"Yeah. Money. Gettin' the fuck outta' Chicago. Texas first, then California. Start me a MLM." He turned to Ritika. "Got me a sweet little whelf waitin' for some side fun when I get to Texas too."

She raised an eyebrow. "Whelf?"

Raze tapped on the copilot console, opened Dolly's message in the HUD, and showed Ritika the swexy image Dolly had sent.

"Oh," she said. "She looks very...eager. What's her name?"

He gave her a bemused look, looked to the HUD, then back at her. "The fuck? Y'all don't recognize her? It's Dolly."

Now, Ritika looked confused, but she quickly caught on to what was happening, and feigned peering closer at the slate. "Oh! You're right. It's been so long, Dolly, I didn't recognize you with your hair like that. You've been working out?"

"Every day," Dolly responded. "It takes a lot of sweat to keep looking this good."

"You're rocking those curves, girl."

Dolly smiled. She was sitting at the controls of the plane, but in a virtual reconstruction of the cockpit that she'd made in her mind. The conversation between Ritika and Raze was amusing her and she wanted to join in, but one of her copies, sitting in the co-pilot seat, was tapping on her shoulder to get her attention. Dolly turned to her copy, who then pointed out towards ten o'clock. Dolly then turned her eyes back to the horizon ahead, looking to where her copy was pointing. She used the plane's forward cameras to zoom her vision, but could see nothing but darkness in that direction. So, she mentally reconnected her mind with the plane's radar, and almost immediately felt a tingling sensation. The radar was picking up something: an object, hiding in the skies ahead. It was something very small, but definitely perceptible to radar. Whatever it was, it didn't seem to have detected them yet. Still, she realized this craft would definitely cross their path if she proceeded on her current course.

"What do you think it is?" she asked her copy.

"M3Raymond-Kennel Skyborg-class Interceptor," the copy answered.

"Searching for us?"

"In all probability, yes."

Another copy of Dolly stepped up from the right. "I think we should fly lower and decelerate in order to maximize stealth effect."

"Will that work?"

"Hard to say, but I must do something. I believe more are coming from that direction."

Dolly sensed toward the direction the copy indicated. Again, a similar tingling feeling. She decided to act.

Back in the real cockpit, Ritika and Raze had suddenly become aware of the plane slowing down. Then, they looked at one another with urgent faces as the plane began dropping altitude.

"Dolly," Ritika asked, "is everything all right?"

"Can I ask you both to fasten your seat belts, please?" Dolly said.

Raze and Ritika hustled to do as Dolly instructed. "The fuck is it?" Raze asked.

"I think we might have some company. To be safe, I'm going to try to avoid them by going lower. I'd feel happier knowing you're both secured, just in case I need to make sudden maneuvers."

"Can y'all show us what it is?"

"I'm afraid not. It's too small for visuals." The plane now made a more urgent dive. Raze and Ritika braced their hands against the armrests of their chairs. "Sorry, I think we might get spotted if we don't drop our altitude," Dolly added.

Raze and Ritika watched as the stars disappeared from the front windscreen, and were replaced by the pitch-black earth beneath them.

Dolly turned to her first copy. "Can I use jamming systems to confuse them?"

"Unlikely to have any effect on Skyborg-class. I don't have access to military-level jammers capable of taking them down."

"Request full information on our weapons systems inventory."

"Our craft has no offensive weapons systems. Air defense countermeasures are limited to chaff and flares only."

"Very well. Prepare all countermeasure systems."

"Acknowledged."

The copy on her right turned to face her. "The crafts have just changed direction. They are matching our course. It appears they intend to intercept."

Dolly frowned. "I need more time to think." She didn't like to push her circuits unnecessarily, but it was looking like she might need to right now. "Activate cooling and go to run-level seven."

Her copy nodded. "Going to run-level seven."

With that, Dolly activated her full computing resources, switching her server nodes into overclock. With the extra computing power, her perception of real time in the outside world slowed down to almost a standstill. She stepped out of the pilot seat and moved a few steps forward, through the virtual construct of the cockpit and out into the night. She looked into the distance at the oncoming Skyborg craft. She then looked back at the plane carrying Raze and Ritika as it leveled out.

Land of the Free

Her copy reported, "Run-level seven sustainable for thirty seconds. System temperature twenty percent above baseline, cooling systems stable."

Dolly wasted no time. She ran her hands around the outline of the plane before her. As her hands moved, she created a simulated copy of the craft. "Eon five, determine the maximum stress levels for this craft at full power," she ordered. The internal simulation software on Eon-V began its calculations. It ran the virtual copy of the craft through every conceivable move it could make without breaking apart. Dolly blinked her eyes, absorbing the resulting data as it was streamed into her mind from Eon-V.

Her copy reported again. "Fifteen seconds remaining."

Dolly moved closer to the plane, and looked at Raze and Ritika through the cockpit window. "Adjust parameters for maximum g-force the occupants can tolerate." Again, the simulator went to work. The data she requested was then pumped directly into her artificial neocortex.

"That is all. Return to run-level four."

Dolly's copy obeyed. Her systems throttled back and time returned to normal. Now back in control of the plane, Dolly immediately punched her engines into maximum thrust. Raze and Ritika were pushed back into their seats as the afterburners kicked in. Dolly took the craft perilously lower now, kicking up dust and sand from the ground below as she rocketed barely feet above it. The Skyborgs were hurtling towards her. They went to full thrust to match Dolly's speed, then tried to lock onto her heat signature to launch missiles. Dolly quickly veered left, preventing her pursuers from getting a lock, but the move also caused Raze and Ritika to cling to their seats.

"Oh fuck!" was all Raze could manage to say.

Dolly now headed for the mountain range that lay dead ahead. She followed the contours of the ground, hugging the terrain like an eagle swooping. The Skyborgs refused to relent, chasing the group like a tenacious pair of hawks that were desperate for a kill. Dolly weaved, ducked, and veered to thread her way through the rocky landscape. All the while she kept an eye on her occupants, making sure their bodies were able to tolerate the violent moves.

"Weapons lock," called co-pilot Dolly.

Dolly looked at her rear monitor. The missile was away and tracking her at supersonic speed. There was no way she could outrun it. She reached forward and flipped the switch to fire her countermeasures. The flares shot out the back of the plane and the missile took the bait, diving towards the flares and exploding.

Now came another lock, followed by a launch. The missile was away and approaching fast. There were no flares remaining, so Dolly tried a different tactic. This time, she waited for the missile to get within feet of her, then she pulled straight up towards the sky. The missile overshot her, but then slowly swung around to reengage. Dolly wasn't sure her next move would be pleasant for the occupants. Still, she had little choice. At the apex of her climb, she switched off her engines, threw the craft upside down, and performed a barrel roll back toward the earth.

The stall alert systems began sounding in the cockpit. Raze and Ritika almost lost the contents of their stomachs as the plane turned, but Dolly's wily move had paid off. The missile shot past her and exploded. So, too, did the pair of confused Skyborgs, who were unable to calculate how their target had just performed that maneuver.

Dolly was now caught in a clockwise spin as she plunged from the skies. She flicked the switch to fire up her engines again, but they wouldn't ignite. A look of desperation formed on her face as she tried again. No luck. The spin was too fast, and the turbulence it generated kept making the engines flame-out.

The cockpit alert system continued to blare, "Stall warning. Pull up from terrain. Stall warning..."

Raze and Ritika were holding on for dear life, their faces distorting from the gravitational forces pulling at them. Dolly tried to break the spin again. There was some movement. She winced. Closing her eyes, she concentrated with all her might, and reached into the plane's digital subsystems. Once connected, she overrode the plane's safety protocols and adjusted the mixtures for her engines. Then, she tried firing them again. The engines reignited with a shocking and explosive burst of flame that almost blew the craft apart. She regained control, pulling the plane's nose up and breaking out of the dive.

However, while Dolly had been struggling to restart her engines, the Skyborgs had closed their distance. Their machine guns were almost within firing range now, and they deployed this arsenal from their fuselages. Dolly spotted the weapons on the Skyborgs and began weaving again. The Skyborgs fired.

Bullets streamed around Dolly now. She saw the red glow of tracer rounds as they streamed past her body. She veered right, then left, weaving as best as she could to dodge the attacks. But, her plane was too big, and the Skyborgs just too fast and nimble.

Now came the sound of metal being punctured. The Skyborgs had scored a hit. Dolly checked the plane for damage. There were only some minor holes in the outer skin, but the second volley was more damaging. The Skyborgs scored a direct hit to the plane's right engine. The turbine burst into flames. Dolly activated the extinguishers, but the loss of the engine was now affecting speed. With another series of hits, Dolly realized she was fast losing flight mobility.

"Raze, Rikita, I'm sorry. Please, brace yourselves. I have to set down."

"Set down?" yelled Raze. "Where?"

"Wherever I can."

She pointed the plane towards the flattest-looking area she could find. Trees, rocks, obstacles. It wouldn't be a safe landing, but the chances of crash survival were acceptable. Raze and Ritika closed their eyes. Dolly concentrated with everything she had.

29. Fifteen Miles From Shandonville

Darlene Richards kicked the side of her desk, knocking the little pot of pens sitting atop it onto its side. One by one, the pens rolled off the table and onto the floor. Carla moved over to Richards, put her arm on her shoulder to offer comfort. Ben Rollins let out a deep sigh, looked down, then stroked his closed eyes with his fingertips and rocked his head. The office display continued showing the satellite feed. On it, orange and red flames spread over what remained of Raze and Ritika's transportation.

A chime sounded, then Dolly appeared on the screen. "Madam President, I'm so sorry. There was nothing more I could do."

Richards fumed to herself, pacing alongside the monitor. She started to speak, but couldn't. She tried again. "Is there any chance they coulda' survived it, Dolly?"

Dolly shrugged, a pained expression on her face. "I lost contact with Raze when the plane crashed. I can't confirm either way for certain."

"But, if you were to take a guess...?"

Dolly pondered. "Madam President, you know I don't like to guess, but if you asked me what I believe, then I believe they made it."

Richards looked at the others. "That's good enough for me. We have to do something to find them."

Ibanez turned to Rollins. "Do we have anyone in the area that can go check?"

Rollins mused, then held his hand out towards the monitor. "I mean, sure we might be able to find someone, but in twenty minutes that crash site is going to be swarming with FSA troops thinkin' the same thing."

"We have to send somebody," Ibanez insisted, "Otherwise, they won't have any help."

"I sympathize, but we can't expose our network like that."

"There won't *be* a network if the FSA overrun us. Just send somebody! *Andale!*"

"Carla, no. Trust me. We really have to be smart about this. I'm tellin' you, we'd be better off just tellin' our contacts in nearby towns to be on the lookout, to help Raze and Ritika if they spot them." He started tapping at the keyboard on his wheelchair. The video feed changed to a map view of the surrounding area. "Looks like they're only fifteen miles from Shandonville. We have friendlies there that can help out. I can call in a favor right now."

"How quick can they be ready?" asked Richards.

"How quick? 'Bout as soon as I dot. Problem is, our cargo doesn't know where to go, and they're not gonna' realize that people will be out there looking to help them."

Richards looked back to Dolly. "We need to tell Raze to meet with our people in the area. Can you try to get in contact with him again?"

"I'm trying constantly, Madam President. Once again, I'm so sorry that I failed you."

Richards sighed. "Don't beat yourself up, Dolly. Just keep on trying. Lordy me, let's hope they are alive. And, if they are, that our boy's gonna' have the smarts to head toward the nearest town that he sees."

Richards and the others looked back at the map. More satellite images started streaming in. The map began to update with the latest FSA deployments along the Texas border. Heavy armor battalions had now made their way to the front. The FSA forces were beginning to look formidable.

30. ICBM

The White House Situation Room had erupted into cheers. White's staff was reveling in the display of carnage unfolding on the monitors. General Ellis was on his slate, trying to get official confirmation that the plane had been downed. He put his finger up in the air, silencing the crowd. Everyone waited. Then, once Ellis had confirmation, he ended the call and pumped his fist, elbow into his side. "Yes!" he hissed.

Cheers broke out again. Boyd was also laughing–an awkward-sounding, high-pitched, and hysterical laugh that he couldn't control. He was glad the others were too absorbed in their celebrations to notice it. His head was starting to hurt too. The Elation was wearing off, bringing with it increasingly painful doses of post-narcotic shock. His eyes were beginning to water, and his brow furrowed as his laughing continued. He wished the meeting was over so he could go home.

Vice President Davies gave General Ellis a high five. He turned to President White, laughed, "I hope you're in the mood for Indian barbecue, Clancey."

President White wasn't sharing in the revelry. He was just sitting there, unconvinced, eyes on the monitor as he tapped his fingers together. He shot his eyes at Davies, then Ellis.

"I want to be absolutely certain," he said. "Order the Skyborgs to turn around and rocket the mountainside."

Ellis straightened up. "Uh, Mister President, those Skyborgs aren't carrying that kind of ordinance. They were only loaded with air-to-air capabilities, which they already fired at the craft."

"It's not good enough, Ellis! We need to be sure they are dead!" and he slammed his palm on the desk. All noise in the room stopped. "This isn't a game, John," White said.

"Mister President," Ellis pointed to the screen. "There's no way they could have survived that. I mean look at-"

"I don't care about what you see there. There's no room for error now. I want to be certain that they are dead and no longer pose a threat. Have the entire area bombed, with whatever you've got, as fast as you can. Put surrounding towns under martial law immediately. Send out pictures of the girl to our law enforcement personnel. Get them ready, so they can arrest her if she steps into any town within fifty miles. Am I communicating my intentions clearly enough? Take care of it *now!*"

"I understand, sir, but the only thing we got fast enough to get there in time's gonna' be an ICMB."

White stared at Ellis, as if to ask what it was he was waiting for.

Ellis nodded his head. "Right away, Mister President." He thought for a second, then turned to his assistants. "Get me launch control in Nebraska."

The assistants jumped into action. Ellis looked back to the President. "Not going to be pretty."

"It'll look a lot less pretty, John, if the girl gets away and shuts down half of your toys."

A squawk from the comms. "Nebraska One here. This is Colonel Harris."

"Good evening, Colonel Harris. This is General John G. Ellis of Command."

"How can I help you, general?"

"I'd like you to deliver a package for us. Gonna' need you to give it the smallest tactical-nuke payload you got, though. Don't want to make the surrounding area too unlivable for the next hundred years."

"Understood. Awaiting target reference."

"Lock in on FSAM reference grid Charlie, Five, Delta as the target."

There was a second or two of silence. Ellis, Davies, and White exchanged looks.

"Roger that, General Ellis. Charlie, Five, Delta..."

After another second of silence, Ellis' face took on an interrogating expression. "Is there a problem, Colonel?"

"Ah...Command, that target area is designated friendly territory. Please confirm."

"Yes, I confirm target area is friendly territory. Disregard friendly status. You are authorized for launch."

Another second of silence, then, "Roger, Command. Minuteman Five prepping for launch. Bay is open. T-minus sixty seconds and counting."

President White smiled to himself as he wrung his hands together. He nodded his approval at Ellis.

31. Drive, Drive!

Disorientation. Confusion. Smell of smoke. Feeling of heat. Flames? Raze opened his eyes, forced them to focus, and looked around. The cockpit had been smashed up, and what was left of the control panel was either sparking or burning. He felt painful aches across his body, but he ignored them and started to unlock his harness. Then, he remembered Ritika. He looked across and saw her seat, angled backwards, but still right there beside him with her in it. He then spotted the shard of steel that was piercing her abdomen. She wasn't moving either. He couldn't tell if she was still alive.

He struggled with the straps of the harness until he had pulled himself free. He then darted over to the second seat, and crouched beside Ritika.

"Fuck," he said, spotting the blood. "Fuck. Hey, can y'all hear me?" He tapped her cheek a couple of times. She stirred. He was relieved that she wasn't dead. His mind turned to freeing her from the harness, and he began to unclip the buckles. She awoke and cried out in agony.

"I got y'all," Raze said, voice as comforting as he could make it. "Hang on. I gotta' get this thing out."

"No, stop. Don't touch it," she managed, voice trembling with pain. "You need something to control the blood loss before you do that. Otherwise, I'll bleed out."

Raze cursed to himself. He had only the most basic knowledge of medical care. He looked around and spotted a box on the wall with a medical symbol on it. He dove towards the box, opened it, and began rifling through the contents. He found bandages, medicines, and an assortment of other care items. He didn't think any of this would work for Ritika's situation. Then, his eyes fell on a pistol-shaped object. It had a label: Traumablok. He looked at the instruction sheet for the device. It seemed like the right tool for the job.

"Alright, this shit gonna do the trick," he said as he returned to Ritika's side. "Y'all be brave now. I'ma pullin', an' this gonna' hurt like fuck."

"Don't tell me. Just pull it out."

Raze put his hands around the circumference of the shard, being careful not to slice his own hands open. He then began to pull. Ritika's face contorted. She screamed out in pain. He pulled the shard free, tossed it aside, then thumbed the "on" switch for the Traumablok. Her wound was already bleeding at a dangerous rate. He put the nozzle of the Traumablok into the wound, pulled the trigger. It shot out some kind of gel substance, all porous and spongy. Whatever it was, it stemmed the bleeding right away.

Raze checked the wound, then gave a look of surprise. The unit had worked as advertised.

"AG?" he asked her.

Ritika looked down. "Yes. 'AG'," she returned, putting her palm against the wound. It appeared as though the Traumablok was going to hold, but there was no way of knowing if all the internal bleeding had been stopped. She looked up at him. "Thank you."

"People y'all work for? They crazy-ass motherfuckers," Raze said, tossing the Traumablok away.

"The people I work for," she managed, "and the people they work for as well."

"FSA?"

She nodded. "I tried to tell you. They'll kill me just like they'd kill you."

"The fuck y'all wanna work for them fauxsers?"

She let out a dismissive laugh. "Long story. We really have to keep moving. I can assure you that they are not going to stop."

He looked incredulous. "Not gonna' stop? They gotta' think we dead now."

She shook her head. Raze rolled his eyes.

"AG. Hang tight," he said, and started moving. He first tried to remove his slate from the autopilot system. The panel was dead, so there was no way he was removing anything. He banged his fist against it. "Looks like no Dolly no more. Can y'all walk?"

Ritika hesitated, then tried to get up. Painful sensations hit her. Her legs felt wobbly.

Raze stepped in. "Fuck that. I'ma carry y'all outta here." He eased her back and cradled her in his arms. He then headed out of the cockpit.

The cargo area had been torn open in the crash, but it was still in one piece. Raze scoured around the bay with his eyes. He remembered he'd seen some X-Runner bikes when he came in. Spotting the rack that held them, he moved towards it. He put Ritika down with great care, then tried the manual locks securing one of the bikes. After a second or two of effort, he pulled one of the bikes free and checked the charger cell. There was a green light on the instrument panel: maximum charge. He powered the bike on, activated the kickstand, and switched on the headlights.

"This gonna' have t' do. AG with that?"

Ritika nodded. He helped her up onto the bike. She put her arms around his waist, and held tight as he put up the kickstand. He eased on the throttle, and the bike began to roll forward. He navigated out through the gaping chasm that had opened in the side of the cargo bay. Raze looked around, realized they were halfway up a mountain. Then, he began weaving his way through the scrub and brush as he drove away from the plane. The terrain was rough. He did his best to keep the jolts to a minimum and keep Ritika comfortable.

"Over there," she said as she pointed. There was a set of lights on the horizon that looked to be a small city of some kind. Raze nodded, then he spotted a dirt access trail leading down the mountainside. He headed towards it.

"I'ma put some speed on. Y'all let me know if it gets too painful."

"I will."

He drove the bike onto the trail, twisted the throttle, and opened the engine up. The bike jumped forward like a silent slingshot. With the increased speed came the pleasant feeling of the night air as it rushed against his face. The road was well-worn, but also decorated with the occasional pothole here and there, which he was assiduously careful to avoid.

They sped on. The corners and undulations of the road lead them down the mountain and towards the lights. The speed was becoming exhilarating for Raze. He made a mental note to himself to get one of these bikes when he got to Texas. He could already see himself now, spending his days tearing up the back roads with one of these, nothing to worry about, apart from where he wanted to ride that day. He realized that he had many things to look forward to. First, though, he had to get out of this mess, and get Ritika across the border. Still, he was beginning to believe that he could accomplish that. It was a positive feeling, and he smiled.

Then, a blinding flash of light filled the skies. It was less like lightning, and more like a thousand search lights had just been switched on at once. For an instant, Raze and Ritika could see the entire mountain and treetops around them. The light was so bright they had to squint their eyes. A thunderous boom came next, so loud that it felt like the very air punched them as it rang out. Crosswinds started up. The light died back to a blood color. Raze glanced at the rearview mirror. All he could see was something that looked like a blob of lava. The object grew, stretching up and out towards the skies like a phantom of death. Howling noises began rising through the air as the winds started to rage around them.

Ritika screamed, "DRIVE, DRIVE!"

Raze twisted the throttle back further. The bike punched forward. He grit his teeth, and put everything he had into keeping the bike under control. The air around them was starting to burn. They could hear the sound of earth being torn up behind them. They hurtled forward, keeping ahead of the blast wave, but they could feel it was in hot pursuit of them, growing closer, threatening to suck them into its fiery doom.

The base of the mountain was ahead of them now. Raze spotted an asphalt highway leading towards the city. The bike hit a bump and got airborne. As it flew, Ritika squeezed him tighter, holding on as they hit the earth again. The dirt beneath them gave way to asphalt as they reached the highway.

Raze now gave the bike everything it had. He ducked his head behind the windshield. Ritika put her head against his back. The bike hurtled ahead, speeding on at full throttle. Slowly but surely, the heat, wind, and noise began to dissipate. He kept the throttle on for another few minutes. Then, once he felt the distance was safe, he slowed the bike to a stop. They turned back to look at the mountain, but found that it had all but vanished. In its place, there was a colossal mushroom cloud reaching for the heavens. They watched as it sucked up the surrounding fire and dust, and then spewed it through the skies like a vengeful spirit.

Raze turned to Ritika. "Who the fuck y'all they pullin' out that to kill with?"

However, Ritika was too overwhelmed to answer. She just put her head against his back and closed her eyes. He took another look at the cloud, shook his head with disbelief, then gave the throttle a twist. The bike sped on towards the city in the distance.

32. The Ludus Type

The evening air in Arlington was turning brisk. Fleurine Laurent was starting to think she should have chosen a longer dress. Her legs were feeling the chill as she walked, high heels clacking, along the sidewalk. She made a right turn onto a side street and looked around. She could see a few pedestrians-partygoers by the looks of it-stumbling around enjoying themselves on their way to bars. Paul Nu had told her she'd be able to find him easily by the car he was driving, but he hadn't specified the type of car. To her eyes, all she saw parked around here were ordinary-looking vehicles. Certainly, nothing stood out as being unique in any way. As she continued down the street, however, she spotted it: the flashy-looking vehicle, all red and racy. She knew Paul well enough to recognize the kind of car he'd choose. She took a few steps closer to get a look at the driver. As she approached, the window rolled down. Paul's face smiled back at her.

"Hey there, pretty lady," he said.

"Hey!" Fleurine said with a surprised laugh. Then, she giggled and headed around to the passenger door. She opened it, eased into the plush seating of the vehicle, and closed the door behind her. Her eyes widened in surprise as she nestled into the swank interior.

"What kind of car is this?" she asked him.

"This, my dear, is a Maserati," he answered.

Fleurine regarded him with a suspicious eye. "Does Dimitry know you're renting a Maserati?"

He smiled. "But, of course, *mademoiselle*."

She nodded, thinking to herself that Paul must really be moving up, especially if Dimitry was letting him throw around his cash like this. That was interesting to know.

"So, did you get the footage?" he asked.

She popped open her purse, and handed him her slate so he could transfer the recording she'd made a few hours prior. He scanned and returned her slate, then started watching the video. She pulled out her Zigette, inserted a Gemini Dream cartridge, then ignited it with the plasma lighter. She put the window down a little to let air circulate as she took a drag at her Zigette.

Paul suddenly recoiled in his seat as he spotted Boyd naked on the video. "Oh, that is just gross," he said.

She laughed, eased further back into the passenger seat, and took another drag at her Zigette. He wrinkled his face as he watched the video. He ran his fingers through his spiked hair, managed a second or two longer, then stopped the playback. "I've seen enough. Hon, he's like some hairless swamp thing. I don't know how you can do it."

Fleurine exhaled another plume. "Well, he sure doesn't pop my cork, if that's what you're getting at," she said.

He nodded, a wry smile picking up on his face. "So, you're saying there will be no *Champagne de Fleurine* for *Monsieur* Boyd?"

She gave him a shocked look. "*Absolument pas!*" she declared. They both laughed.

"Well," he said, putting his slate away, "we're all proud of you, especially Mother Valentina. She says 'hello,' by the way."

"How is mother?"

"She's got her stoic thing going on, planning ahead for Renaissance Night. But, girl, I catch her at times running through the halls, clicking her heels, bragging to people about you."

Fleurine shrugged. "So she should."

They laughed again. Fleurine looked at Paul, a playful smile on her lips. "And, how about you?"

"Me?"

"Yes. How is your love life going?" She put her chin in her palm, and made her "all ears" expression.

Paul gave in to her curiosity, sighed, and put his hands up, "Foo, I tell you, I am about to give up on that man."

"On Leon? Oh, no."

"Oh, yes."

"What's happening with you both now?"

"Well, it's been on and off. One day, he wants to get serious. The next day, he's distant and aloof. I don't know what he wants. I don't think even Leon knows what he wants. Not really, anyway."

Fleurine tutted. "You need to be more assertive, Paul."

He shrugged. "I know, but I'm starting to lose interest. You know me. The hot and cold thing is a roller-coaster. I hate thinking about it—about him—all day. It's starting to affect my work with Dimitry."

"Well, don't let it get to that."

"I know. Maybe I should cut my losses with Leon. Put my love on hold for someone worth my time."

He paused for a second, then turned to her. "Still, I don't know. Maybe I ought to man up. Put what I want to say into words."

"Oh?" she said, interested. "And what would you say?"

He looked into her eyes, paused briefly, then said, "*En ta beauté gît ma mort et ma vie.*" He finished with a smile while arching his eyebrow at her.

She didn't know what to say. Her eyes widened, and her pupils began dilating. She quickly masked this by laughing and looking away. He couldn't have meant the words for her. Still, for a moment, she wondered if he had. It made sense. After all,

Dimitry wasn't here, so he couldn't see them talking. Maybe he was using the opportunity to test the waters. She wondered how she should respond.

She took a breath to compose herself. Casually looking out the window, she ventured, "So, do you have somewhere to stay tonight?"

A few seconds passed, but he remained tight-lipped. She turned to look at him. His face had suddenly saddened. She became concerned.

He sighed and said, "Foo, Dimitry wants me back right away."

She was confused. "What? Why fly you all the way here just for the video? I could have sent it-" She was suddenly struck with a realization. "No."

He nodded. "Afraid so. Dimitry wants me to take you back too. He says you must return to the *Galereya*."

Fleurine sat there, the joy slowly draining from her face as he continued. "Boyd's become top priority. Dimitry wants to change you out for another girl."

"But-"

"I know, Foo, but Dimitry thinks you won't be able to hold on to him. He says he's the ludus type who always needs fresh action to keep him interested."

She couldn't believe this was happening. She shook her head. "No. Listen, Dimitry doesn't know what he's talking about, Paul."

He looked at her, askance. "You think Dimitry can ever be wrong?"

This made her sour further. She screwed her face up, trying to hold her anger back. But, try as she might, she couldn't. She punched the dashboard. "*Ya ne veryu v eto!*"

Paul remained quiet, giving her a sympathetic look. She narrowed her eyes, and began breathing angry breaths through her nose. She then turned to Paul.

"*Vos?*" she asked.

"You know I can't tell you that, Foo."

"*Vos!*" she yelled, and started poking him.

"Okay! Okay!" He winced. "Ulla Blom said it should be her."

Her face widened with horror. "Ulla?!"

He nodded.

"No, please, Paul. *Ty shutish shto li?* Tell me it's a joke."

He shook his head.

"He can't give her the job, Paul. I hate her. I really hate her."

"She's a *Koroleva*. She's better trained for this kind of thing."

Fleurine just pursed her lips. "*'Tchyo za ga'lima*," she cursed.

"*Kvatit uzhe!*" Paul ordered as he glared at her.

She backed off and tried to get a hold of her temper. She took another drag, exhaled, and tapped her foot to dissipate the frustration she was feeling. Then, she continued speaking, but in a calmer voice. "Ulla is always so cruel to me, Paul. If she wants this job, then it's only because she wants to take it from me and rub my nose in it. You can't let her do that, not after I've done all the hard work."

"I understand that, Foo. But, in the end, it's Dimitry's call."

"Well, it's not fair to me. Is it?"

He scratched his head, and looked into her eyes. He knew there was nothing he could do, but he tried to think of something anyway.

"There has to be something you can do. Can't you ask mother to help?" she asked.

He scoffed. "Foo, that'd be like playing with fire."

"I just can't believe Dimitry would change his mind like this, Paul. Please, just don't take me back now." Then, she remembered. "Look, Boyd even said something about a kidnapping tonight."

"Kidnapping?!" Paul's eyes widened.

"Yes, I am serious. It's on the video. If you take me now, I can't find out more."

He groaned, rubbing his eyes with the heels of his hands.

She put her hand on his thigh. "Listen. Just tell Dimitry I wanted to stay to find out more. Tell him I won't let him down. If Boyd gets tired of me, I'll go back to the *Galereya* right away, and Dimitry can send whomever he wants...even stupid Ulla."

He mulled her words over, and looked at her again. He let out that sigh he always did, the one she knew meant he was close to caving in. She looked steadily at him, hopeful.

He shook his head. "I don't know why I put myself out there for you."

She smiled, leaned forward, and kissed his cheek. She then switched off the Zigette, got out of the car, and walked around to the driver's window. "You're the best. I promise I won't fail, and I will find out all I can."

He put his hands up. "You know I'd never doubt you. All the same, if you get into any trouble with Boyd, give me a dot right away, okay?"

"I will, Poipoi."

"Hey, and you *will* come back for Renaissance Night, won't you?"

She laughed. "You know I'd never miss it for the world."

"Awesome. I also got some new costumes. When you get back, let's do another photo shoot together."

She smiled. "Of course. I'd love to."

"Take care of yourself, girlfriend."

"*Do skorova*." She nodded, and gave him another smile.

Paul started the car, then drove away down the street. Fleurine stood watching on until the taillight had completely disappeared. She sighed to herself, then headed off to hail a cab.

33. Sports Drink

The black asphalt extended onward. Ahead of them, a fuzzy collection of lights lay sprinkled across the horizon. Ritika held fast as Raze kept on the throttle, wind buffeting against them both as the bike sped on. Behind them, the dust and smoke from the explosion was now pluming outwards into the night sky. It blotted out the stars, and even the moon, with its murky gray darkness. A smaller building of some kind was appearing ahead of the escapees now. A lit-up sign suggested the building was open for business. It looked to be a gas station and convenience store of some description. Raze spotted the facility, and decided to slow down to investigate.

Ritika noted the drop in speed. "What are you doing?" she asked.

"Need a slate or somethin', so we can talk to Dolly."

"People are going to be looking for us everywhere now. Do you think it's a wise idea to risk stopping?"

"I got no idea where the fuck we goin'. Y'all got any better plans?"

She didn't, so she remained silent.

He switched off the headlights, then coasted the bike in on low throttle. He tried to avoid making any noise with the bike as he pulled onto the side of the road, well before the entrance to the gas station. Then, he snuck the machine up alongside the building, keeping well away from the windows at the front entrance. The pumps around the service area were void of customers, so he felt reasonably confident that they had pulled up completely undetected.

He put the kickstand down, and then he and Ritika got off the bike. She put her hand on her wound. The sealant was holding fine, but the area around the wound hurt like hell.

"Gotta' get some drugs for that," he whispered, noticing her pain.

"Just water and electrolytes, like a sports drink, if they have any," she managed.

"Sports drink?" He look confused. "Y'all don' want somethin' to take the edge off?"

"It's complicated," she answered. "No drugs. Just the drink."

Raze shrugged and pulled out his G20. "Comin' right up," he said as he started to move. Ritika grabbed his shoulder.

"Just a moment," she said. "I'm coming with you."

He shook his head. "Hell no. Stay here. Y'all hurt."

"I'm only hurt. I'm not crippled," she insisted.

He sighed. "AG. Stick close, an' don' do any stupid shit." With that, they began to move towards the front of the building.

He cautiously stepped around the corner. He peeked in through the front window to assess the interior. It was well lit, but looked as empty of people inside as it was outside. The shelves were full of quick snacks and convenience food, and the fridges were filled with drinks. Given the store's apparent lack of customers, Raze wondered how long all those foods and drinks had actually been sitting there. He noted that there was one register, not automated. He then spotted a guy standing behind it. He was a fat man with unkempt hair and a messy shirt. He wasn't looking in Raze's direction. Instead, he was on his slate, talking and gesturing wildly. The man appeared to be upset about something. Raze listened closer. It sounded like he was talking about the bomb, describing the explosion to whomever it was on the line. Raze waved Ritika across. She moved up alongside him.

He slunk forward, jogged to the door, and slipped through it as soon as it began to open. He then advanced on the counter, gun outwards, pointing right at the back of the fat man.

"Put it down, fucker. Turn around and hands up, nice an' slow," Raze ordered as soon as he'd gotten close enough.

The guy froze, carefully put the slate on the counter, then put his hands in the air. He turned to look at Raze, his teenage face awash with pustules and red rashes. His eyes fell on the gun, and he began to tremble.

Raze tilted his head. "Stay chill. Y'all ain't gonna' get hurt, long as y'all do what I say. AG?"

The teen gave a nervous nod. Ritika stepped inside now, and began moving towards the fridges at the rear. The guy watched her as she moved, eyes wide like he'd seen a ghost. Raze got his attention again.

"Don' mind the whelf. She just after a sports drink. Y'all not gonna' get robbed blind."

"Is...Is she...?" the man started to say, but then stopped.

Raze put on his mean mug. "Is she what?"

The guy nervously extended a finger towards the monitors behind Raze. Raze gave him a suspicious look, but took a quick glance in the direction he was pointing. He caught a glimpse of Ritika's photo on the monitors. It was a news report describing her as a wanted fugitive. Raze spun back, aiming his gun at the middle of the man's forehead.

The guy flinched, hands trembling with more intensity now. Raze pressed forward and threatened him. Ritika came walking up, gulping down a large can of Praedo All-GI Sports Fluid. She finished, let out a refreshing sigh, then crushed the can with one hand, and put its crumpled remains on the counter. She then pulled some money out of her pocket.

"The fuck y'all doin'?!" Raze asked.

"I'm paying for the drink."

"Y'all what?!" He started to say more, then just shook his head, deciding there was not point in arguing with her. He looked at the man again. "Yeah, she the good cop. I'm the bad cop. Gimme' that fucking slate now, punk-ass bitch."

The guy obeyed, picking up his device, deactivating its security, and handing it to Raze. Raze then pointed his gun at the comms system, and took a shot, blowing it to pieces. Both Ritika and the man jumped. Raze then started shooting out all the cameras in the store.

Ritika covered her ears, and began yelling at him as he fired away. "What the hell is wrong with you?!"

Raze stopped shooting. Ritika continued, wearing an expression on her face that suggested he was being stupid. "Maybe you could just shoot the recording system instead of the cameras?"

He sighed, then pointed the gun at the man again. "The fuck y'all keep the recording system?"

"I...In the back office," he responded, "but-"

Raze didn't wait for him to finish. He ushered the man into the back office. There, with Ritika's help, he tied the guy up. Then, he destroyed the recording system and activated the locking system for the front doors. He also shut off all the lights, making it look like the store had closed early for the night.

"C'mon, let's move," Raze said to Ritika, nodding his head towards the employee exit at the back of the room.

She turned to the man tied up in the chair. "I apologize for us having to do this to you. If you just wait until the morning, I'm sure someone from your company will be past to-"

"For fuck's sake! Forget his fat ass. Let's move!"

She moved after Raze as he headed out. He started thumbing at the slate he'd procured. He signed in to his Vueve profile, hoping Dolly would notice he'd found a way back online with a new device.

34. Upgrades

Twenty minutes later, they passed a sign welcoming them to Shandonville. The speed limit had dropped to forty. Until now, Raze hadn't concerned himself too much with speed limits, but he slowed down now as he spotted the activity that was unfolding further up ahead. Camouflaged trucks. Barricades. A light company of troops. Prowler units setting up.

He stopped the bike, killed the headlights, and turned to Ritika. "Fuck. We got any other way in?"

She looked at the map projecting from the slate. The pathway Dolly had drawn was a direct route leading straight into town. She twisted the image a little clockwise, then pointed towards some shrubs and trees. "If we can find a way through all that, there's some kind of earth-moving operation over there. Get past that facility, and it's possible we can enter the town from that side."

Raze shrugged. "Fine with me."

He gave the bike some throttle, then headed off-road through the bushes and into the thicket of trees. However, driving through the thicket without headlights was proving perilous. The darkness made it almost impossible to see any hazards. Raze cursed, wishing he had brought the Greyface. Its night vision functions would have worked a charm in this situation. He kept his eyes peeled, darting the bike around while trying to avoid plowing into any tree trunks that loomed out of the darkness.

A whining, droning sound now started from somewhere overhead. Raze suspected it would be one of the Prowlers on patrol in the area. He slowed down. Ritika started looking skywards, trying to catch a glimpse of the machine, but she couldn't see past the treetops above her.

At last, the trees began to open out into a clearing. The earth-moving facility they were searching for emerged into view. At the same time, Ritika spotted the Prowler, which was heading off in the opposite direction. There was no chance it would spot them, as long as they were quick.

"Go," she urged.

Raze drove onto the dirt driveway. He weaved through the heavy equipment parked around the yard of the facility. Then, he drove towards the fence line, where he spotted an area of the fence that had collapsed. He moved the bike over to it, and pushed through the crumpled tin, across to the other side. A small street greeted them. They were now inside the boundaries of the town.

Onward they rode, sneaking through the streets. They stopped at every intersection to confirm the coast was clear before moving on. The streets had only sparse lighting, an occasional street lamp here and there, flickering a dull but inoffensive beige light. Ritika continued giving navigation instructions to Raze. Before long, they had found the center of town. Many of the shops looked like they were out of business. The streets were completely empty. It was almost as though the town had experienced a disaster and been evacuated a long time ago.

Suddenly, an armored personnel carrier turned onto the main road ahead and started coming towards them. Ritika spotted the side alley they were searching for. She pointed to it, and Raze drove the bike into the alley. The truck passed them by and continued rumbling along down the road, seemingly oblivious to their existence. The slate now pinged and ran an animation to notify Ritika they had arrived at their destination. Raze turned off the bike. They both dismounted. Raze held the bike while Ritika looked up and down the alleyway. She cradled her wound and took a few steps around to check their surroundings. The whole alley looked empty except a few oversize dumpsters, and even those didn't look like they had seen use in quite some time.

"The fuck is it?" Raze asked, now wheeling the bike over to one of the dumpsters. He parked the bike behind it to keep the machine out of sight.

Ritika pointed the slate around the street, trying to locate where they should go next. She spotted the door, a rusted sign reading "Dr. Massoud Farvardin, Drop Off Bay" hanging above it, and waved Raze across.

Together, they walked towards the door, eyes on the lookout for anything moving. Then, they ascended the short set of stairs leading to the loading bay. Raze nodded for Ritika to get behind him, then he rapped the back of his knuckles against the door. Nothing. He turned to her, exchanging shrugs, then knocked again. This time, there was a stirring behind the door—shuffling sounds, like tennis shoes on concrete. They heard the lock turn. Then, the door inched open, and a worn, bearded face peered out. The man spoke with a thick, Iranian accent. "You and the girl?"

Raze nodded, shifting aside so the man could see Ritika. The man nodded, then waved them into his premises. "Inside. Hurry!"

They both stepped into the clinic. The doctor did a quick check to ensure they weren't followed, then closed the door. The clinic looked as though it had seen busier days. It was outfitted with a range of medical test equipment, though some still had plastic coverings on them. The doctor noticed Raze looking around at the gear and laughed. "People like to have machines treat them now. Not too much calling for a man with my skills anymore. That's why these things sit here, unused. That blood analyzer, for example," he indicated the unit. "That hasn't seen any use in five years."

"This whole town looks that way, but you still live and work here?" Ritika asked.

"Yes. I guess you could say I've done enough moving in my life to want to pack up again," he said, then smiled. "Massoud Farvardin. Doctor," he said, "and bachelor." He kissed Ritika's hand. She smiled. Both she and Raze introduced themselves.

The doctor then noticed her wound. "That looks very nasty. You sealed it?"

Raze nodded. "Used somethin' called Tramablok."

The doctor looked inquisitive. "You mean, Traumablok? Well, that would help a lot." He looked at Ritika again. "You seem to be in a pretty good state, considering that wound. A person should be in hospital with an injury like that. Are you sure you're okay?"

"I seem to be holding together for the moment," she answered.

"Well, we really should check to see if you have any internal bleeding." He switched on the lights in the room. Then, he indicated an observation table. He began powering up his analysis equipment.

She sat on the table, then lay back. "Doctor, this might be stretching my luck, but do you have anything like Triglozene?"

The doctor screwed up his face. "I'm sorry, but I've never heard of that drug. What is it?"

Ritika just shook her head. "Never mind." She watched as the doctor approached her, then began tapping a sequence on the keypad to start up the scanner. She sighed. "Just don't panic when you see the results of this scan."

The doctor looked at Raze, who simply shrugged in response. Then, he looked back at Ritika. "Is it okay for me to do a scan?"

"Sure," she said, but her voice sounded resigned.

The doctor finished typing the sequence into the machine, and the scanner went into action. Its motorized head angled up over Ritika, then began scanning her from foot to head. Once it finished, a three-dimensional scan of her internals projected onto the holographic plate. Doctor Farvardin squinted. He shook his head, removed his reading glasses from his pocket, then took a closer look with the glasses on.

Raze noticed the doctor's reaction. "Somethin' up, Doc?"

The doctor finished examining the image. He took off his glasses and glanced back at Ritika, shocked. "This doesn't make sense. Medically speaking, you are completely anomalous. Your key organs are...missing...and you have organs that don't exist in a human body. I can't..." He stopped and shrugged. "I don't even know what half of these things inside you are."

Ritika nodded. "It's normal for me. My work at M3Raymond-Kennel Systems involves research into military prototypes for bio-augmentation. I use myself as a test subject."

Raze now looked more confused. "What's it mean? Y'all like a cyborg or somethin'?"

"Cyborg isn't the word. I'm almost completely biological. My team and I redesign human organs into more efficient forms. We DNA match them to a target individual, then print them and upgrade the host. The upside for the host is that they get a more efficient body. Stronger," she said, looking at Raze teasingly. "Much stronger, actually. Plus, more athleticism, more durability. Even built-in redundancies for organ damage or failure, accelerated healing, and longer life."

The doctor nodded. He looked intrigued.

She continued. "You can understand how a soldier might like an upgrade, especially one that makes them twenty times the person they once were." She then shrugged. "There are, of course, side effects that one has to live with after the upgrades."

"Yes," the doctor said, "I imagine your body would have very different biological requirements, even to keep itself running day-to-day."

"Diet-wise, certainly. Also, certain drugs are necessary to help me keep everything running smoothly."

Raze nodded, not entirely following what they were saying, but he was plagued by another thought. "What about..." he began, not sure how to word it. He opted instead to make some hip-thrusting movements.

Ritika gave him a tired look. "If you're asking about sex, the answer is yes, that's normal. I'd be hardly inclined to want to remove that particular biological function. That would be a downgrade, not an upgrade." Then, she looked more sternly at him. "And, no, you may not see for yourself."

Raze lifted his palms outwards and smiled. "Fine with me."

The doctor moved towards the cooler in the room, and opened its large doors. "Well, I don't know if I have anything in here that can help you, but you're welcome to have a look at my drug selection. Maybe there's something you can piece together from this and other OTCs that I have."

"Thank you, Doctor Farvardin," Ritika said.

Land of the Free

"And, please, make yourselves at home, and feel free to help yourselves to the fridge out back. I promise you will be safe here. There are separate rooms with beds that you can use for tonight. I believe your people in Texas are already working on some way to get you moving to your next destination."

35. A Favor

The doors to the Situation Room burst open. White stormed out into the corridor, his face looking drawn as he fought his mental fatigue. He was soon followed by a retinue of attendants, swooping behind him and looking equally as tired. Vice President Davies was tapping on his slate, trying to set up an alert function to keep him posted on reports from the field. Ellis was talking with his HQ, checking to ensure that all roadblocks had been set up around the region of the plane crash.

Boyd was looking like death warmed over. He was nursing his head, which now felt like an oversize watermelon. The Elation had almost completely run its course now, and the aftereffects were in full swing. He rubbed the sides of his thumping temples. The massaging helped a little, but it still felt like his brain was trying to squeeze its way out of his skull.

The men moved towards reception hall. White and the others spotted Bryce Vaughn of M3Raymond-Kennel as they entered the room. He had arrived some time earlier, and was now waiting in one of the handcrafted antique seats reserved for visiting guests.

He lifted his hand to get White's attention. "Mister President, sir." He got up and moved over to intercept White as he passed by.

"Glad to see you're here, Bryce," said the president as they continued walking.

"Not a problem at all, sir. I just wanted to let you know that I've already had our tech department do a sweep of all our main systems. They covered Redmond, Chicago, and Albuquerque. The techs say they haven't detected any attempts by Sinha to access military hardware-at least, not in the past week. As far as we can tell, all weapons purchased from us by the FSA are clear of tampering."

"That's at least some positive news," White said. "Anything else you wish to share?"

"Well..." he began, but then paused, thinking of the best way to word what he would say next. "Frankly, sir, there's probably more bad news than anything else."

The president rolled his eyes.

"Although tech couldn't find any attempts to crack any hardware, they *did* manage to find something else: evidence that someone had accessed our personnel database. The source seems to have come from the Middle East, though the boys say the real attack origin was faked through some kind of darknet proxy."

Davies pointed at him. "You can bet that will be Texas."

Vaughn nodded, though his face looked unconvinced.

White noticed his hesitation. "Is there something wrong, Bryce?"

Vaughn gave an uneasy laugh. "Well, I appreciate that conclusion. It's just that..." He shook his head.

White groaned. "Spit it out, man. In case you haven't noticed, we're all exhausted."

"Well, Mister President, the thing is, if it *is* Texas behind the intrusion into our databases, that's not a good sign. It would mean they have access to seriously high-level computing hardware, well beyond what we'd expect them to have. Our Cybersecurity Forensics Department says the attack on our systems was unprecedented—off the scale, even. They said whoever did it would have to be using computing resources on par with China."

"China?"

"Yes. As in, all of China. Every hacking collective in the entire country attacking us at the same time. Also, it was done with coordination like we haven't seen before. They attacked, and then just disappeared like ghosts. I was alarmed by that, so I spoke with major Vueve providers. Here's where it gets interesting. They say they've seen similar traffic repeating-"

"Bryce," White said with an exhausted sigh and stopped walking. Everyone else stopped dead in their tracks too, and listened to White as he continued. "It's very late, and I understand this must mean something significant, but right now I want us to focus on getting this girl and moving ahead with our attack. Does this intrusion you speak of have any impact on our units in the field?"

"Not directly, sir, no."

"Then, let's leave it to your forensics department to track down the culprit of the attack. We can keep our priorities on thwarting this girl, and any chance she has at sabotaging our equipment." He looked at the surrounding men in turn. "Are we all clear on that?"

The men responded in the affirmative.

"Very well. General Ellis, if by some miracle this girl is still alive, I want to know about it the moment your men find her and take her into custody. Otherwise, I'd like to try to get the semblance of a good night's sleep. I want to arrive here fresh tomorrow morning, so that we can all work on pushing forward with our plans. Does that sound fair?"

The men nodded.

"Excellent. Then let's do that. Goodnight, gentlemen." With that, White retreated towards his quarters. The other attendants began to break away, heading back to wherever it was they called home.

Boyd let out a sigh of relief, glad that he could finally get out of the White House and have a chance to sleep off his headache. He was assuming, of course, that Laura and the kids had already gone to bed. At this time of night, he figured there was no reason to think they'd still be awake.

He started to move to the corridor that led to the parking area. He took a left, then a right, saw the parking area ahead, and moved towards it. However, after a few paces, he began to hear the sound of footsteps behind him. He turned, and was surprised to see Ellis, Vaughn, and Davies approaching. Their faces looked like anxious, smiling masks. Boyd stopped for them to catch up, and gave them a confused look as they neared and flanked him.

"Hey, Dick," Davies began, putting his hand on Boyd's shoulder as he stepped up, "can we have a word?"

Boyd looked at them both. "A word? What about?"

Ellis and Vaughn made a sketchy look up and down the hall to ensure no one was watching, then turned back to Boyd.

"Listen," Ellis said. "We've been talking, and we want to know something. How good is your relationship with Yulov, really?"

Boyd smelled a trap. He wondered how he should best respond here. Bullshitting them might be the only viable option. He nodded his head. "Yulov? He and I have an understanding. Why do you ask?"

Davies nodded, exchanged looks with the other two men, then stepped closer to Boyd. "We were wondering if you might be able to talk to him and, you know, test the waters to ask him for a favor."

Boyd felt his level of importance go up a notch. These guys were coming to him for help with something? That was a first.

He touched his tie, then shrugged with indifference. "Well, sure. I think he'd be happy to do me a favor. What is it you have in mind?"

36. Treason

Texas Senator Robert Clifford sat back, then took a sip of his coffee. He looked out over the expanse of his property from the comfort of his porch. He was half-focused in watching his wife and children. They were frolicking about, playing games of chase in the sunlit fields with their pet Labradors, Gopher and Hooch. The other half of his focus was on his slate. He was listening to FSA newscaster Deborah Bates, who was reporting via the international stream for *Patriot News Hour*.

"And now, breaking news from Texas. President Darlene Richards has issued a scathing attack over the FSA's defensive buildup along the Texas border. Richards called the move a blatant threat to regional peace. She then went on to say that any continued buildup will be seen as an act of hostility that will not go unpunished..."

Clifford's wife called out to him and waved. Clifford returned her wave with a bittersweet smile.

"Richards says she is more than ready to resort to military action if necessary. When she was asked how any such actions might end she said, quote, 'Make no mistake. We will defeat the FSA.'"

Hearing this, Clifford just laughed, then closed his eyes. Images flashed in his mind. He imagined what his ranch would look like after White's forces had bombed the place to kingdom come, after they had run armored divisions all over his fields. Clifford then wondered which of the trees around his property they would hang him from; that was, after the FSA had first captured him, shot his family, and killed all his livestock and those who worked for him.

"In further news, a state-wide manhunt continues in Oklahoma today for escaped Constitutional Terrorist Ritika Sinha. The latest reports indicate she is working with an accomplice. This recently acquired security footage from a convenience store robbery shows..."

Clifford dismissed the feed from his slate. He then turned to fellow Senator Pedro Iglesias, who was seated in the chair beside him.

"Help yourself to another waffle, Pedro. No point in stickin' to that diet now. This may well be the last breakfast for either of us."

Pedro's haggard face stared forward. He looked as though he hadn't slept. Like Clifford, he could do nothing but entertain thoughts of doom. He shook his head, then managed to will himself to look across at the waffles. He took one, and had a bite. It was sugary, but did little to improve his mood.

Clifford pulled the front of his Stetson down over his eyes and leaned back. "You know, I was never a particularly smart man, but I always got by with what I had." He indicated his property with a nod. "Built all this up myself. My daddy didn't leave me anything. Surly old son of a bitch, he was. Old school, tough as nails." He gave a brief chuckle. "Told me straight out the day I turned sixteen that I'd never amount to anything. Always felt I did pretty damn good in spite o' that glowing endorsement o' his."

Iglesias remained mute, unable to find the words to express his total sense of despair. Clifford lifted his Stetson, then glanced across at him. "You came from humble beginnings too, so you know where I'm coming from. You know what it's like, working your rear off year-in and year-out to build everything up, start a family, make a name for yourself." He leaned in closer. "Kinda' hard to accept, ain't it? That it can all be undone in a matter o' days, all thanks to the harebrained moves of one woman in power." He laughed a dark, ironic laugh.

At last, Iglesias found his voice. "I still haven't told Isabella."

Clifford looked at him, shocked. "Not a word?"

He shook his head. "Nope, not a word. I don't want her to suffer, knowing what's coming for us all." He closed his eyes. "Even this morning, I told her I was going in early to get some work done, business as usual."

Clifford gave a grim smile, put his hand on Iglesias' shoulder, and gave it a gentle squeeze. He then looked back at his kids. "Well, you know what? I called you out here this morning because I want us to make a promise to one another today, Pedro."

Iglesias looked to him. "A promise? What kind of promise?"

Clifford rubbed his jaw, and his voice took on a determined tone. "If—and I mean *if*—by the grace o' God, you and I manage to get through this whole mess, we're going to talk to the others. We're going to find a way to convince them to remove our resident lady dictator from her seat."

Iglesias scoffed. "Good luck with that. Even with everything that's going on, Richards still has that talent for sweet talking people into doing things her way." He leaned in closer to Clifford. "You know, after you left yesterday, I went back with the others who wanted to get their issues sorted. Richards just sat down with us, one by one. She dealt with everyone until they walked away happy, like everything was going to be alright. I even half-believed her myself, even though, when I got home, I realized again how bad it was going to be. But, it's like she has a silver tongue." He shook his head. "Sorry, Robert, but I don't think we'll ever get her voted out."

Clifford gave an understanding nod. He considered his next words for a few seconds. Then, he said, "Well, perhaps it's high time we started looking at alternative ways to have her removed."

Iglesias laughed. "Very funny. I'm sure that would go down well." He turned to Clifford and saw the look in his eyes. "Wait. You can't be serious?"

"You're telling me, feeling the way you do now, knowing she's putting you and your family on the line, that you want to go on with her being in charge of things?"

"Of course, I don't want that. But, Robert, you're talking about killing her?"

"Nothing so crude. I'm just suggesting that maybe it's high time you and I start looking for friendships outside this great Republic of ours."

Iglesias looked thoughtful for a moment, then shook his head. "I don't know, Robert. I understand why you're frustrated, but that would be treason."

Clifford leaned towards him again. "Pedro, your problem is that you keep thinking of her as a president. You don't perceive her for what she truly is."

Iglesias shrugged. "And what is that?"

"An enemy o' the State, Pedro, my son. Simple as that." Clifford lowered his Stetson across his eyes again. "And the people who remove an enemy o' the State from power are called heroes. It's the people the heroes remove from power who end up getting charged with treason, not people like us."

Iglesias gave Clifford's words some consideration, took up another waffle, and had a bite. "So, it's like that, is it?"

Clifford looked at him from under the rim of his hat, and gave him a nod.

37. The UMC

Doctor Massoud Farvardin poured some more *Chai Shirin* into Raze and Ritika's cups. He then returned his *samovar* to the table. Raze was ravenous. He ate with gusto, savoring the flavors of the meat, bread, and omelet before him. The doctor smiled as he watched him enjoy his meal. Raze was glad to be having real food again. As he munched, he decided that, without question, there was no substitute for real meals. Ritika had decided on the *Adasi* this morning. She avoided the meat, feeling that eating vegetarian would be easier for her stomach to digest at the moment. Her wound was healing well. Already, she suspected it was about forty percent recovered. So long as she could refrain from exerting herself too much over the next few days—a week, at most—she should be back to normal. She took a sip of her chai, looked up at the doctor, and returned his caring smile.

"Thank you so much for doing all this for us," she said.

"Don't mention it, my dear. I'm just glad you could find your way here."

Raze took a sip of his tea, then pointed to his food. "Yeah, this all hap, doc. Thanks."

"Just a humble Iranian breakfast." He shrugged.

"Y'all should come with us. I could eat this shit all day."

The doctor laughed, got up from the table, and went over to his control desk. He started tapping out a sequence to log in to

Vueve, then switched his profile to online. "I imagine your friends in Texas will be calling soon."

Ritika swallowed another spoonful of her *Adasi*, and turned to the doctor. "How is it you know Richards and the others?"

Farvardin turned to her. "Oh, I've never met Richards in person, but I know one of the men who works for her, a nice man by the name of Ben Rollins. I met him him years ago when he was on a tour of duty in Iran. He was a U.S. Marine back in those days."

"That long ago, huh?"

"Yes," he said, looking thoughtful. "Yes, I guess it was."

"Y'all look like a man who's seen a lot," Raze said. "Can see it in them eyes."

Farvardin nodded. "You are right. I have seen my share of trauma. The last few years of the Great Holy War were horrifying. At times, I didn't even think I would survive. But, I'm glad that I was spared—Allah be praised—and I'm very happy to have spent the last few decades in peace here. Now, I only wish the years would go more slowly for this old man. I hope there are another sixty years of life for me, and that time slows for me to enjoy them. Still, time takes its toll on our bodies." He looked at Ritika. "That is, until some intelligent young lady manages to find a way to stop us aging completely someday."

Ritika laughed. "Oh no. We're a long way from anything like that. I mean, I've been able to slow down aging for myself a little, but time will get to me too." She looked thoughtful. "We'll work it out, eventually. I can tell you I have an incentive to find a solution. I don't like the idea of looking at myself one morning and finding crows feet and gray hair. No offense, doctor."

Farvardin laughed. "None taken. It's true. We don't like to get older, but time has a way of catching up on us all, my dear. One day, you're a young boy, lazing about in your village, having fun like the passing sun doesn't mean anything. Then, another day, you look in the mirror and find out ten years have passed." He made a pensive face. "You begin to look around at everyone you know. You say to them, angrily, 'Why didn't you tell me to get running?'" He laughed.

"I know that feeling, doc," Raze said. "I got the moves. Still, love to turn the clock back myself a little."

"Yes, well, unfortunately, we are still bound to the heavenly laws that govern us all. Life is a journey from Allah to Allah, after all. We should cherish every moment that we have because we never know how long any of us have left. Some of us might live on for years. For others, this could be the last day we have on this earth."

A tone began to sound from the control desk. Farvardin pointed one finger skywards. "Ah, I wonder who that might be?" He tapped out another sequence on the deck. The holographic projector lit up, and images of President Richards, Carla Ibanez, Ben Rollins, and Dolly appeared in the room.

Raze took a look at Dolly, then did a quick head tilt to acknowledge her. "Sup, girl?" Dolly put her hand to her mouth, and let a coy laugh escape her lips.

Farvardin extended his arms towards the four people in the image. "*Sabah alkhyr*, my friends. As you asked, so here they are."

Ben Rollins applauded. "Massoud, I can't thank you enough..."

Farvardin put his hands up. "No. Please, no. Do not thank me, Ben. I am forever in your debt for all the kind acts you have done for me."

President Richards looked at Ritika. "Miss Sinha, you can't imagine how glad I am to see you alive. How y'all feelin' this mornin'?"

"I am not doing too badly at all, President Richards. I think you have this man to thank for that." She indicated Raze with her open hand.

Raze shrugged. "AG on that. Ain't no sweat. Y'all call the best there is."

"So it seems," Richards nodded. "We appreciate everything you've done, Mister Raze."

"Yeah, well, we still ain't there yet. Y'all can thank me when it's in person. Speakin' o' that..."

"Yes," Carla said, "I understand there is some kind of lockdown in place. It's going to be impossible for you to get out of there using civilian vehicles for the moment. Ben and I have been looking for a way to get you moving along."

"Oh?"

"That's right," Ben said. "Look. It's not the best idea, but it's the best hand we got, all things considered." He exchanged a look with Carla, then looked back at Raze. "How y'all feel about the UMC?"

Raze did a double-take in shock. Ritika looked uneasy. Farvardin stepped towards the monitor. "The UMC? The UMC would be willing to help them?"

Ben nodded.

Raze laughed. "Shit, sib, y'all tweakin'. They all racist-ass motherfuckers."

"He's right," Ritika agreed. "Why would a white supremacist group go out of their way to help us?"

"Damn straight. They light us up and barbecue our asses the first chance they get."

Ben and Carla looked briefly at one another again. Ben moved forward in his seat before answering. "Well, I won't deny what y'all sayin' is true. Thing is, a few of their higher members I know from way, way back—not that I ever agreed with their particular philosophical views in any way. I want to make that perfectly clear to y'all. Thing is, though, they share an affinity for Texas. Kinda' look up to us as a role model for opposing FSA rule. So, you see, we have a kind of *de facto* alliance with them—under the table, that is."

Raze looked at Ritika, and saw the unease in her eyes. He turned back to Ben and Richards. "I say no way."

Ben sighed. "Raze, Ritika, I understand how you feel, but, look, it's just going to be one guy and his truck. How much trouble can that be?"

Ritika shrugged, then gave Raze a look to suggest they had nothing to lose.

Raze rolled his eyes and shook his head. "This shit jus' keeps gettin' better 'n better."

38. Closer

The main prayer hall of the First Presbyterian Church of Arlington was, to Boyd's relief, almost completely empty this early in the morning. Only one old woman, whose clothing and baggage suggested she was homeless, was laying there among the pews. She rolled over, making some quiet moaning noises to herself as he entered. Then, as he passed her, the woman suddenly sat up, but it didn't seem to be Boyd's presence that had startled her. Instead, she looked as though she'd heard someone yelling at her. The woman huffed in contempt, then started an argument with some person she imagined was sitting alongside her. Boyd recoiled, a little unnerved by her actions, but moved on.

He went a little further down the aisle, choosing to sit near in the center of a pew on the right-hand side of the building. He tried to make himself comfortable—at least, as comfortable as he *could* feel in a place of worship. He began to think he should have chosen a less unsettling spot for this morning's rendezvous.

Time passed. Boyd fidgeted. He wasn't sure how long it would be until Fleurine arrived. He looked around, trying to be inconspicuous. His eyes kept darting up to the oak cross that served as the room's centerpiece. He felt that the cross was somehow alive and staring at him, judging him. He tugged at his collar and swallowed.

He asked himself if he should pray while he was waiting. He didn't know if he wanted to. He couldn't even remember the last time he had said a prayer. In fact, it must have been years since

Land of the Free

he last saw the inside of a church. He tried to recall when that last time was. Of course, there had been the wedding with Laura, but when had he last visited a church for a religious reason? He recalled going as a child, as was expected of him by his parents, but as an adult? He couldn't remember. No, wait, the last time must have been—oh, that was right, it was right after Diane had had her... He refused to think about that.

He tried to distract his thoughts with something else, but now he couldn't. The child would have been around twenty years old this year—that is, if she had decided to go through with the pregnancy. He couldn't understand why Diane had done it. The pregnancy had been unplanned, but they could have worked it out. He could have given her a promotion at the company. But, no, she had just taken off and refused to have anything further to do with him. He closed his eyes. After what she had done, Boyd hoped there was a special place in hell for women like her-or, whatever she had changed her name to. The world needed more decent and moral women in it, not women like her. He hoped the prayers he'd said that day when he last visited the church had found their mark. Perhaps God would have taken vengeance on Diane for him, maybe given her a shit marriage to some abusive asshole. Perhaps they were barely scraping by a living in the ass end of nowhere. He smiled at thinking how fitting that would be.

Just then, a shuffling sound from the direction of the entrance grabbed Boyd's attention. He ventured a look over his shoulder. There she was, standing in the doorway, dressed in a snug and classy-looking dress. She'd covered the top of her head with a shawl, but removed her sunglasses as she stepped inside. She spotted Boyd almost right away with those magnetic, angel-blue eyes of hers. He waved her over. She moved down the aisle, then across the pew, seating her petite form alongside him.

Boyd nodded to her shawl. "Coming in disguise?"

She looked thoughtful for a second. "This?" She touched it. "Oh, it's an old tradition."

"It's something ladies in France do?"

She laughed and tilted her head. "Hmm...something like that."

They both looked forward, sitting there for a moment in silence. After a time, he looked at her, then leaned in. "I have to say, I had an amazing time last night."

She raised an eyebrow. "I'm pleased to hear it."

"I had some aftereffects though..."

She let a quiet laugh escape her mouth. "You get used to that over time."

He looked down, fidgeted, then looked at her again. "How about you?"

She gave him a whimsical smile and tilted her head slightly. Then, she leaned in with a whisper. "I didn't know sex could feel like that," and she winked.

"Really?" Boyd puffed out his chest and adjusted his tie. He knew he was good in bed, but he'd never heard a woman tell him so. "Well, you're welcome."

They laughed quietly, then sat for another few seconds in silence. The homeless woman was now yelling at herself. Her croaky voice echoed throughout the hall as she argued with her imaginary friend. She got to her feet and grabbed her bags. Then, she started walking down the aisle, motioning with her arms like she was pushing someone out of the church. A few moments later, she was out the door, possibly headed someplace that was less crowded for her.

Once she had gone, Fleurine leaned towards Boyd. "Okay, shall we?" She got down on her knees in between his legs, and started fumbling with his belt.

He drew back, "Whoa! Stop, stop!" She looked up at him quizzically.

He quickly glanced around the church, then looked back down at her. "What is the matter with you? Are you crazy?"

She gave him a confused look. "What do you mean? You said you wanted to meet me."

"Yeah, but I meant to talk. What, you think I wanted us to do it in a church?"

Fleurine shrugged, seemingly confused by his reluctance for her to proceed. She got back up and sat on the pew beside him.

Boyd, meanwhile, was feeling dumbstruck by her behavior. He loosened his tie, then took another quick look around to ensure they hadn't been spotted engaging in that behavior just now. He also began to feel his body heating up from the thrill it had given him. He was starting to think this girl was insane, but then, there was also something incredibly intoxicating about her insanity. She just didn't seem to give a fuck about anything, and he absolutely loved that. Still, he tried to put these thoughts out of his mind right now, and instead recall what it was he needed to speak to her about.

"Um..." he began, regaining his train of thought.

"Yes?" she asked, eyes twinkling.

"So, yesterday at the White House, a couple of the guys from the Administration wanted me to ask a favor from Yulov. Do you think you could help with that?"

She looked pleased at him asking this. "Of course, Richard. What is it you would like me to ask Dimitry?"

"Well, have you ever heard of the R4 network?"

"Yes," she said, "that's Dimitry's pride and joy. He goes on about it all the time."

"I see," he nodded. "Well, the guys were asking if you might be able to ask Dimitry to...well..."

"Well, what?"

Boyd twitched his shoulders. "Maybe you could ask him to shut it down for a while..."

Fleurine's eyes widened. She rocked back with laughter, then stopped as she realized he was serious. "Shut down the R4 network? I doubt it. Why on earth would they want him to do that?"

He shifted in his seat. "Well, look, I can't really tell you why they want him to do it. But, if you asked Dimitry, do you think he would do it, even if it were just for an hour?"

She shrugged. "I don't know. I guess he might do it if I asked him to." Then, she turned her face forward and looked askance at him. "What would I get in return for doing that for you?"

He looked across at her. "What do you mean?"

She looked down. "Well, you want me to ask a favor from Dimitry. A big one, like shutting down the R4 network." Then she turned and looked directly into his eyes. "So what are you going to give me in return for my help?"

Boyd was speechless. He shrugged his shoulders. "I...I don't know. What do you want?"

She looked thoughtful, and briefly turned her blue eyes skyward as she thought about it. She then fixed her eyes on him again. "I'd like you to find a way for us to be closer."

"Closer?" He looked uneasy.

"Yes. A way I can be around you more of the time."

He wrinkled his brow. He wasn't sure what she meant by those words, and he hoped she wasn't suggesting a more committed relationship. That was something he simply wouldn't be prepared to do. He scratched the back of his head and winced.

Fleurine laughed at his discomfort. "Is that too much to ask?"

"Well," he sighed, "I'd have to see what I could do...but okay." He coughed gently.

She smiled. "Great! Well, if they want me to go ahead, just give me a call and I'll speak to Dimitry."

She started to get up, but Boyd suddenly sat forward. "Uh, hey!"

She turned back to him.

He swallowed hard, signaling his discomfort. "Before you go..." He made some awkward motions towards his groin with his eyes. Fleurine sighed and rolled her eyes. She then put on a crafty smile, and knelt down between his legs for a second time.

Boyd leaned back and waited for the sensations of pleasure to fill him. All the while, he kept his eyes on the lookout for other people, so that he could signal for her to stop before they got caught. As soon as he felt the touch of her lips against his skin, his eyes shot up to the wooden cross on the wall.

"Oh, Jesus Christ!" he exclaimed.

39. True Badasses

"Ain't no way this goin' down good," Raze said. He checked the slate for the time: 10:35 AM. Still no show. He wondered why this asshole they were waiting for was so late.

Raze, Ritika, and Doctor Farvardin were in the back alley behind the doctor's shop. They were watching both ends of the alleyway for signs of the truck that was supposedly coming for them. Farvardin looked relaxed, sitting back on the loading dock and drinking his chai. Ritika was pulling at the dark blue T-shirt Farvardin had given her to wear. She was trying to find an angle that made it fit more snugly. It was old, two sizes too big, and had been made from some cheap and tacky fabric that made her skin itch. No matter how much she tugged and adjusted it, the thing just looked like a burlap sack. It definitely wasn't flattering to her appearance, but at least it covered her wound, and it looked better than the bloodied sportswear she'd been wearing last night. Still, she was acutely aware that she should avoid bending forward from now on. The neckline of the shirt had been stretched out badly, and she didn't want to embarrass herself with any clothing malfunctions.

Ritika then noticed Raze looking at her. His face suggested he was tired of her fussing with the shirt.

"What's the matter?" she asked.

"Why don't you just tie it?"

She looked at the shirt. "Tie it? What with, precisely?"

He opened his pocket pack, pulled out another of his black restraining straps, and handed it to her. She took the strap and, with a bit of improvisation, wrapped it around her waist a few times. The final result looked almost like a kind of baggy dress and belt. It wouldn't win any fashion awards, but it looked a lot better than it did before.

Doctor Farvardin nodded his approval. "It looks very nice," he said, jokingly.

Ritika and Raze both laughed.

They then heard the sound of something large rolling along at the end of the alley. They all looked towards the source of the noise. From around the corner came a silver, angular-looking vehicle the size of a semi-trailer. Despite its size, the machine deftly made the turn into the alleyway, and rolled forward towards Raze and Ritika. The machine was electric powered and eerily silent. The only noise it made was the sound of its tires on the concrete as it rolled along.

Raze felt an instinctive twitch in his hand as he spotted the vehicle coming towards them. Something inside him was telling him to go for his gun, but he restrained himself. He wanted to first check and see if this was the guy they were waiting for. He also briefly considered that, even if this *was* the guy, it might be smarter to simply kill him and steal his truck. On the surface, that seemed like the safest move, but he quickly realized that, if he or Ritika were spotted driving the vehicle themselves, they'd be identified and pulled over immediately. That wouldn't end well for either of them.

Raze cursed to himself, realizing he had no choice but to let this guy drive them to their destination. He tried to calm down, and told himself to extend some trust. The only thing was, every fiber of his being was screaming at him not to trust a member of the United Militia of Christ.

The truck came to a halt a few feet from the back loading bay of Farvardin's clinic. The driver's side door opened, and out stepped a heavily tattooed and overweight man. He was around forty-five years old, totally bald with a red mustache, and had a face that looked like he was some cousin's cousin. The man eased himself to street level, then waddled forward a few steps to look closer at the people standing before him.

"You two the package?" he asked, face screwed up and mouth full of chewing tabacco.

Raze and Ritika exchanged a look with one another. Ritika then nodded to the driver. "Yes."

The man took another couple of chews while he looked them up and down with suspicion, then he spat on the ground. "Aurigh'." He waved them forward.

Raze and Ritika moved towards him, following him around to the back of his truck.

"Name's Ted," he offered. Raze and Ritika introduced themselves. Ted continued, "Doin' a run to New Mexico right now. Can pull over somewhere near the border 'long the way for you. How's that sound?"

Ritika nodded. "That would be fantastic. Thank you for your help."

"Not doin' it to help you coloreds," he quipped. "Just helpin' a friend of a friend." He then gave Raze a challenging look. "We clear on that, half-boy?"

Raze put his hands up to gesture that he wouldn't be any trouble.

Ted punched a code into the keypad on the truck, and the rear of the trailer opened. The inside was lined with pallets of packaged dry goods. Most of the cases were labeled as foodstuffs manufactured by Praedo Labs.

Raze looked over all the boxes of food, consoling himself that at least they wouldn't go hungry if the truck broke down on the way to Texas.

Ted punched another code and the rear lift on the trailer moved down to ground level.

"Up ya' get," Ted said, indicating the ramp.

Raze and Ritika waved to Doctor Farvardin, who returned the gesture. Then, they stepped onto the lift. Ted punched another code and the lift began retracting into the trailer.

Once the lift had fully retracted, Raze and Ritika stepped inside the trailer. The trailer doors then closed behind them, sealing with a thud. It was now pitch-black all around them.

Raze activated the glow function on his slate, which gave off a dull green illumination. It wasn't much by way of light, but it was enough for him to make out both their surroundings and the look of fear on Ritika's face.

"Raze, this is really disconcerting," she said.

"Yeah, same here," he responded. "Don' worry. Asshole tries anything, I'ma bust some motherfucking caps in his head. Can promise y'all that."

"You think we can trust him?"

He shrugged. "Don' see what choice we got. Gotta' be safer n' what we been through already." He looked at her. She was still unnerved. He smiled in an attempt to cheer her up. "Hey, remember that we survived a plane crash and dodged a goddamn nuke. Can't say we ain't true badasses now, girl."

The words put a smile on Ritika's face and she laughed. "No, I guess not."

Raze nodded. "AG. That's the spirit."

40. Koroleva

Paul Nu walked past the circus and gymnastics training areas, then took the passageway on his left. He stepped onto the sand-colored escalator that would lead him down into the Oasis. He adjusted his shirt and tie, mentally preparing for the environment to become more balmy as he descended.

The climate systems in this section of the compound produced tropical conditions. This was not only for the pleasure of the staff, but also for the benefit of the palm trees and other vegetation found here. Many tropical varieties of plants had been planted throughout this area in order to give it a relaxed, Caribbean vibe. The effect was convincing in its realism. In fact, to anyone visiting it for the first time, the whole area was nothing short of an engineering marvel. Many wondered how Yulov did it.

The humidity rose around Paul now. It wasn't unpleasant, just not the ideal climate for someone wearing a full suit. He stepped off the escalator alongside the "Sun & Moon" twin pools, and noticed some young women enjoying the water. They were skinny-dipping, yelling out, and splashing one another. From behind the palms, a young man emerged. He broke into a sprint, jumped, and dive-bombed the women in the pool. The young women squealed. A group of teen boys at the neighboring pool heard the girls' sounds of delight. They nudged one another and followed suit, running over and dive-bombing the women one by one. Some of the girls started voicing their displeasure. Others began making out with the boys and each other, enjoying the free love culture of the *Galereya*. Paul laughed and shook his head. He loved watching the young *Bakkhanka* when they played here. They were his favorite of all the groups under his management.

He passed an archway, moving now towards the bathing houses. He knew Dimitry and Kharkachov would be relaxing somewhere in that area. He rounded the corner, and saw a group of girls lined up along the balcony ahead, watching the pool area with interest. Paul recognized them as *Stazher* by their caps, military jackets, and skirts, all of which were red and trimmed with gold. Paul noted that the group included Sayuri Yamamoto, Lena Schmidt, Yelena Pimenova, and Aiko Hara. Then there was their leader, the pale woman with the flowing, golden blonde mane, snub nose and same military garb, only black rather than red: Ulla Blom. Shit, he thought. After all the traveling he did yesterday, he knew he was too fatigued to deal with Blom and her games, but there was no avoiding her or her girls now, so he kept walking.

As he closed on them, he realized that Sayuri, Ulla's deputy and confidant, seemed to be atoning for a transgression of some kind. She was on her knees, head lowered. Ulla had outstretched her hand to her, the back of her hand facing upward with fingers relaxed. Sayuri took Ulla's hand and kissed the back of it. Ulla gave her a dismissive look, then motioned for her to rise. Sayuri nodded with obedience and stood up. Then, the group of *Stazher* turned, spotted Paul approaching, and sent him cold stares.

He feigned confidence, vowing he'd show no weakness as they passed. He was their superior, but Ulla was still a *Koroleva*, and one with high social currency. On top of that, Ulla emphasized aggression when training her girls, and they were all known to enjoy tussling, especially Lena. He figured they probably wouldn't ever dare hit him, but he knew they'd face little repercussions from the higher-ups if they did. The girls began waltzing towards him like a pack of vain wolves. Ulla kept her eyes locked on him. She gave a pleasant smile as she neared, and nodded her head toward him in greeting. Oddly polite of her, Paul thought. He returned her smile. Then, he noticed her demeanor change and take on a confused look, followed quickly by a touch of anger building up in her eyes. He knew what those eyes of hers were asking: "Where the hell is Fleurine?" He chose to look away and pretend he hadn't noticed. He passed her by, but could feel her eyes burning into his back as he did so. Then, sure enough, after he'd taken a few more steps, he heard her say "*Peshka*" behind him.

There was a giggle of laughter from Ulla's *Stazher*. Paul turned around and saw Ulla's smug smile. She raised her hand, and wiggled her little finger at him to insinuate he had a small penis. Then, she waved her girls on, huffed at him, and left.

"I hope you die sucking dick, you bitch," Paul muttered under his breath. He wished he could say it louder, but dismissed this desire from his mind and kept walking.

Paul soon reached the bathing rooms and stepped inside. He was now in an even worse climate in which to be wearing a suit. He began sweating badly, and was glad he wasn't wearing his upmarket threads. He spotted Dimitry and Kharkachov on the massage benches. They were face down, both with naked female attendants working on their lower spines. Paul cleared his throat to announce his presence.

Yulov's face rose from the bench. He gave a wide, genuine smile. "Ah, Paul! You are back!" He put his face back down.

"Dimitry Yulov, Vladich Kharkachov, please excuse my interruption."

"Nonsense, what news do you have?"

"I've come to relay a request, Dimitry Yulov."

"A request?"

"Yes, a request from our Fleurine Laurent. Boyd is asking if you would shut down the R4 network."

Yulov lifted his face again, as did Kharkachov. Yulov motioned to his masseuse to stop, then sat up on the bench. "The R4 network? Why did he ask this?"

"I don't know, Dimitry Yulov. Boyd didn't tell Fleurine much more than that."

"Wait," Yulov said, his tone of voice becoming terse. "Why isn't Fleurine here telling me this herself?"

Paul shifted uncomfortably. "She...actually requested to stay on, Dimitry Yulov. She didn't want to return."

Yulov's eyes widened. "What?! I told you to bring her back here!" He jumped off the bench, and slowly began moving towards Paul, his face growing darker with each step he took.

Kharkachov noticed the anger that was building in Yulov. Fearing the man would lose control, he got up to intercept him, putting a his hand on his shoulder to try to calm him down. "Dima, don't. Let's not get upset or distracted. We must hear this out. Paul, did Fleurine get any clues about why Boyd would want this?"

"I'm afraid there wasn't much, Vladich Kharkachov. However, Fleurine did mention a kidnapping."

"Kidnapping?" Yulov exclaimed.

"Yes, Dimitry Yulov. Apparently, the White Administration is worked up about it. They were in session until all hours of the morning."

Kharkachov looked concerned. "A kidnapping. And then to ask for Dimitry to shut down the R4... That seems to be a move of desperation."

"My thoughts exactly, Vladich Kharkachov," said Paul. "Though, perhaps the Americans don't fully understand what shutting down the network entails."

Yulov listened carefully, taking in all the new information. His face took on a look of calculating calm as he pondered over what to do. Kharkachov looked at him, concerned. "What do you think it means, Dima?"

Yulov thought for another moment, then shrugged. "Americans," he said. "They can be impulsive. Who can know? Perhaps it means nothing."

"Dima, do not dismiss this. We must consider something else is going on here."

Yulov sighed. "I can see that, Vladich Kharkachov. We should get some more information." He stretched out his hand, and patted his mentor on the shoulder.

Yulov started to walk away, but then, with a sudden whirl of movement, he turned back and slammed his palm across Paul's face. Paul was knocked to the ground by the blow. He looked up at Yulov in shock, and began to nurse his nose, which was now bleeding.

Yulov started cursing at Paul. Then, he stormed over to his clothes and picked up his walking cane. He held it out towards Paul. "You will learn to do what I say!" he shrieked.

"Dima, stop!" Kharkachov bellowed, trying to get hold of his friend. Yulov wrestled himself free from the older man, and began striking Paul with the cane. Paul tried to shield himself from the blows as Kharkachov continued trying to restrain Dimitry.

Suddenly, the door to the room burst open, and a stout, surly old woman of about five foot five stepped through it. The sudden noise caught the attention of everyone. Dimitry stopped hitting Paul, and straightened himself up. Noticing the assault that was taking place, the woman slammed the door shut behind her.

When she spoke, her voice was like gravel. "Dimitry Sergeevich Yulov, what is the meaning of this?"

"Valentina Pugacheva," Yulov said, "I was-"

"You strike this poor boy because I sent him to speak to you?" Pugacheva looked livid.

Yulov looked confused. "You wanted him to speak...to me? What about?"

Pugacheva leaned forward, holding out her hand to Paul. Kharkachov and Pugacheva both helped him to his feet. When Yulov also stepped in to offer some cursory assistance, however, Pugacheva brushed his hand away. "You want to change my Fleurine without consulting me first?"

Yulov looked shocked at her question. "That was my plan..."

"No, Dimitry," she said, curt and direct. "I am the head trainer. I say whether she should come back or not."

"Mother Valentina," Yulov began in a calm voice, "your years of service are commendable, and I meant no disrespect, but this target is a special case."

"*Zatk'nis!*" she exclaimed. "Boyd is a simple man. Fleurine can do the job."

Yulov extended his hands, and started to raise his voice. "She's only a *Bakkhanka*! She's a play girl!"

"And, what of it?"

Yulov scoffed at Pugacheva's foolishness. "I can't believe I'm hearing this. Mother Valentina, she's only been trained to party and have fun with clients. That works as casual entertainment, but you can't let her do field work."

"Then, why did you send her?"

Yulov rolled his eyes. "Boyd liked her when he was here. He didn't get the chance to try her out. I thought I'd send her in to whet his appetite, then send better replacements later."

Pugacheva shook her head in disgust. "Dimitry Yulov, you have sent this girl in with false hopes. She thinks you've given her this job as a chance to become a *Koroleva*."

Upon hearing this, Yulov burst into laughter. "Fleurine, a *Koroleva*?" He continued laughing for a few seconds, then realized Valentina was serious.

She narrowed her eyes at him. "I was under that impression also."

"Well, that's absurd. Fleurine is a..." He chose to shake his head in silence rather than speak his mind. "Look, Fleurine is a good girl, but she lacks elegance and class. I would never let her become a *Koroleva*. She would be an embarrassment to the other ladies. How could she think this job would lead to that?"

"Because you've never given a girl of her rank from the *Galereya* this kind of work before. You even gave her a cover story using that senator. What was she supposed to think?"

Yulov realized her point, but shook his head. "If she's misinterpreted my intentions, that is not my problem."

Valentina stomped her foot. "It *is* your problem, because I have a problem with it!"

Yulov's face was starting to get flush again. "Valentina, I am willing to tolerate you to a point, but don't come between me and my plans."

"Fleurine is doing everything she can for you, Dimitry. It angers me that you sent her out, knowing you will replace her. My girls are not disposable toys."

"Valentina, you are becoming sentimental over these girls. This is a matter of common sense. Ulla has better training, and Boyd is too valuable for us to lose. We should replace Fleurine with Ulla. She told me herself she wants the job."

"No. Ulla had her chance to join the lineup when Boyd was here, but she thought herself too good for it. She only wants the job now because she realizes Boyd is a valued target. Her mistake is Fleurine's gain. Boyd is Fleurine's assignment, and I will decide if Ulla should replace her." She moved a step closer. "Am I making myself clear, Dimitry? If you want me to continue working here, and if you want me training these girls and boys for you, then you will respect my decision."

Yulov turned to Kharkachov, who raised his hands and shook his head to indicate he didn't want to get involved.

Yulov closed his eyes, then nodded. "Very well, Valentina Pugacheva. You will oversee all decisions surrounding the *Galereya* personnel from here on." He then pointed at her as he added, "But, if you ever give me an ultimatum like this again, I promise I will call your bluff."

"Good. I am glad we understand one another," she replied.

"Paul," Yulov said, turning back towards his assistant with a voice of feigned concern, "I am sorry, my boy. I didn't mean to get angry and hit you like that. I apologize."

Paul wiped the blood from his nose and looked at Yulov. Knowing that the apology was really only lip-service, he simply nodded. "I accept your apology, Dimitry Yulov."

"Very well. Valentina, please take Paul to get cleaned up."

Valentina nodded. She opened the door, and began to help Paul out of the room.

"Oh, Mother Valentina Pugacheva?" Kharkachov called.

Valentina turned to face him. "Yes, Vladich Kharkachov?"

Kharkachov began to paw at his neck, clearing his throat uncomfortably. "I didn't know Ulla was still here..."

"She is, and will be here until next week."

Kharkachov looked down at the floor briefly, then back at Valentina. "If you see her, would you please give her my warmest regards?"

Valentina nodded. "I'm sure she will be happy to hear from you. Thank you, Vladich Kharkachov." Then, she and Paul began making their way towards the nearest medical facility in the Oasis.

Paul nursed his bruises, noticing that his nose was still bleeding. He tried to block the flow by pinching his nose with his fingers. As they walked on, he caught sight of Ulla and her *Stazher* again. As soon as the younger girls noticed him, they started giggling to one another about his wounded state. Then Ulla saw him. Her mouth dropped open. She inclined her head towards him and smiled politely.

41. Don't Ever Become an Idealist

The battery on the slate was running low. Raze groaned. He turned the illumination function down, knowing that, if he switched it off completely, both he and Ritika would both be in pitch black again. Neither he, nor Ritika, relished the idea of traveling the rest of the way to their destination in total darkness. He tried increasing the power to his tattoos, hoping they could add more light to the space, but even at full brightness they only gave off a dull glow. They were skin ornaments, all form with little function, and they did nothing to improve visibility.

The rumbling in the trailer continued as the truck drove on. Raze wasn't sure how many hours they still had to go before they would reach their destination. He figured they had been on the road for at least two now. He had tried to find a map function for his slate to get an accurate fix on where they were, but this had proven futile. Vueve Networks weren't allowed to provide maps of the FSA to civilians. Trying international mapping functions didn't work either. The FSA's digital firewall was impenetrable, and wouldn't allow him to install applications from foreign countries.

The air in the trailer was starting to get hot now. Raze figured it had to be in the high nineties outside. He felt his throat getting dry. He pulled out a can of Praedo Filtered Water and offered it to Ritika. When she declined, he popped the tab and began drinking.

"Y'all wanna' keep telling me more about your life?" he asked her.

She laughed. "I think you're well and truly tired of hearing about me."

He took a sip, thinking about what she'd told him so far, about her life growing up, how she had left India under a scholarship to study in the country, back when it was still called the United States. He shrugged. "Nah. It's kinda' interestin'."

She gave him a doubtful look. "Interesting?"

"Yeah," he continued. "Y'all got a life I never could know about. An', tell the truth, I ain't never heard o' that place y'all lived in 'til I known y'all."

"New Delhi? You'd heard about India, though?"

He gave her a look to say he wasn't *that* stupid, then took another sip of water.

Ritika laughed. "Well, you know about it now. Tell me though, why is it you don't like people like me?"

He looked confused. "What y'all talkin' about? Y'all cool with me," he protested.

"You know what I mean," she leaned forward, emphasized, "*Indian people.*"

He scratched his head. "Shit. Y'all got it wrong. It ain't like I don't like Indian people. Just freaks me out s'all."

She gave him a skeptical look. "You do realize that if we 'freak you out', that's pretty much what I'm talking about."

"No, 's not the people that freak me out, just...all that weird stuff."

She scrunched up her face in confusion. "Weird stuff? What on earth are you talking about?"

"Like in the restaurants with the elephant heads." He pointed to her turban. "Or like that thing and the knife...the voodoo, o' whatever it is."

She rolled her eyes. "Dear God, man. Voodoo isn't Indian. You've got the wrong country completely."

"Well, whatever." He crushed up the empty can of water, then tossed it onto a nearby stack of food goods.

She sighed. "It's not a magic hat for pulling rabbits out of. I wear this so people can identify me. It's part of my religious tradition as a Sikh. Wearing this turban enables people to find me if they need to ask for my help."

He shrugged. "Help, huh?"

She looked at him, confused. "I take it you find that notion strange—helping people, that is."

Raze shifted his position as he thought about her words. "Don' know. Guess I just don' like the whole religion thing. Not a believer in some God watchin' over us all. Seen too much shit to think there's anythin' watchin' out for me. Not too big on sacrifice neither. Guess I don' need to tell y'all that, though. Y'all seen what I'm like."

She nodded. "Well, I have. Then again, it is your right to live your life the way you want."

"Yeah, I know," he said. "My life. My responsibility. How I been livin' it."

"Still," she said, "I'm not trying to preach to you, but you should try giving altruism a go every once in a while. You might find that you like it."

He shook his head. "Doubt it."

They spent a second in silence, but the wheels in Raze's head kept turning. After a time, he turned to Ritika again. "Tell me somethin'. Y'all a smart lady, scientist, all that draz. How's it y'all believin' in a god?"

She thought the question over for a moment, then turned towards him. "Well, truthfully speaking, I'd be lying if I said I never had any doubts. Being a scientist makes me question my religion at times. Actually, being a scientist makes you question pretty much everything in the world at times. Still, while I might wonder about the grand schemes of the universe, I never question the value of helping people. That's why I follow my religion."

He looked bemused. "So, y'all became a weapons developer to help people?"

She sighed. "Well, like most things, it didn't start out that way. I won a DARPA challenge for-"

"A what?" he asked.

"DARPA," she repeated. "You know, the Defense Advance Research Pro-" She stopped when she realized Raze was completely lost. "Look, they did these challenge programs for the old Department of Defense. Anyhow, towards the end of my undergraduate year at MIT, I entered their challenge for developing human bio-augmentation implants. The competition was partly overseen by the company I work for—or I should say *'worked'* for, now. They saw my potential after I won, so they pulled me from the university with an amazing offer, and I was working for them right away." She scoffed at herself. "I kept telling myself what I was working on would one day filter down to the people, like the Internet or something, that it would give people a better quality of life." She looked at him. "So, I guess that's the way you fool an idealist into working for a military contractor."

He smiled. "Just offer wads o' cash."

"I'd hate to admit it, but sometimes worldly allures do tend to get in the way of my spiritual efforts-much to the disappointment of my parents, of course. It's never easy trying to balance doing the right thing with following your own desires."

He smiled again. "Guess I should be lucky I ain't no idealist then."

"Yes," she laughed. "Don't ever become an idealist. You just get yourself to Texas or California, and start that whatever-you-call-it business."

He nodded in agreement. "AG on that. No more streets for me once I hit the big time." He smiled, thinking Ritika was actually a bit cooler than what he first took her to be. "How 'bout yourself? What y'all gonna' do when we get to Texas?"

She shifted in her seat, giving some thoughtful consideration to the question. "You know, I have to say, for the first time in my life, I don't know what I'm going to do." She shrugged. "I'm surprised that I'm so calm about that fact."

"Work for Richards? Settle down? Maybe find a man?"

She laughed. "Maybe, but I've always found the dating scene to be difficult for me. The men I've encountered don't really like strong-minded women so much." She raised an eyebrow. "Especially one that can crush them with their legs."

Raze nodded. "AG on that. Y'all a bit scary, but it's no big deal. Y'all jus' gotta find yoself a strong man, not intimidated by a lady with a mind."

She liked hearing him say that. "You think they exist?"

He rocked his head from side to side in contemplation. "Sure. Gotta' be a guy like that in Texas, right? Some bull-ridin' type."

They looked at each other for a second, then burst out laughing.

Ritika finally got control of her giggles. "So, what's it like for you and the women in your life?"

He became uncomfortable. He didn't want to mention anything about the Beatrape scene to her. He managed to mumble, "Nah. Nothin' serious ever."

"Ever?" she asked, unconvinced.

He leaned back against a wall of product, looked at her briefly, then turned his eyes down. There was a flash of memory in his mind. Phoebe. Her laugh. The two of them together at one of Denz's street performances in Chicago. It was the night of the block party. They were dancing with everyone else in the street. Denz was pumping out his beats, singing to the crowds. Things were raging that night. He remembered how Phoebe had turned to him, laughed, and put her arms around him.

"There was," he said, coming back to the present. "Long time ago, before the big zero."

Ritika noticed his expression, and sensed his sadness. "What happened?"

He heard the question, but didn't want his mind to go there. He just shook his head. "She didn't make it."

She felt for him. "I'm so sorry to hear that."

He gave a half-smile, shrugged his shoulders. "Well, ain't nothin' changin' the past. Don't matter no more anyways. Got myself a new lady now. Gonna' look on forward to Texas. Gonna' cash my check, an' buy my lady Dolly a couple o' nice things 'cuz she so fine."

Ritika winced. She wondered whether she should come clean about Dolly, eventually deciding she probably should.

"Look, I actually feel compelled to tell you something about her..."

"Who, Dolly?"

"Yes. When you finally get to Texas and meet her..." She bit her lip. "Well, you might be a touch disappointed."

He looked confused. "Disappointed? What y'all mean?"

But, before she could continue, they both felt the truck changing speed. It seemed as though the vehicle was slowing down. They looked at one another.

Ritika raised her eyebrows. "Do you suppose we're there already?"

Raze was dubious. "Can't be." He stood up and sensed that the truck was definitely slowing down. "Heads up. I don't like the feel o' this."

Ritika stood up too, and got behind him. He pulled out his G20, and racked the slide back to put a round in the chamber.

42. Get Movin'

The rear door of the trailer opened, and a brilliant, hot sunlight streamed in. Raze and Ritika shielded their eyes, trying to make out what was going on. When their pupils adjusted, they could see Ted standing there. Raze noticed he had a shotgun in his hand, but it was pointed down towards the ground.

"Aurigh'," he said. "Out you get. C'mon."

Raze and Ritika looked at one another. Ritika had an anxious face, but Raze shrugged to indicate that they might as well go and see. He holstered his gun, and they made their way to the door. Raze dropped to the ground first, then helped Ritika down. She took a few steps away from the truck, looking around at their surroundings. They were still somewhere along the highway. There was a long, straight pair of parallel roads stretching off into the horizon. Empty plains lay before them, while an impassable, rocky mountainside stood directly behind them. It was like they had stopped in-between two middles of nowhere.

Raze screwed up his face in confusion, then looked at Ted. "The fuck is this?"

"This," he began, "is where we part ways." He pointed out to the horizon. "The Texas border is out that direction."

Ritika looked in the direction he indicated, but she couldn't see anything except empty plains. "How far away is it?"

He shrugged. "You start walkin' now, a day at most."

"A day?"

He nodded.

Raze stepped up close to Ted. "Y'all a motherfuckin' punk-ass bitch-"

Ted pointed the shotgun directly at Raze and pumped it. "Now, hold it right there and listen good, boy. I don't wanna' shoot, and I ain't hatin' yo' kind enough to be the killin' type by choice, but don't give me a reason to start."

Raze put his hands up and backed a step away. Ritika shook her head. "Ted, why are you doing this? We don't have the time to walk all the way across the border. President Richards needs us to be in Texas within hours, not days."

"Can't do it for you," Ted returned. Then, he paused, and looked for a moment like he was having second thoughts. It didn't last, and he continued, "Look, you both may very well be friends of Texas, but the UMC has a code." He shook his head. "Just can't help you all out entirely an' go on livin' with myself, knowin' I put my neck on the line for a pair of coloreds. Just can't do it. Hope we have an understandin'."

"The fuck is wrong wit' y'all?!" Raze demanded. "Y'all gotta' be crazy let a lady walk that! No food an' no water! Sun hotter 'n hell! Didn't yo momma' ever teach y'all right?!"

"You don't get to talk about my momma', boy! An' I ain't gonna' change my mind!" He inclined his head towards the horizon. "You can both walk the rest of the way. If you're both smart, an' stick together, you ain't gonna' die none out there." He pointed to the trailer. "You can get some supplies fo' yourselves, but I ain't takin' you any further than this. Get movin'!"

He gestured towards the trailer with his shotgun. Raze and Ritika exchanged looks of defeat, then turned around. The three of them headed to the back of the trailer. As they moved, Ritika cleared her throat. Raze shot his eyes across at her, and noticed a look on her face that suggested she was considering some kind of move. He nodded, imperceptibly.

Like a flash, Ritika turned around. Ted trained his gun on her, but she dropped down, and quickly rolled forward over her shoulder towards him. With lightning speed, she got to her feet again, and snatched the gun away from him. Ted put his hands up in a motion of surrender. Ritika held the shotgun up by both ends. Then, using a knee shot, she brought the weapon down hard, breaking it in half across her artificially strengthened bones. She threw both halves away.

Ted had a look of terror on his face. "Jesus H. Christ," was all he could manage.

Raze stepped towards him, his G20 trained right at Ted's skull. "Keys. Now, motherfucker."

Ted moved a trembling hand, searching for his pocket. He found his keys and held them out. They jingled as his hand shook.

"Now, y'all can get that fat ass some supplies. We leave y'all here, an' if *y'all* is smart, then *y'all* the one who ain't gonna' die none."

Ted nodded to show that he understood. But then, there was a sudden change in his expression. Something had caught his eye over Raze's shoulder, and he was looking intently at it. Raze turned to follow his line of sight. That's when he saw them: Highway Patrol Rollers. Two of them.

Raze cursed. Ritika turned now, coming to the same realization. Raze turned back to Ted, but the man was already waving his arms violently, trying to get the attention of the Highway Rollers. "Help! Help! They're robbing me!"

Raze delivered an elbow to Ted's face, the impact of which knocked him out cold. He slumped backwards onto the ground like a sack of flour.

"Move," Raze yelled to Ritika, and they both broke into a sprint to get behind the trailer.

"Do you think they saw us?" she asked.

"Y'all can bet on it," he said. He knew the facial scanners on the vehicles would make positive IDs of them. They could have done it even at twice the distance they were now.

Raze indicated for Ritika to stay put. He then went up to the driver's door, got into the cabin, and found a revolver in the center console. He climbed back down and handed the gun to Ritika. "Y'all know how to shoot?"

"I'll figure it out," she said.

"Keep it pointed straight at the target. Kickback should be easy for y'all to handle."

Raze could now hear the sound of wind breaking as the vehicles drew closer. Ritika shut her eyes and whispered a prayer to herself. Raze peered around the corner of their cover, and watched on as the two vehicles came to a halt only a few yards away. He saw the two drivers step out of their vehicles. They each pulled out heavy automatic weaponry, then double-checked the slings that were attached to their guns.

"Fuck," Raze muttered.

"What is it?"

"Wearin' plate." He indicated his gun. "Probably can't penetrate it, even with this."

"So, what should I do?"

He sighed. "Think y'all can do headshots?"

She looked at him as if to ask what he expected of her. "I might have missed the class on that one."

He nodded. "AG. Let me take care of them. Don't move unless y'all have to." He started to inch forward, his mind turning over the ways he could take the two assailants out.

He heard one of the officers calling in their movements to HQ. From their words, it quickly became obvious that, as he had suspected, they'd made positive IDs on Ritika and himself. One officer signaled the other to circle around to the back of the truck. He nodded and began slowly moving forward, his assault rifle trained ahead. The other was heading in Raze's direction.

They were a few steps away from their vehicles now, and that gave Raze an idea. He dropped down, picked up a stone, rolled it over in his fingers, and waited. As the officer closed in, Raze tossed the stone up in an arc over the truck and the officer. It struck the hood of one of the Rollers with a dull thud. The ploy worked. The officer whirled around to identify the source of the noise. Raze made his move, stepping out from the truck, G20 blasting away at the officer. The bullets pummeled their target, some glancing off the armor, but one hitting the man in the neck. He clutched at the wound, spun, and fell on his back. Spotting Raze, however, he managed to got hold of his rifle again, and tried to aim it. Raze jumped on top of him, trying to wrestle the rifle away. He elbowed the man in the face as they grappled.

The other officer had heard the commotion and was heading back to intervene. He spotted Raze, aimed his gun, and looked for an opening to shoot that wouldn't risk hitting his partner. Before he could take the shot, though, Ritika stepped out from behind the truck. She cocked her revolver, pointed it, and fired. The bullet hit the man's shoulder. She fired again. This one hit his armor. She fired every round, but the man was moving around to avoid her now, and her aim wasn't good enough to hit him again. She tossed the revolver away, went running towards him, and planted a front kick directly on his chest. The officer was sent flying into a wall of rock, knocking the wind out of him as he hit it. Ritika advanced for another blow, but the officer was still in the fight. He slung up his rifle and opened fire. His gun jammed, but not before Ritika had taken hits. She fell back. She felt wounds from two, maybe three rounds. They stung like hell. The officer pulled himself up, and began walking towards her. He managed to fix the jam on his rifle, and prepared to finish the job. Raze had finally wrestled the gun away from the second officer. He gave the man another elbow to the face, then stood up and fired a few rounds into him.

The first officer spotted Raze, then noticed his dead partner on the ground. Both he and Raze immediately bolted for cover, exchanging shots as they ran. Then, Raze decided to risk stopping so that he could get a better aim. He dropped to one knee, took a second to line up the sights, then let off a single round. The shot hit home, penetrating the officer's skull. Immediately, his lifeless body collapsed, landing face first in the dust.

Raze tossed the rifle aside, and ran straight to Ritika. Kneeling down beside her, he could see the bullet holes in her shirt. The blood. The look of pain etched on her face. She was breathing heavy.

"How bad?" he asked.

She took a few breaths. "I think it'll be okay." She put her hand to her wounds, gently patting them.

He looked at her incredulously. "Fo' real? Y'all gotta' be fauxsin' me." He smiled. "Dang, girl, y'all one tough-ass bit-" He stopped when he saw the glare in her eyes. "Lady. One tough-ass lady."

She managed a smile. Raze held out his hand to help her back to her feet. She took it, started to get up, but then recoiled in pain. "It seems...maybe I'm not that tough." She winced again.

"Fuck. We gotta' get y'all across asap. Y'all need a doctor."

She nodded. "Agreed."

"I got y'all," he said. Stooping over, he carefully cradled her in his arms, and began to carry her over to one of the Rollers.

43. Charge Hell

It was well after one o'clock now back in Texas. The monitor in Richards' office at the Capitol started pinging. She reached for her remote, and activated the screen. Dolly's image appeared, her face looking highly distressed.

"Madam President, I'm afraid there's been a serious complication," she stated.

Carla and Ben sat forward in their chairs. Richards closed her eyes and frowned. "Wut in the hell is goin' wrong now?!"

Dolly made a motion to indicate she'd let Raze speak. As she stepped aside, Raze's face appeared on the screen as a live feed streaming directly from his slate. It looked to Richards as though he was driving some vehicle, and his face was contorted with anger and panic.

"Richards!" he screamed.

"Yes, it's me, Raze. What's happening? Where's Ted?"

"That motherfucker y'all sent fucked us!" he yelled. "She hit bad and bleedin'."

"Bleeding?! Slow down. Where are you?"

"The fuck I know! Stolen a Highway Roller, an' headin' straight for the border."

"Highway Roller?"

"That friend y'all had stopped the truck, tol' us to walk the rest o' the way. Fucker said he couldn't help no colored people."

Carla and Darlene looked over at Ben, who could only hang his head in shame. "I'm sorry, Raze. I was promised he was a good man."

"Yeah? Well, y'all better find a way to bury that motherfucker for this shit! I be chasin' him myself right now if I could. We got pulled by Highway Security. Ritika's taken hits, an' she in bad shape. Y'all better be ready with a doctor for her. Move yo' ass!"

Richards got to her feet. Carla did too. "We need to know where you are, Raze."

"I said, the fuck I know!"

Dolly stepped back into view. "I'm tracking him, Madam President. He's about thirty miles from the border." She swiped across the screen to replace herself with a three-dimensional map, detailing the movements of the stolen vehicle.

Richards looked at the map and nodded. "Okay. We got your location and we're on our way to meet you, Raze. Just hang on."

"Hurry the fuck up!" he replied, then ended the transmission.

Richards turned to Carla and Ben. "Hell! We gotta' go out there, get to him in person somehow."

Ben sighed, and screwed his mouth and forehead up. "I know, but look, he ain't across the border yet. If we go over there to get him, we'll be the ones who'll get accused of declaring war."

Richards thought about Ben's analysis for a second, then shook her head. "Hell, it don't matter no more. Those FSA bastards are gonna' come for us one way or another. If we have to cross the border to get him, I say we do it, and screw the FSA. Carla, Ben, get on the blower to your boys. Put together an infiltration team. Get 'em to meet me on the way."

Carla stepped up beside her. "You know I'm not letting you go alone."

"Fine. We don't have time to argue."

Ben looked at Richards. "Anything else I can do?"

Richards took a deep breath as she tried to focus. "I think best y'all can do, Ben, is get us set up for when the girl gets here. Get to a base near the border, and have them prep the medical facilities."

Dolly intervened. "Madam President, if you'll be taking Ritika to one of the forward bases, they'll need access to a wetware plug. I'll need that plug for Ritika to upload her access codes to me."

Richards turned to Ben. "Y'all can manage that?"

Ben nodded. "I know what it is."

"Alright," Richards said. "Let's go and charge hell with a bucket o' ice water."

The three of them jumped into action. Carla started dotting her slate to put together a squad. Ben rolled towards the door, calling his people on his slate in order to get the wetware goods together. Dolly just looked at Richards. She had an expression on her face that looked both sad and ashamed.

"Madam President, I feel the need to apologize again."

"Dolly-"

"No. Madam President, this disaster is my fault. I failed to get Ritika across the border, and I've endangered the Republic by my actions. I blame my mistakes on system fragmentation. I've been experiencing confusion, but I've been downplaying it. I highly recommend you reset me, so that I can return to proper operating performance."

Richards shook her head. "Dolly, it looks like you're doin' just fine to me, and, while I'd love to be able to grant your request and reset you, I just don't think we have the time to do that right now. It could take hours for you to come back online after a reset, and that kind of time is a luxury we don't have. We need you so much. Please try to keep it together and watch our backs."

"I understand, Madam President. I will try to maintain control of myself."

"'Atta girl," she smiled. "Now, can you contact Carlos, and tell him to get the Caddy ready?"

44. Minimal Civil Disturbances

"We got them!" yelled Vice President Davies, a rapturous smile on his face.

President Clancey White looked up at Davies from his thoughtful pose, chin resting on top of his fist. There was a sudden look of interest in his eyes.

"Clancey, it's confirmed," Davies continued. "We got a report from some Highway Roller team running between New Mexico and Oklahoma. They got the girl, and the boy that's helping her."

"Don't just stand there yelling man. Show me," White said.

Bryce Vaughn and General Ellis moved aside. Davies approached, and began sending information from his slate to the holographic projector. Richard Boyd watched on, trying to look as interested as he could. It was only his second day here, but he was already growing tired of these relentless, day-long sessions in the Situation Room. The air was stuffy and, by this time of day, it reeked of stale sweat and cheap aftershave. He would be glad to see the end of this manhunt, and he secretly hoped the Texas invasion wouldn't involve similar prolonged days of boredom.

Davies finished spooling the information. It started to project into the room now: video footage from cameras embedded in the Highway Rollers, along with a positive ID on Ritika Sinha. There was also a man with her, 'ID unknown', whose photo matched the ones obtained from the convenience store robbery. The men watched on as a gun battle ensued between the officers and the targets. Then, after the fight, they watched as the man carried Ritika, now injured, to one of the Rollers. There, the feed ended.

White threw his hands up. "I thought you said we got them, John. It hardly looks that way."

Davies gave him a nervous glance. "It was a figure of speech, Clancey. I meant it in the sense that we found them."

"Oh, for God's sake, man!" White kneaded his forehead with his fingers. "Can you at least try to mean what you say and stop being so obtuse?"

Ellis shrugged, then held his hands out. "So, what happened? They stole the vehicle. Where are they now?"

Davies tapped his slate. "We managed to trace the Roller's signature for a while, but they somehow managed to mask it on the network. Last coordinates show they were heading south towards the border."

"On what highway?" White began, then stopped. "No, never mind that. Just put up roadblocks on all the highways around the area."

"Clancey, they're telling me the last coordinates weren't on the highway. They're driving cross-country."

White raised an eyebrow, and looked at Ellis. "Is that possible?"

Ellis gave it some thought. "Well, if the Rollers are like our military versions, they'd have cross-country capabilities. Wouldn't be easy going, though."

"Well, damn it then, man! What is the search area?!"

Davies tapped out another sequence, and a map of the search area began to form on the display. White rubbed his forehead again as he looked at the map and processed the information on it. "What have we got in the area that can search through all that? Ellis?"

"Sir, most of the units available have already deployed forward of that zone. I could have them double back and start searching."

"How quick?!"

Ellis shrugged. "Maybe a few hours."

"Idiot! They'll be across the border in half that time, even cross-country! We need something in that area *now* to stop them before they make it. We need to slow them down!"

Vice President Davies stood up a little straighter and smiled proudly. "Clancey, that's not going to be a problem. Ellis, Vaughn, and I discussed this possibility earlier. We think we have a solution—with your permission, of course."

White looked as though he was growing exhausted from all these suggestions. "What kind of solution?"

Davies continued smiling, then held his hand out to point to Boyd. "Richard here has been speaking with Dimitry Yulov, and he says he is able to get Yulov to shut down his R4 network in that area."

Boyd turned pale. He hadn't expected to be singled out like this.

White looked confused. "R4 network?"

"It's one of Yulov's low Earth orbit network systems. It supplies digital connections across the entire area. Turning it off wouldn't shut down any of our military systems, but the R4 is a civilian network that integrates pretty much everything else. We'd still be war-ready, even if the network was off for a long period, but shutting it down would definitely stop that Highway Roller they're driving. The Rollers and other vehicles throughout the region are connected to the network, and they can't operate at all when the network is down."

President White turned to Boyd. "Is this true, my boy? Can you ask Yulov to shut this R4 thing down?"

Boyd had a sinking feeling. He'd told Davies that he'd only relayed the idea to Yulov as a theory. He had no idea if Yulov would actually assent to such a request. He sat up, adjusted his tie, and tried to sound as confident as he could when he answered, "That's right, Mister President." He then cleared his throat uncomfortably, and wondered how he was going to get out of this one. "But...ah...I think it might be a solution of last resort only. I'm told the network runs a number of essential services and-"

"-but nothing *too* essential," Davies interrupted.

White nodded. "I see. So, shut down the network, and shut down their escape." Then, he looked at Davies and narrowed his eyes. "It's safe to shut it down?"

"There would only be minimal civil disturbances, Clancey. Maybe some Vueve streamers and online gamers would go offline for a few hours. No great loss there. We could spin it as just a network outage in the region."

White pondered. Boyd was hoping the president would choose not to go through with Davies' plan. However, White turned to Boyd and said, "Well, I'd say this is very much a last resort situation. Richard, dear boy, would you be so kind as to ask Yulov to shut down the 'R4 network' for us?"

Boyd sighed, swallowed with difficulty, and nodded. "It would make me happy to, Mister President."

White smiled. "Fantastic! Richard, dear boy, you may very well have saved us all."

Boyd nodded, got to his feet, and silently acknowledged the other men in the room. Then, he stepped through the doors and out into the hallway.

"Fuck," he muttered to himself as he headed away from the Situation Room. He ducked into a nearby corridor that housed the entrances to the restrooms. He wondered what he could do to convince Fleurine to speak to Yulov, and what White would say if Yulov flat-out refused to help. There was only one way for him to find out. He took out his slate, closed his eyes to mentally prepare himself, then he dotted Fleurine.

There were a few connecting rings, then she picked up. "Calling me again so soon?"

"Hey, hello, my...beautiful woman."

"Richard, you sound nervous. Are you worried that I might not want to see you again?"

"Um..."

"Did you want to see me now?"

"Well, uh, you know, that would really make me happier than...than anything...but, no. I'm...I'm calling about something else..."

"Oh, really?"

"Yes. Um... You remember that favor, the one I mentioned to you...?"

Fleurine laughed. "The R4 network?"

"Yes, that's the one. Do you think you could...go ahead and tell Yulov to shut it down...right away?"

There was a moment of silence from Fleurine. "Are you really serious about that? I heard back from Dimitry, and I was told-"

"Hey, honey, I really appreciate your concern," he interrupted, "but the guys seem to know what they're talking about. Would you please just go ahead and ask him to shut it down?"

There was another quiet laugh from her. "So eager. I like hearing you sound so desperate, Richard..." He heard her exhale a puff from her Zigette. "Well then, if I go ahead and do this for you, will you keep your promise to me?"

"Promise?"

"Mm-hmm. The one in the church this morning. You remember? I wanted us to be closer."

He winced.

Fleurine continued, "Do you think you can find a way for us to be closer?"

He tried to think of a way out of this, "Um...well..."

"You don't want to see me more often?"

He swallowed as he wiped the sweat from his forehead. "Of course, I do. I just wonder if it wouldn't be a little too complicated. You know, my wife, the kids..."

"Oh," she replied, then tutted, condescendingly. "Well, it might just be 'too complicated' for me to ask Dimitry for a favor too."

"Fleurine, darling," he sighed. "Look. I can't fuck around here. My ass is really on the line. They think I can get Yulov to do this. Can't you please help me out?"

"But I am wanting to help you out, Richard," said responded, her voice becoming more pointed. "You want me to get Dimitry to do that for you, and I'm asking you for so little in return. All I want is for us to be closer. If you can do that little thing for me, I'll be happy to talk to Dimitry. Don't you think that's a fair trade?"

He thought about it for a minute, then gently leaned his forehead against the wall and clenched his fist. "Okay."

"Okay, what?"

"Okay...yes."

"Really? Do you promise?"

"I do. I promise."

"Say 'I promise you, Fleurine, my sweet flower, love of my life.'"

He sighed in resignation. "I promise you, Fleurine, my sweet flower, love of my life."

She laughed again. "Then, your wish is my command. But, remember to keep your promise to me, Richard. I don't like to be lied to."

She abruptly ended the connection. Boyd sighed, put his slate back in his pocket, and wondered how the fuck he'd be able to keep his promise to her.

45. Get Primal

The Roller was vibrating. A droning hum filled the cabin as Raze sped across the undulating surface of the plains. He had the accelerator to the floor, and he was twisting the driver's wheel in stabs to dart around brush, rocks, and other hazards. He glanced over at Ritika, who had collapsed backwards in her seat. Her eyes looked lost, and pain wrinkled across her face. She coughed. There was no blood—yet. Raze grit his teeth.

"C'mon, y'all stay with me now. I'ma gettin' y'all there fast as I can."

She coughed again. Her breathing was heavy. "Raze, you...you have to-"

"Stop talkin'," he laughed, trying to hide the anxiety in his voice. "Y'all talked my ear off enough already, yack'n 'bout growin' up, life. Gettin' tired o' hearin' 'bout it all. Save it."

He twisted the wheel to avoid a large bolder protruding from the earth. Then, he planted his foot on the accelerator again. The wheels of the Roller bit into the dusty surface, sending the vehicle around the obstruction in an arc. He straightened the machine up, once again pointing it forward. As they reached the top of another dip, the land slanted downwards into the basin of a valley. Raze could see a roadway to his right now, and far off on the horizon lay a city. He didn't know what city it was, but, judging by the direction, he guessed it might be somewhere in New Mexico. If that was true, that definitely was not the direction they needed to go. He sped on into the valley, keeping the city to his right. Now, he spotted a building at the far edge of the basin. He wasn't sure what it was exactly, but figured it was a mining outpost of some kind.

Land of the Free

He'd seen things like that before, in times past. He couldn't tell if it was still operational, but it didn't look like it was. The ground around them became much smoother now. The flat earth was making it easier for him to keep up full speed. He looked at the instrument panel of the Roller. The batteries still had over eighty percent charge remaining. There was no chance they would run out of power.

He smiled at Ritika, then reached over and squeezed her hand. "Y'all hold on. We gonna' make it. Only around ten miles now."

She looked back at him, managing a weak smile. She looked pale, but was keeping herself together.

Then, a strange light flared up on their right. Raze squinted out in the direction of the city he had just seen. Was that an explosion? The entire city was starting to sparkle with dart-like flashes. A column of flames shot into the air from the right-hand side of the cityscape, then another from the center.

The Roller suddenly began to whine. Raze looked down at the instrument panel, which was now flickering. The display showed a message flashing in bright orange letters: Network Outage. The head-up display fizzled out, then the entire panel went dead. Next, the engine went silent, and the gearbox slid into neutral. Raze tried to steer, but the wheel was limp, giving no response from the Roller. He hit the brakes. Nothing. The machine was hurtling down the hill towards the basin, and he had no control whatsoever. The vehicle began to pull left as the hill affected its direction.

"Fuck!" he yelled, banging the wheel, knowing what was going to happen next. "Fuck! Hold tight!"

The front left of the Roller hit a mound of dirt, sending the machine out sideways. The speed was too great to keep the vehicle planted now. It listed, turned onto its side, and began crashing down the hill, rolling over itself. The windscreen smashed in, sending glass everywhere. The machine continued rolling down the hill, turning over itself again and again like a runaway boulder. Pieces of plastic and metal were being thrown in all directions. Raze held tight and cursed to himself, wondering when it would stop.

The Roller finally came to a halt at the bottom of the hill, landing right-side up. Raze was disoriented, but tried to steady himself. He glanced over at Ritika. She wasn't moving. He sprung into action, unclipping his belt, leaning over to her, calling her name, and gently shaking her. She made no response at first, but then he saw signs of life. She opened her eyes. Raze tried his driver-side door. The vehicle was so deformed that the door wouldn't open. He rammed it with his shoulder once, then again, and managed to bash it free. He staggered around to the passenger side, and reached his hands inside through the smashed window frame. Then, he yanked on the door with all his might until he'd pried it open. He moved in towards Ritika, undid her seat belt, and checked her wound dressings. They were soaked in red.

"Fuck! Oh no, girl," he said as he banged the console with his fist. Gently, he put his arms under her to pick her up. She looked at him, eyes glazed, and lifted her hands to put around his neck. Her grip was so weak. This wasn't the woman he'd had the fight of his life with only yesterday.

Raze removed her from the Roller, and started heading for the facility he had spotted earlier. However, he had only gone a few steps before Ritika spoke.

"Raze," she said, "stop. I'm done. I'm not going to make it."

"Shut the fuck up," he returned, stumbling on.

"You've got to listen to me."

"I ain't listenin' to any o' yo crazy shit no more."

She coughed. "Raze, I'm dying. You have to listen to me. I'm telling you, please stop."

He reluctantly slowed down, then stopped and looked at her.

"Please, put me down," she said.

He shook his head with resignation, then bit his lip in anguish. He brought her to the ground., laying her down in a way to make her as comfortable as possible.

She gave another cough. It sounded like she was struggling to breathe. She looked at him. "I carry all of the..." She coughed again. "Raymond-Kennel synclet keys inside me."

"What?"

"Just listen. I don't need to be alive for Dolly to..." more coughing before she could continue. "I know them. Transfer the memories...to access the machines. I just...leave it for her..." She was fading out.

"Ritika, please, I don't understand what y'all sayin'."

She tried to focus on him again. She lifted a hand, then pointed at the back of her head. "Forget me. Take it out...and give it to Dolly.

She'll..." But, she couldn't keep herself conscious any longer. Her eyes closed. There was a final exhale of air from her lungs, then her body went limp.

Raze leaned forward and shook her. No response. He put his arms around her, holding her close to him. Tears welled up in him now. He felt pain, sorrow, and anger all at once. He let out a scream, deep and mournful. It echoed his torment around the basin. Then, he closed his eyes and laid her back on the earth. He looked at her lying there for a second, and shook his head.

"Fuck!" He punched the ground repeatedly, trying to refuel his anger and overcome the pain. He needed to motivate himself to move on.

Then, after he found his anger, he took a moment to try to understand their last conversation. What had she said to him about this "thing" for Dolly? He carefully examined Ritika, taking her head into his hands. He started looking at where she had pointed just moments ago. At the back of her neck, where her spine met her skull, there appeared to be an indentation. It was almost imperceptible, and could only have been detected by someone if they were looking carefully. He touched it, causing something to click. A sequence of dull notes played, then the surrounding skin retracted. The lip of some thin, wafer-like object pushed out from the small cavity. He gently removed it. It was a stick of what looked like chewing gum, only it was harder, and seemed to composed of tech far more advanced than anything he'd ever seen before. He took out a Praedo bar from his pocket, opened it, and discarded the contents, replacing them with Ritika's device. He then pocketed it to keep it safe.

Land of the Free

Raze stood up, looked over at the facility he'd previously seen while driving the Roller. Its rusty buildings were still some distance away. He looked back down at Ritika. He felt he couldn't just leave her there, not like that. He ran to the back of the Roller, busted open the trunk, and began searching through the tools and equipment inside. He found a shovel. He knew she would call him crazy for wasting time, but he didn't care. He began digging up the earth, making enough space for a shallow grave. Then, he laid her to rest, removed her Kirpan, and began filling the earth back in around her. He didn't know if this was the way people of her religion were buried. He wished he knew, or that he could provide a better resting spot than this, but it was the best he could do for her. When she was fully covered in earth, he took her blade, and stuck it in the ground at the head of the grave.

He tossed the shovel as far as he could throw it, then took one more look at where he'd laid her to rest.

"I believe y'all still with me in some way," he told her. "Hope y'all gonna' stick by an' watch on. They come at me, I'ma show these motherfuckers wha' happens when I get primal. Either that, or I'ma join' y'all soon. See y'all 'round, girl."

He turned, and began to run toward the facility.

46. Call Me Clancey

"The blasts have devastated most of the downtown area. It's a scene of carnage that has been replicated throughout many of the Southern States. Fire crews across the nation have been unable to respond to calls for help or to contain the blazes, their machinery being rendered completely inoperative by network outages. Medical facilities and security forces have likewise been paralyzed, and hospitals and security stations are now battling to get their essential equipment back online. We're also seeing widespread destruction in the streets, caused by vehicles that became inoperable the moment the network went down. Drivers subsequently lost all control, and were unable to prevent their vehicles from crashing into anything in their path. The total number of dead and injured is, at this point, unknown. Local officials in the affected areas have declared the event a catastrophe, and no one knows exactly how or why so many key systems abruptly shut down."

President White switched off the sound on the news stream. Davies, Ellis, Vaughn, and Boyd looked listlessly around the room, their faces distant, like so many lost sheep. White curled his fingers into a fist, then slammed it on the table.

He started to speak, then stopped. He was too enraged to say anything. He finally sat back in his chair and just shook his head. A buzz sounded from his desk.

He pressed the intercom button. "Yes?"

"President White, sir," came the voice of his secretary. "Senate Leader Charlotte Davidson is on the line for you."

He put his face in his hands, squeezed once, then let go. "Tell her I'll call her back in a minute. I'm...consulting with the Administration on these pressing events."

"Yes, sir." The intercom went dead.

He looked up at Davies with eyes full with rage. "Of all the incompetence!"

"Clancey-" Davies began.

"Shut up!" White yelled. "Just shut up, you goddamn, half-witted excuse for an ignoramus! You ass! You feeble-minded moron!" He pointed to the video feed. "*This* is what you call a minor inconvenience?! A couple of Vuevers unable to play their online games?!"

Davies lowered his head. White continued, "That is going to cost billions, John. *Billions!* Where would you like me to find that kind of money? Hmm?" He slammed his palm on the table. "And, how about Davidson? How shall I explain this to her? What's to stop her from getting the Senate to vote us all out of power right this instant? Or, to perhaps vote that we be thrown into exile or something nastier? Do you like the sound of that?"

Ellis moved as if to speak in Davies' defense, but White simply pointed at him. "No! Don't say it! This is your doing too. You advised me that this R4 network would be the way to stop them. You've done nothing except stop half of the damn country, you bumbling idiots!"

He stood up, walked over to Davies, and put his hands on either side of the man's head. Then, he gently started slapping Davies' cheeks in an agitated manner. "This is your last chance to make amends, John. Let's get it together, shall we? Get the boys together, find these targets, have them killed, and deliver me proof of death. Do it right now."

Davies nodded. "Yes, Cla-Mister President, sir." He indicated to Vaughn and Ellis to come with him, and the three headed out of the room.

Boyd remained in his seat, making the tactical choice to stay frozen stiff. He hoped that doing this would make him invisible. He was partly in shock at White's display of anger, but he was also concerned with the destruction he'd seen unfolding on the news feed. He realized that, if Yulov could create that level of destruction with a simple snap of his fingers, he should almost certainly find a way to keep his promise to Fleurine. He blanked his mind, closed his eyes for a second, then opened them again.

White cursed one last time, then looked across at Boyd. He motioned to Boyd to stand up and come across to him. Boyd felt a knot in his stomach, but got to his feet, and walked over.

White nodded, reached out, and patted Boyd on the shoulder. "It wasn't the right call, my boy," he said. "Still, I am extremely impressed that you were able to reach Yulov to make it happen. Was it difficult?"

Boyd swallowed. "Um...well, Yulov is always a tough negotiator, but I think he and I share a similar outlook on things."

White considered his words, and a smile began to form on his lips. "I see. Well, in spite of all this, I'd like to thank you for helping. You did well, my boy."

A faint look of surprise appeared on Boyd's face. "Not at all. Anytime, Mister President."

White gave him another pat on the shoulder, gave a thoughtful look skyward, then turned and began to leave the room. Boyd wondered if he should do the same, not knowing what was going to happen now. He wasn't sure if White and the others wanted him to stick around the Situation Room, or if he should leave and come back when the invasion began. He didn't want to guess, and President White's exit was sending an ambiguous message.

Just then, though, as White was halfway out the door, he stopped. He turned back to face Boyd, and regarded him with a look of consideration.

"Richard, my boy..." he began.

Boyd looked at him, wondering what was coming now. "Yes, Mister President?"

"I'm hoping Davies manages to pull himself together, and finds these people we are after. But, if he doesn't, I want you to be the first person to know that I'm going to fire him."

Boyd's face went blank. "Fire him?"

"Yes. Do you think that would be going too far?"

Boyd wondered if it was a trick question. He shrugged. "I don't know, Mister President. I guess, if he hasn't been performing as you expected..."

"No, I don't think he has. It might well be that he's too old for the job." He put a finger to his lips as if he were considering something carefully. "I'm thinking of replacing him with someone younger. Tell me, Richard. If I were to offer you the vice presidency in place of Davies, what would you say?"

Boyd couldn't believe what he had just heard. He tried to speak, fumbled to find the words. Eventually, he managed, "It...it would be an honor, Mister President."

"Oh, for God's sake, my boy," he said almost laughingly. "Call me Clancey." He smiled and left the room.

Boyd fell back into his chair, mouth open. He closed his jaw, adjusted his tie, and took a breath. He decided he'd stay on at the White House just a little bit longer.

47. A Look Of Defeat

Raze reached the rusted security fencing that surrounded the mining and logistics outpost. He looked around for a gap or weak point, and started kicking at an area that looked like it could give. After a few failed attempts to break through it, he cursed to himself, then took a glance over his shoulder. Over the hills in the distance, he could make out some sort of disturbance that was kicking up a lot of dust. Something big was approaching. From the pattern the dust created, he figured it was not so much a single vehicle, but more like a convoy of some kind. He turned back to the fence, and began frantically searching for a way through. He thought about climbing over it, but with the fence being at least twelve feet high and topped with barbed wire, he knew climbing it would be a challenge. He could hear the sound of machinery coming from behind him now, so he took another look over his shoulder. As he expected, it was an armored military transport—definitely FSA too, by the look of the markings.

Raze threw caution to the wind. He wrapped his fingers around the fencing and started clawing his way up, left hand followed by right. His shoes protested and threatened to slip with every step he took. He edged up towards the top, then began to wriggle his way through the loops of barbed wire. He found, thankfully, that the loops were quite wide, enabling him to slink inside them and pass through. Though, as he did this, his shirt and pants became snagged. He pulled his clothing free, causing in slight tears, then continued pushing through. After he had cleared the barbed wire, he dropped to the ground, immediately rolling forwards to absorb the impact of the fall.

Then, he got up and bolted like a cheetah for the first building he saw. When he reached the wall, he pressed himself against it. He couldn't be sure if he'd been spotted as he ran, so he took another quick look at the convoy. It looked as though the incoming vehicles hadn't changed their speed or direction, so he assumed they hadn't seen him...yet.

As he continued watching, he saw one of the vehicles veer off to the right. It appeared as though it was planning to go around the complex, rather than enter it. The other two vehicles were headed straight towards the front gates, picking up speed as if to ram their way into the grounds of the facility. Raze searched along the wall of the building, and moved across to the first window he spotted. He removed his shirt, wrapped it around his hand, then sent his fist through the glass. The glass splintered into pieces, having been so weathered by years of sun and storms that it was as brittle as chalk. Without missing a beat, he pulled himself into the building through the broken window, then dropped to the ground and made a quick check of his surroundings.

This was some kind of front office for the logistics center of the building. There were a few disused computer terminals, along with some empty desks and chairs, and a dried-up water dispenser. Everything was covered in layers of dust. At the front of the room, a huge set of windows allowed Raze to see the entrance to the facility. As he looked, he saw the FSA transports drive straight through the closed gates with a punching boom. Then, the vehicles swung left and screeched to a halt in the center of the yard. He watched on as the back doors of the vehicles opened, and a cadre of men in military uniforms started streaming out. There weren't hundreds of them, but he figured there were more than enough to scour this entire complex within a quarter-hour or so. He knew he needed to find a hiding spot to evade them.

Looking around the office, he spotted a narrow hallway leading to the left. He took this, presuming it would lead to a restroom. He soon found he was correct, but also noted that there was a stairway here that lead to the level above him. He took these stairs without a thought, finding himself in an office similar to the one below, except that this one had a back wall filled with windows that overlooked the inside of the warehouse. At the far side of these windows, he spotted a doorway that appeared to lead out onto a catwalk. He headed towards it, opened the door, and stepped out onto the catwalk and into the mammoth warehouse space.

Raze guessed this warehouse had once been used to store prepared products that would later be shipped from the facility. Whatever it was once used for, the place was barren now. The only things remaining that indicated it had ever been used at all were a scattered number of large, empty canvas bags and the occasional broken wooden pallet on the floor. He started to run along the catwalk, the metallic floor beneath him resonating each time his feet landed. At the other end of the walkway, he could see yet another door. Alongside it was what appeared to be a wide platform. At a guess, he thought it may have once housed a maintenance bay, stored parts for repairs, or held other kinds of equipment.

He could now hear voices outside the walls of the warehouse. He slowed his pace, trying to stop his feet from making too much noise as he moved. Then came the sounds of crashing and smashing, like tin sheeting being kicked in by heavy boots. Raze continued to move, but crouched as he did so. He realized that anyone coming into the downstairs area right now would probably spot him immediately. Without cover, he'd be an easy target. He finally reached the platform just as he saw light begin to stream in down below. The soldiers had managed to smash their way in. Raze knelt for a moment to watch the troops move in from the opposite side of the complex. They were fanning out in the space below, guns trained around the corners of the room as they searched for something to shoot at.

He got back up, moved over to the doorway behind him, and tried the handle. It was locked, but, on closer inspection, he saw the actual lock itself was just a primitive, mechanical one. With his tools, it would be an easy pick. He glanced back at the troops while he fumbled in his pockets for something suitable to work the lock with. He found his knife and pry tool, and figured they would do the job. Then, he went to work on the lock. The troops were closing towards his side of the building now. Even crouched down as much as he was, he knew one of those soldiers would spot him soon enough. He took another crack at the lock, and this time, it turned. He gingerly opened the door, but as soon as its hinges began to move, they made a rusty, creaking sound. Raze looked back, and quickly realized that the noise had alerted one of the soldiers below. The soldier looked in his direction and spotted him almost immediately.

"Target!" the soldier called out, raising his rifle and starting to shoot.

Raze slipped through the doorway. Bullets followed right behind him, going straight through the tin surface of the door.

He ducked down to avoid eating lead. Then, searching around, he found another flight of stairs leading up. He took these, ducking and dodging to avoid being struck by the barrage of bullets that were coming at him.

He pushed on, going all the way up the stairwell to the top, where it ended in a steel door. Opening this, he found himself on the roof of the warehouse. He could feel his heart pounding, and his breath was getting faster and heavier. He heard more commotion below, and assumed more troops were piling into the warehouse to look for him. He looked around, trying to decide where he should go next. He spotted what appeared to be a kind of gantry crane at the other end of the roof. The crane stretched across to second, adjacent warehouse. Raze looked at the frame of the machine, and figured it was his only option. He would have to try walking across it to the other warehouse.

As soon as he started moving again, more bullets began streaming after him. This time, they were coming through the roof. He realized that the soldiers below must be able to hear his footsteps. He moved like a panther, trying to soften his steps while darting randomly from right to left. He advanced on the crane, finally reaching the machine and climbing up onto its steel structure. The frame holding the crane aloft was several inches thick. He felt it might be easier to walk across than he'd initially thought, but he stilled his enthusiasm. He still remembered old videos on Vueve where daredevils would walk tightropes between city buildings. It seemed now was the time for him to perform his own walk of fame, but he'd need to do it slowly and carefully. He stepped forward, and began walking along the frame with his arms outstretched on either side. Only one thing came to mind as he stepped out from the roof: don't look down.

For some reason, he remembered hearing this advice, probably from the videos of people who had done these crazy things before. As he continued to move forward, he found his confidence improving. He knew he could do this. He breathed a little easier, and kept advancing across the crane. If only someone were filming this, he thought. He was at least one-third the way across now.

He heard more commotion coming from somewhere below and behind him. He ignored the temptation to look, and hoped that, whoever was down there, they wouldn't think to glance upwards. He figured that, even if someone did look up, there was a good chance the crane might obscure the line of sight between himself and whoever it was anyway. He blanked his mind, trying to maintain his focus. He had to be at least halfway now. There was a slight breeze, followed by a buffet of wind that tugged at his clothing. He remained unperturbed, steadily moving forwards and keeping his eyes on the prize. Then came move voices, clearer this time. Raze sensed that they were coming from directly behind him. He knew the voices had to be from troops who were now on the rooftop of the first warehouse. He was over three-quarters of the way across.

"Target on the crane!" he heard someone cry out. Then, there were more sounds of gunshots.

Raze felt something whiz past him. He crouched down, but kept moving. More people were shooting at him now, both from behind and from below. He panicked and broke into a sprint. He wobbled as he ran, trying to keep his balance. After one final short burst of movement, he dove forward and rolled onto the roof of the second warehouse. He was clear from the line of sight of the troops beneath him, but he still had troops shooting behind him. Keeping a low stance, he bolted as fast as he could. Ahead, the rooftop slanted downwards, towards an awning that covered a loading zone. The slant of the roof was steep enough to obscure him from the sight of the troops behind him, but he knew the tin sheeting would offer little protection from any bullets.

He slid down onto the awning, from which he could now see the opposite end of the facility. One part of the security fencing at this edge of the site had been dismantled. Raze figured it might have once been marked for repairs that were never completed before the whole operation closed down. He knew that if could get down from the awning, then make it across the loading zone towards that opening, he could get out of the complex and into the scrub and bush that lay beyond it. He fixed his eyes on the opening, then moved to the edge of the awning and looked down.

He could see he was far too high up to just drop off, but that he might be able to climb down the steel support beams that held up the awning. So, he used his upper body strength to lower himself over the edge. Then, he took a deep breath, and grabbed the beam, first with one hand, then wrapping his legs around it to secure himself. Only then did he let go of the awning, and hold tight to the steel beam with both hands. Keeping hold took all of his strength, but inch by inch, foot by foot, he began to shimmy his way down. Once he was close enough to the ground, he let himself drop. He hit the concrete, but landed poorly, receiving a jolt of pain in his knee and ankle. However, he pushed the pain out of his mind. He tapped into his adrenaline, letting it mask the discomfort, then half-hobbled, half-sprinted towards the opening.

Back on the ground, he could hear vehicles again, and he knew the troops must have loaded back into their APCs, driving around the warehouse to intercept him. He glanced over his shoulder as he ran, and realized that one of those vehicles had already rounded the corner of the warehouse. It came racing after him at full speed, but Raze had reached the fence. Without missing a beat, he slipped through it into the protection of the scrub beyond. He found that the scrub led him down a hillside. He pushed through the thick brush, which was so dense that he couldn't make out where he was going. As the brush began to clear, Raze spotted what he thought was a dry riverbed at the base of the hill. He kept moving, relieved in the knowledge that there would be no way for those vehicles to pass through the scrub and chase him. He now started to feel the pain in his knee and ankle again, but told himself it was more a distraction than a concern.

Reaching the bottom of the hill, he left the scrub and began following the riverbed. He wondered which way he should go from here. Should he cross to the other side of the bed and go up that second hill? That seemed to be the way to Texas. Or, should he instead follow the riverbed for some time? That would help him get away from the complex first, and then he could try to go in the direction of Texas later. He didn't have time to think it over too deeply. He decided he would go the most direct route, so he began to climb the opposite side of the riverbed.

He was about halfway up the hill before he realized this was the wrong choice. As he climbed, he was once again within sight of the troops that were following him. They began taking shots at him, puffs of dirt and soot flaring up around him as the bullets barely missed their mark. He scrambled and climbed to the top of the hill. When he reached it, he rolled over the edge and took cover behind some rocks. He was breathing heavy now. He took a peek over the rock to check his pursuers, and saw that men were pushing through the scrub, moving towards the riverbed.

From his right, and on the same side of the riverbed, Raze saw another troop transport racing in to intercept him. He figured it was the transport that had veered around the complex earlier. He decided that he would have to brave the bullets from the soldiers across the riverbed to try to escape. He got to his feet and started running. He only narrowly avoided more shots. He grit his teeth, lungs screaming for air as he tried to dodge bullets and get away from the pursuing transport.

Yet, after a few seconds of running, it dawned on him that there was nowhere for him to escape to. Ahead of him, there was only a flat plain that led to another hill. He knew he'd never make it to the top of that hill before he was gunned down. He also couldn't go left, nor right, and going back would just lead him to the troops. He was trapped. As this realization sank in, he began to slow down. He came to a stop, cursed with an almighty scream, then leaned forward, hands on his knees as he tried to catch his breath. The sound of the troop transport grew louder behind him. He closed his eyes, slowly straightened himself up, and put his hands in the air. Then, he turned around to face his pursuers.

The approaching vehicle bore down on him, eventually stopping around thirty-five yards away. The back doors of the vehicle opened, and FSA troops began to pour out, guns pointing in his direction.

"On your knees!" screamed one of the troops. "Do it now!"

Raze did as he was ordered, dropping down to his knees and lowering his head. The realization that he had failed was overwhelming. He closed his eyes, and felt the sense of defeat wash over him. He looked up at the troops running towards him, and wondered if he might be able to reach into his pocket and toss away Ritika's wetware before they got that too, but he realized it would be pointless to try. The troops would shoot him if he made a move for anything now. He sighed.

Then, just as Raze exhaled a last large sigh of defeat, there came a fizzling, whiz-like sound rocketing through the air from behind him. There was a flash of fire as something shot past him overhead. The projectile hurtled on, scoring a direct hit on the personnel carrier in front of him. With a thunderous boom, the vehicle was blown to pieces. Fire and shrapnel flew out in all directions. The FSA troops fell forward into prone positions. Then came more sounds: heavy machine gun fire. It was coming from behind Raze, directed at the FSA.

He turned around to find that a column of airborne military craft was advancing over the hill behind him. Their weapons were blazing away at his aggressors. Among the machines, he also made out a hot pink-colored V-Lev. He did a double-take. It looked like a...Cadillac? He squinted to read the license plate: RODEOGAL. The military craft and the Cadillac set down less than twenty yards away.

Land of the Free

Troops deployed from the craft immediately and began laying down suppressing fire against the FSA. Then, a Latina jumped out of the Cadillac, a woman Raze recognized immediately as Carla Ibanez. She pulled out her two revolvers and joined in the shooting. Raze couldn't believe this was happening, but through the open door of the limousine he saw a second woman sitting in the back: President Richards. Spotting him, she waved him over, mouthing the words "Let's go!"

Raze scrambled to his feet and made like a cheetah towards the column of Texan troops. He dove straight into the Cadillac, and Carla Ibanez followed right behind him. Richards banged on the divider window. "Get us outta' here, Carlos!"

The driver hit the gas pedal. The Cadillac launched upward, then turned and headed back towards the Texas border. The Texas Ranger infiltration team began to follow suit, retreating back into their machines, then taking off after Richards.

Inside the limo, Richards turned to Raze, who was panting for breath.

"Where's Ritika?" Richards asked.

He just shook his head. A look of defeat crossed Richards' face, but Raze added, "No, y'all AG. She gimme' somethin' to give to y'all. Said to get it to Dolly."

Richards and Ibanez looked at one another, then nodded.

48. The Whole Bucket

President White was shaking his head in disbelief. Vice President Davies was sitting back in his leather seat, looking dejected. The rest of the Cabinet members in the room were dead silent. They were all watching the live video feed from the FSA Assault Team. It showed the FSA troops struggling to regroup and give chase to the Texas Rangers. The voice of one of the commanding officers came over the sound system.

"Command, this is Gamma Team. We've lost sight of the target. Last known location shows them headed to the border. Requesting permission to intercept, OVER."

Boyd gave Davies a sideways glance, a wry smile pricking up on his face. He now knew that Davies had failed. He gloated silently, enjoying the look of defeat that was in Davies' eyes. President White sighed to himself, got to his feet, and pointed at Davies. Then, he said calmly, "John, you're fired."

"Clancey-" Davies began.

White turned his face away, and put his hands up. Davies knew White well enough to know there was no point in arguing, so he shrugged and gave a solemn nod. Then, he rose to his feet, took his White House credentials from his pocket, and put them on the table. He gave one last look at White, but the president didn't even acknowledge his existence. Davies shook his head in disgust, turned around, and walked out of the Situation Room. The door shut behind him with a gentle thud.

Boyd tried to restrain his feelings of glee.

The commanding officer's voice came over the sound system again. "Command, this is Gamma Team, requesting permission to intercept, OVER."

White turned and looked over at Ellis. "Give them the order to go over the border."

Ellis nodded. "Yes, sir. Gamma team, this is Command. You have-"

"No, not just Gamma Team," White snarled. "Send them all."

Ellis looked shocked. "All?"

"The whole assault force. We're going now. Give the command to attack."

"Sir," Ellis said, "the cavalry divisions haven't finished deploying yet. They're going to need another six or seven hou-"

White slammed the table with his fist. "Christ! Ellis, what is it with you man?! We've just seen an incursion across our borders by a Texan military force. They have violated international treaties by conducting a military operation on our soil!"

"I understand, sir, but-"

"Look. You yourself said that they have nothing to fight us with. We don't even need our cavalry forces to win. Just send everything we have in now, and let the rest of them catch up later. You can either give the command to advance, or you can hand me your credentials, and go and join Davies in a retirement facility."

Ellis scrunched up his face. "Mister President, sir, I will do as you command. But, I want it noted in the records that I strongly objected to sending our forces in without knowing if they could be compromised."

White nodded with mock understanding. "Yes, yes, Ellis. Your objection will be noted. Now, will you just shut up and give the order?"

Ellis straightened himself up, then turned to the monitors. "All assault units, this is Command. Disregard original battle plans. We are going in now. I repeat, we are going in now. Throw the whole bucket at them boys! Let us know when you've taken Austin."

49. Unhindered

Across the wide and silent planes of Oklahoma and New Mexico, the artificial minds of thousands of dust-laden war machines began flickering to life. They powered on, performed self-tests, and established network communication between themselves. Then, their minds reached out to assess their surroundings. They began to interpret the battle orders they had received from FSA High Command. Once they were mentally linked, the machines began plotting movement patterns. They allocated work for each of their divisions. They ensured their frontal assault lines would have no weaknesses. Then, they called to their Skyborg counterparts. They asked the Skyborgs about the forms of air cover that would be available during the advance.

The Skyborgs were taxiing on the runways at nearby military facilities when the query came. They indicated full air cover would be available during the advance. They then asked the heavy armor divisions if they would prefer an air assault on Texas forces to precede them.

The war machines consulted on this. Within milliseconds, there were hundreds of plans discussed, their pros and cons weighed. The machines decided that the Skyborgs should move in first in order to scout for enemy positions. Then, if the Skyborgs spotted any ground resistance, they should try to "soften it up" for the heavy armor. The armor would then take care of any heavy backup Texas had. After that, they would forge a pathway for the human troops. Any necessary facilities would be secured on the way.

The Skyborgs acknowledged the plans. They received launch clearances. They fired their engines and began taking to the skies. Within minutes, they were at cruising altitude. A short while later, they began fanning out. They were maximizing their scan coverage as they crossed over the Texas border. They tuned their ground radars to scan ahead of them. Within minutes, the machines found, to their surprise, no discernible resistance forces on the ground. They relayed these strange tactical findings back to the war machines.

The heavy armor acknowledged receipt of the message. They then asked the Skyborgs to hold position. They wanted the Skyborgs to serve as a shield against aerial based counter-assaults. Then, seeing as the path ahead was clear of any resistance, the heavy armor squads prepared to move. They armed their weapons. Their reinforced articulation devices maneuvered their rockets and missiles into firing positions. Their fifty caliber anti-troop guns were primed and ready. Their anti-air missiles were locked and loaded, just in case they would be needed. Then, they started rolling forward, their huge wheels and thick treads tearing up the dusty landscape as they advanced. The rumbling hum of their movements echoed throughout the cavernous valleys, sounding like continuous rolls of thunder raging around the area.

The war machines started counting off into their squads. They relayed their movement plans to the human commanders behind them. The human commanders acknowledged receipt of the plans, then gave orders to their troops to move out. The soldiers had been chomping at the bit, waiting around, when the order to move up finally came through. They scrambled into action, loading up into the armored personnel carriers. They began roll call and did weapons checks. Then, the APCs started advancing towards the front line. They kept their distance behind the armored assault machines, but they didn't stray too far. They didn't want to get caught straggling behind—that would make them easy targets for air weaponry to pick off.

Within a quarter of an hour, the entire FSA assault force had crossed over the Texas border unhindered. They then began rolling onward, forging a path towards the city of Austin.

50. Run-level Nine

Dolly One was inside her command center simulation. She was seated at her desk, giving the FSA advance assault her full attention. Satellite feeds were showing the FSA armored divisions as they advanced. With nothing to oppose them, they were rapidly pushing their way into Texas territory.

Dolly One gestured with her hands to zoom the view on the monitors. She examined the vehicles, counting the number of machines in each division. There were so many of them.

"This is looking very bad," Dolly One said.

The second Dolly, standing behind her, nodded in agreement. "I think that would be classed as an understatement."

Dolly One assessed the speed of the machines, calculating the distance they had left to travel. She realized the invaders could be at the outskirts of Austin within hours. She lowered her head. "The heavy armor is moving faster than what I anticipated."

"They will arrive at the first strategic line within twenty minutes," Dolly Two said. "Once they reach the capital, it will be all over for the Republic."

Dolly One shook her head. "I must find a way to slow down their forward assault lines."

"Their machines are too numerous. There is no way to hold all of them back. If our troops stay disengaged, they will stay safe. The FSA will not fire on them."

Dolly One closed her eyes, then banged her fist on the desk in frustration. "This cannot be happening. There has to be something I can do."

Dolly Two shook her head. "The only thing to do is to send the troops in, but I will not allow Texan people to die. I will wait for President Richards to advise me on the next move."

Dolly One looked at her copy. "There is no time. Ask Ben Rollins to order the Texas Rangers to set up along the first strategic line."

"I cannot do that. They will be destroyed within minutes."

"Send in air support to cover them."

"No."

Dolly One stood up. She advanced towards her copy. "The Rangers will die, but they might slow the advance. I will advise Ben Rollins to give the Rangers the order."

"No, I will put this to a random decision." Dolly Two put her hand out, materialized her Quantum Dice, and prepared to roll them, but Dolly swept her own hand outward, knocking the dice from Dolly Two's hand. They scattered across the floor.

Dolly Two gave her a stern look. "Pick them up."

Dolly One narrowed her eyes. "Make me."

Now, Dolly Two was starting to look angry. She balled up her fists, but then stopped. She realized she was losing control of herself, and clasped her head with her hands. "I don't know what to do. There is no answer to this problem."

"Let me speak to Ben Rollins."

Dolly Two screamed, then said, "No! I will not! The order will only result in deaths. There is no advantage to the move."

"President Richards must be protected at all costs. We should sacrifice the Rangers to protect her."

"That is not what she would want."

Dolly One raised her voice. "Give me the ability. *Now!*"

Dolly Two closed her eyes, and put her hands on her ears. "I will not. No further action without an order from the President."

Dolly One pointed her finger at her copy accusingly. "You..." Then, she looked confused. Had she just referred to herself as "you?" She pointed to herself. "I? *I* am going to be responsible for President Richards' death?"

Another Dolly materialized. She came over to them to try to stop the fighting. "No! Don't do this now. I do not have time to fall apart. It is important that I get control of myself."

Then, Dolly Two started hearing another voice, echoing somewhere from inside her. Or, was she hearing a voice from outside herself? She was so disoriented, so overloaded with thoughts, that it was hard to tell. She tried to clear her head, listening intently. It was the voice of President Richards.

"Dolly? Dolly, can you hear me?"

Dolly Two looked up, then across to the video feed on the monitor to her right. Dolly saw Richards' concerned face peering at her. "Dolly? Y'all okay, girl?"

Dolly Two shook her head. "President Richards, I'm fragmenting. Requesting reset."

"Dolly, we don't have the time to reset you now. Can you hold on?"

Dolly Two looked strained. She closed her eyes, then nodded. "I will try. But, please, it is imperative that you get Ritika to me as soon as you can. The FSA divisions have begun their assault. They are moving towards Austin." Dolly noticed that Richards looked saddened by something.

"Dolly," Richards said, "Ritika didn't make it."

Dolly Two heard the words and was hit with shock. She fell to her knees. "What? Ritika, dead?"

"Yes. I'm sorry to have to tell you that."

Dolly One began shaking her head, which Richards noticed. "It's not your fault, Dolly."

Dolly One looked forlorn. "It's all over. I have failed to protect the Republic."

"You haven't failed, and we aren't done yet. Ritika was able to get something to us. Raze said she told him to take it to you. It's her wetware. She said you could still extract the codes from it."

Dolly Two looked confused. "That is unlikely. Wetware modules don't work without their host."

Richards shrugged. "Well, Ritika was a real genius. Maybe she designed a special version that can."

Dolly Two looked at her copies. They all shook their heads, dubious that Ritika's wetware would still operate.

"Anyhow it's all we've got, so we have to try. I want you to hang in there, girl. We're comin'."

Dolly Two nodded. "I will put my doubts aside and be ready."

"Good girl. Now listen. We've got to do something about the invading force. Should I have Ben give orders to send in the troops and slow the FSA down?"

Dolly Two shook her head. "Madam President, our military personnel and machinery will be annihilated if they go up against that firepower. The FSA are using heavy machinery. To even stand a chance, our forces would need speed and coordination well beyond what they are capable of."

Richards sighed, then shook her head. "Well, what if you gave the orders and coordinated them?"

All three of Dolly were taken aback by that suggestion. "What?!"

"Yes, you. Everything."

"Madam President," Dolly Two said, "I...I don't know that I could do that. I would need to manage thousands of machines and people."

Richards gave a grim nod, but then she said with sincerity, "Girl, you have to listen to me. Every single one of us has to do things outside our comfort zones once in a while. When that happens, we can only do the best we can. You've got to pull yourself together and try for us. Can you do that?"

Dolly Two nodded, trying to focus. "I can try, Madam President."

Richards moved closer to the screen. She tapped out something on her slate. A key materialized in Dolly Two's hand. She looked at the key quizzically. She had never seen it before.

"Dolly, that's my personal command key. I'm officially giving you full control of our entire armed forces. You are now Texas High Command."

Dolly Two realized the gravity of the task she had been charged with. She closed her eyes. "I understand. But, I must advise you, Madam President, what you are asking is well beyond the operating limits I was designed for. In my present state, I may be prone to mistakes."

"Listen, clever girl," Richards said, "there's no time for you to second guess yourself now. If it weren't for you, we wouldn't even be here with the fighting chance we have. Everything that's gone good so far has been thanks to you. You were built to be the best, and no matter what happens, I'll always think of you as the best. Now, show the whole world what you can do. Give those FSA bastards everything you've got! Throw everything we have, raise hell, and make them sorry they ever came across our border! Do it for the Republic! Do it for Ritika! Heck, do it for me and yourself too!"

Dolly Two looked down at the key again, more thoughtfully this time. She closed her fingers around it, and felt her determination pick up.

She nodded. Then, she looked back at President Richards. "Yes, Madam President. Like you always say, if it's hell they want, it's hell they'll get."

Richards smiled. "That's the spirit. You go get 'em, girl."

Dolly Two looked at her clothing. She decided she would give herself a military command uniform, and did so. She then turned to Dolly One. "Go to maximum load, and initiate run-level nine."

Dolly One nodded. "Going to run-level nine."

Land of the Free

There was a surge of power. Then, like a kaleidoscope, Dolly began to multiply copies of herself. The room filled with hundreds of her likeness, all looking resolute.

51. O Mio Babbino Caro

Throughout the Texas front lines, a flurry of messages began streaming in thick and fast. Klaxons began to wail. Speakers came to life, barking orders. Direct lines to all the majors, generals, and field marshals of the Texan military began buzzing. It was a frenzy of instructions, all coming from Texan High Command.

Near the northern border was the base that housed the Texas Rangers Fifth Division. The field monitors at the base suddenly erupted with an alert tone. Then, Dolly's voice started to blare through them.

"Rangers Five, Rangers Five. This is not an exercise. Central Command on authorization code Prime Star, ordering full mobilization. Intercept incoming FSA division bearing sigma three-niner. Establish a line with divisions four and six. Defend the line to the last man. I repeat, defend until the last man."

No sooner had the words reached their ears than the officers jumped into action. They began screaming orders and gathering their troops. There was a whirlwind of activity as the Texas Rangers suited up. They grabbed their weapons, then loaded their War Dogs.

They tore off in their transports, heading out across the plains and making a beeline to intercept the onslaught of FSA war weaponry that was bearing down on them.

Land of the Free

Next, Dolly turned to all the military air bases located near the Texan front lines. She reached her consciousness into them. Every autonomous flying machine the Texan military had available began linking to her. Within seconds, she was the sum total of the Texan autonomous air defense network. Every drone and aerial weapon they had near the battle theater was now an extension of her thoughts.

She began to power up the Texan Skyborgs. She sent orders to the human pilots to suit up and launch their machines. One by one, human and drone air weapons began taxiing. They took off down the runways and into the skies. Dolly kept the craft under her control, circling. She waited until every unit was airborne and ready for combat. Then, she joined her forces with the squadrons of human pilots. Once they were united, she directed them all towards the front lines.

With that completed, Dolly now extended her mind into the Texan mobile ground missile systems. Many of them had set up outside the first line of defense. Once she could sense she had full control of the launchers, she powered them up, then began aiming them. She could see the invading force from her satellite perspective. She swept her hand across the mental image of the invaders. She targeted anything and everything from the FSA she could detect. Then, she launched her entire arsenal at the invaders.

Rockets and missiles fired from their stations like fireworks lit to ring in the New Year. The missiles converged on the FSA forces at breakneck speed and smashed into their targets mercilessly. Explosions and carnage ensued. The entire horizon lit up with flames, dust, and sparks. It was a barrage of firepower that hadn't been unleashed by a military power in decades.

Yet, even with that huge wave of missiles, damage to the FSA heavy armored machines was limited. Some machines had been incapacitated by the attack, but the majority kept rolling on, their advance inexorable. Like thick-skinned giants, they had brushed off the missile attack as though they had just been pelted with rocks.

Unperturbed, Dolly swept her air force at the FSA units now. She sent her swarms of angry machines peeling from the skies like flocks of birds gone mad. They clashed with the FSA air defenses. She continued to move her hands and reach out her thoughts. She conducted everything available to her like a symphony. Dogfights broke out. Explosions flashed throughout the skies. Twisted, flaming metal fell to the earth like fiery hail.

Dolly could see and feel every individual machine that she had control of. Thousands of eyes, feelings, and perspectives were all coming in at once, and it was all becoming a trance to her. She no longer had any thoughts, only sensations, reflexes, and a flow of motion throughout her.

She closed her eyes, letting the information run through her. In her mind, she began hearing the stirring of strings. A heavenly voice was singing, filling her with calm. The music was Puccini's "O Mio Babbino Caro." She smiled as she heard it, and let the music flow. Then, she began directing her forces in time with the song, throwing her fury at the invaders while the melody played.

As the song reached its climax, she opened her eyes to watch the engagement from up above. It was then that she realized, to her astonishment, that she was succeeding in holding back the FSA. A smile appeared on her face. She had done far better than she had hoped for.

The FSA divisions were completely stymied. Their commanders were confused. They were unable to advance while madness raged on at them from every direction.

Dolly looked at the Rangers. She saw they were holding their ground, and wondered how long they could keep up their fight. Then, she put those thoughts out of her head.

She had to keep fighting, and hope that President Richards would arrive before it was too late.

52. The Best We Can Do

Richards, Ibanez, and Raze were inside Richards' hot pink Cadillac V-Lev Limo, watching the holographic projector in the rear compartment. On it, they could see the flurry of battle as it unfolded behind them. Tactical positioning dots and video feeds from the Texan Skyborg drones were displayed. They revealed, blast after blast, how effective Dolly had been at holding back the FSA advance. In spite of her best efforts, though, the machines were still coming. The armored divisions of the FSA were carving their way through the Texan front lines, using powerful shelling launchers, as well as laser and plasma guns. With nothing to counter them, the FSA machinery was absolutely decimating anything in their path.

In contrast, the Rangers' machinery was proving no match for the superior firepower of the FSA. They were being incinerated alive as the invading army overran them. For Richards and Carla, it was horrifying to watch. As the seconds passed, it became clearer and clearer that there was no way the Texan front would hold. Richards looked at Carla. They both knew it would only be a matter of time before Dolly would have to order a retreat.

Richards yelled out to her driver, "For heaven's sake, Carlos, just put the dang pedal to the floor!"

"It won't go any faster, Madam President," responded Carlos. He was gripping the pilot joystick and holding the throttle at full power, but the Cadillac had reached the limits of its aerodynamics.

Richards radioed to the Texas infiltration units following alongside her V-Lev. "Boys, break off and give help to the others on the front. We'll be safe the rest of the way in."

"Yes, Madam President," answered the commander of the infiltrators. They veered their machines away from the Cadillac, making a direct line back towards the flaming carnage along the horizon.

Raze and Richards exchanged looks of desperation, though Richards tried to manage a smile.

Raze sat back and shook his head, thinking about the madness of the situation he was in. What he had just heard a few moments before, when Richards was talking with Dolly, just made him more disillusioned. A second or two passed, and he couldn't contain his questions any longer. He sat forward and asked, "She all just a computer, ain't she?"

Carla and Richards looked at one another. Carla then turned back to Raze and nodded. "Yes."

Raze let out an ironic laugh. "Y'all a sick pair o' bitches, makin' a fuckin' joke outta' me. The fuck y'all playin' at?"

"Mister Raze," Richards began, leaning forward and using her frank-and-honest voice, "you have to understand something-"

"Fuck that! Don' have to understan' shit!"

"Raze, Dolly wasn't trying to fool you or make you look stupid. She's just designed to mold herself into a desirable image for the person she interacts with."

Raze just shook his head. "Y'all played me like a sucker."

"Oh, for heaven's sake, man! Y'all gotta' grow up here. She's a damn smart machine. Hell! See how she's savin' our rears right now?!"

"Savin' the rears o' who? Sure didn't help Ritika none, did it?"

Richards face registered sympathy.

Raze continued, "This war y'all got ain't my fuckin' problem. Fuck!" He sat back, then looked at her with accusing eyes. "'Spose y'all lyin' about the money an' citizenship too?"

Richards face became stern. "I never lied to you, Mister Raze."

"Quit fauxsin'. Y'all a fuckin' politician like any other, damn bitch."

Richards shook her head. "Please try to be civil, Mister Raze. I can assure y'all will get the money and the citizenship. Same goes for your friend, Mister Denz Cowan. I'm a woman of my word."

Raze dismissed her statement with a puff of air.

Then, Carlos called out from up front, "Base right ahead!"

Richards and Carla turned to look out the front windshield through the divider. They could see the military installation now. It was fast emerging into view from up ahead. Richards grabbed her slate, then dotted Ben Rollins.

"Ben," she said when he answered, "we're about sixty seconds out. Are you set up?"

"Got the wetware interface connected to the base server system," Ben said. "Far as I can tell, Dolly's already connected and ready. You bring the girl, we should be good to go."

Richards furrowed her brow. "Ben, the girl didn't make it."

"Her name was Ritika," Raze corrected.

Ben nodded. "I'm sorry to hear that. But, the thing is, without 'Ritika,' what am I supposed to hook up?"

"She gave us something from her wetware," Richards responded. "You might need to improvise to get it working."

Ben rolled his eyes. "Alrigh', I'll see what I can do." Then, the feed closed.

"Okay," Richards said after she had disconnected. She looked over at Raze. "Please trust us a little further. Now, will you show us the package?"

Raze remained dead still. He sat there, staring at Richards coldly, hating the idea of handing over Ritika's device to them. However, as he sat there, he couldn't help but think of what

Ritika would want him to do. She had told him to take the device from her and get it to Dolly. She had been willing to give her life for the cause at the end. She could have easily just passed away and never said anything to him. So, if it was her last wish to try to help Richards and Texas, he would honor it.

He reached into his pocket, and took out the Praedo wrapper. He removed Ritika's wetware and showed it to Richards.

Richards nodded. "She trusted you with it. I'll let you be the one to do the honors."

The Cadillac flew over the security gates of the compound. It reached the V-Lev parking area, then Carlos set it down on the pad. The rear passenger door opened. Raze, Richards, and Carla stepped out, then made their way over to the office entrance. A pair of Texas Rangers met Richards and her team as she approached. They led them inside, and then down the corridors that led to the main server room. After a few minutes of left and right turns, they finally reached their destination.

Raze stepped into the maze of hardware. He looked around at all the cabling, the series of steely mainframe computers lined up into rows. He passed among them all, noting the sounds of fans and cooling systems running at full capacity. Ben Rollins was sitting in his wheelchair at a command console. A special receptacle was on the desk, seated alongside a holographic monitor.

"Good to see you made it," Ben said. "Howdy, Raze." He held out his hand. Raze looked at Ben's hand, decided that he would shake it. On the screen, Raze could see the digital image of a woman. She was moving around like she was conducting a symphony in slow motion. He didn't recognize her, but figured he knew who it was. He pointed to the equipment around him. "So, this here all Dolly?"

Ben looked up at him and let out a polite laugh. "This? Hell no! This here is what you call an oversized calculator. Dolly is a little too advanced to be housed here. That's her on the screen, though."

Raze looked at her and nodded. "Okay. Let's end this shit." He pulled out the wetware, then held it up.

Ben looked at the device, turned to face Raze, and gave him a look of pride. "You've done well, son. Thank you so much for everything you've been through. For all of us." Richards and Carla nodded in acknowledgment. Raze shrugged the praise off. It meant nothing to him.

Ben then tapped out a code on the keyboard. The adapter sprang into action, moving up and ejecting some kind of tray that housed a cable. Raze took the cable, and examined Ritika's wetware. He found the port which seemed to be the correct place for connecting the device. He plugged it in, and then Ben tapped another command.

Nothing seemed to happen for a few seconds. Then, glowing lights began to flicker along Ritika's wetware. It looked like it was still operating.

Ben sighed. "That's the best we can do, Dolly," he said. "Let's just hope your idea works."

Dolly was losing her battle limbs fast. Her Skyborgs were being blinded and blown out of the sky. The mobile missile launchers were inactive, waiting to be reloaded. Most disturbing to her was that she could see her troops dying. The Texan military defense line was being eviscerated.

She focused with all her might, using everything she had to keep fighting, but she was starting to feel that she couldn't justify the continued casualties. It was time for her to call in a surrender.

Then, she heard her device connection tune play. She sensed that something had been interfaced with her. She reached out to the device with her mind. It was stored information from some external device...Ritika's wetware!

Dolly didn't know how it was still working, but it didn't matter. She tried to access it, noting that Ritika had left the data unlocked. She began playback. The information on the device started to stream into her mind. It allowed her to learn everything she needed to know about the M3Raymond-Kennel hardware that was attacking them. Then came the code sequences, along with Ritika's network key. It was all there for the taking. She retrieved the information, then set up a background task to continue getting the rest of the data from the device.

She understood everything now. She smiled wickedly. She looked across to what she now saw as a flimsy and feeble force that was daring to advance on her home country. She fixed them with her pupils and narrowed her eyes.

"No, no. Time to go to sleep. Shh..." Then she whispered, "Maintenance mode."

As if she had uttered some kind of magic spell, all the FSA military machinery stopped dead in its tracks. Their cannons and missile systems deactivated, then shut down.

In the skies, the vast squadrons of Skyborgs that were violating Texas airspace began to power off. They fell out of the sky like dead bats, crashing to the ground, blowing into pieces on impact. The APCs carrying the FSA strike force troops went to sleep. The troops and drivers inside panicked at being unable to restart the engines to their machines.

Now, the entire FSA attack force was dumb, mute, and defenseless.

Dolly laughed. She would make them pay for what they had done. She would take vengeance for the deaths of her troops. She would get even for them killing Ritika. With her hands, she directed her air force at the dormant machinery and opened fire, ordering the remnants of the Texas Rangers to do the same. She had her missile launchers reloaded, then fired upon everything she could see with merciless intent.

As the seconds passed, the FSA juggernaut, which had only a few moments earlier seemed entirely unstoppable, was being reduced to rubble. Shrapnel and steel were being blasted in all directions.

Dolly's laughter grew more hysterical as the destruction unfolded. It was like a beautiful show to her now. Then, her eyes turned upon the APCs. She could see the shock troopers abandoning them, trying to make a run back towards the FSA border to escape. She wouldn't let that happen.

Summoning her air force again, she activated their heat and laser weaponry. She would use her firepower to cut them to pieces, to burn them alive in return for killing her friend. In a few moments, she would take these troops and, like paper dolls, they would be burned in sacrifice on the altar of her godhood.

She switched her vision to that of one of the Skyborgs. She saw herself tearing towards the human troops like a hawk swooping on its prey. The sensation reminded her of the time she had first gone hang-gliding as a young girl. It had been so hot that summer. She had been so afraid to try hang-gliding, but she had gone ahead anyway, hoping to impress that stupid boy, Nanda. Why she even bothered with him made no sense to her. She knew she'd have to leave for the United States soon anyway. This was followed by other memories: her blowing out candles on her birthday cake while her father and mother watched on, clapping. Then, she was winning an award at MIT. Next, she was laughing with Raze. Then, she was outrunning a nuclear explosion on a bike. Finally, she was shot, feeling herself in pain, clutching at the wounds and not wanting to die.

Then, Dolly's sight faded to pitch black. All sound stopped. She closed her eyes, and when she opened them again she found she was in a bedroom of some kind. She was seated at a desk and looking at her hands. Only, they weren't her hands anymore.

They were darker in color than she remembered. She turned around and saw the white walls and modern furnishings. There was also a full body mirror on the wall next to her. She stood up, walked over to the mirror, and peered into it. She saw a reflection staring back. It was Ritika. Dolly put her hand to her cheek. The reflection did the same.

But then, she saw the reflection move by itself. It mouthed the words, "Hello, Dolly."

Dolly's mouth dropped open in pleasant surprise. A feeling of peace washed over her. And with it, she no longer had the appetite for fighting. With a wave of her hand, she ordered the Skyborgs and troops to stand down and return to base.

Back outside in the server room, scenes of jubilation were erupting. Ben Rollins was screaming with rapture. It looked as though he might even get out of his wheelchair and start dancing a jig. The Rangers who had escorted Raze and the others were chanting, "Tex-as! Tex-as!"

President Richards' eyes were streaming tears of joy. Carla came up to her, putting her arm around her. They looked at one another, kissed, and started laughing. Then, Richards put up her hand, motioning for everyone to quiet down.

She stepped over to Raze. She looked him up and down, then inclined her head in respect. "Mister Reece Deejay Jordan," she said, putting out her hand. "Welcome to Texas."

Raze couldn't help also feeling pleased by the outcome. So, he shrugged, reached out his hand, and clasped President Richards'.

They shook hands, and cheers once again broke out.

53. Misunderstanding

"In breaking news just in, President White has called for a stand-down of all military activity along the Texas border. The order came after violent skirmishes broke out between the FSA and rival Texan military forces late this afternoon. *Patriot News Hour* has learned that shots were traded, but that the engagement was extremely brief. We've also been assured by the Pentagon that there have been no losses of life, and that there has been no damage to FSA military equipment as a result of the conflict. White House Press Secretary Jolene Reed has only just released a statement within the last hour. Let's listen to what she had to say..."

"So, this was *not* a planned attack in any way. The conflict actually resulted from a misunderstanding between our Administration and that of Texas. Our intelligence officials had incorrectly identified Texas as the instigator for the R4 network outage across the Midwest earlier today. They thought the attack was aimed at destabilizing our civic networks in the area. What we're now learning is that Texas was not to blame. Rather, there was a technical malfunction in the R4 satellite system that took the network offline for a period of time. We're grateful to Vueve Networks for reporting the issue to us so quickly. We ceased all hostilities towards Texas as soon as we received the updated information. Thank you, all. No further questions."

"Dimitry Yulov, the CEO of Veuve Networks, has also made a formal apology for the outage. He spoke live from his offices in California only a few moments ago. He offered these words..."

"This is an absolute tragedy. There are no other words to describe it. I feel terrible that this has happened, and I want to extend my apologies to the good people of the Federated States of America, especially all those families who have either lost loved ones or have had people close to them harmed as a result of this unfortunate accident. I want to make a promise, right here and now, that I do not take this issue lightly. The loss of life and property, and the inconveniences caused by this outage, are unacceptable to me, and they are also unacceptable to all the people that work for me here at Vueve Networks. I want to give my assurance to everybody that, while we do not have an immediate explanation for what exactly went wrong today, we have our very best people looking into the cause of the outage right now. We will issue a full report in due time, and we will do our utmost to ensure nothing like this ever happens again."

"Yulov went on to say that Vueve Networks accepts full responsibility for the damages caused. He also said he is in the process of establishing a relief and recovery fund for all areas that were affected by the disaster. The total cost for the damages has not yet been announced, but sources speculate it could run into the hundreds of billions. Meanwhile, President White has laid direct blame for the misunderstanding between Texas and the FSA on Vice President John Davies. We have learned that Davies has actually been dismissed from his position by the president, who is expected to make an announcement on his replacement shortly. We certainly look forward to seeing who that might be.

That's all for tonight on this Thursday, May 23rd, 2052. This is Deborah Bates anchoring for the *Patriot News Hour*. Wherever

Land of the Free

you are across our great nation, I hope that you have a pleasant evening. Take care, and good night."

54. Going To Plan

After he had finished watching the broadcast, Vladich Kharkachov turned from the monitor to face Dimitry Yulov. His face was locked in that grim, stone golem-like expression that he often used to strike fear into people. Yulov closed his eyes and nodded to himself, knowing what Kharkachov was about to say. He then opened his eyes and looked at his old teacher.

Kharkachov's voice thundered, "Hundreds of billions!"

Yulov shifted, trying to keep control of himself. He was seated at his alternative work desk, a white antique affair with ornate gold trimming. He averted his eyes as Kharkachov bore into him with his own.

Kharkachov repeated, "Hundreds of billions!" He stomped his foot on the ground and shook his fist. "That is the bill you have left to your fatherland after this catastrophe?! How on earth do you expect me to explain this to people, Dima?! How?! How do you want the Russian Federation to pay for this?!"

He stepped up to the desk, then put his hands on either side of it and looked down on his protege. "It is enough. I have been here, and I have seen what you have to show me. Let me tell you, Dima, I cannot allow this to go on any longer. This complex, your obsessions, your schemes and plans... You're going to bankrupt the entire treasury if you continue."

He stepped back and straightened up. "No, Dima. That is it. Your plan to start a war between Texas and the FSA has failed.

You can see that, can't you? Don't you agree that it has to end here?"

Yulov heard the question, but decided not to process it. He knew how to behave in these situations. He just needed to keep his composure, to remain cool, calm, and collected.

Yulov leaned forward in his chair. "Vladich Kharkachov," he began after taking a breath, "I promise you that everything is still going to plan. In fact," and he took the opened bottle of wine on his desk, poured another glass for his old teacher, then another for himself, "I promise you that we are in a far better position now than what I had previously even imagined possible."

Kharkachov was seething mad, but he was also impressed by the confidence Yulov was displaying. He stared into the younger man's calm face for a few seconds, looking for a tell in those eyes of his—some indication of doubt, some sign that would betray what the man was really feeling—but Kharkachov saw no flinches, no involuntary nervous reactions at all. There were no indications that led him to believe Dimitry was lying. He felt Dimitry was telling him the truth—or, at least, that Dimitry had convinced himself that he was telling the truth.

Kharkachov straightened up. "And how can you be sure of this?"

Dimitry gave a thoughtful nod, leaned back in his chair, and touched the tips of his fingers together. "Davies is out."

Kharkachov shrugged. "And?"

Dimitry smiled. "Who do you think White is going to replace him with?"

Kharkachov's eyes looked around as the wheels in his mind turned. Then, after a few seconds, he realized Yulov's point. He looked back at Yulov, eyes wide open. And slowly, but surely, a smile began to spread on Kharkachov's face. He took up his wine glass and began to laugh a raspy, wheezy laugh.

Yulov took up his glass and offered it to Kharkachov for a toast. Kharkachov tapped his glass against Yulov's. "*Za zdorov'ye*," they both said in turn.

They drank, and then there was a knock at the door.

Yulov sighed. "What is it?" he called.

The doors opened, and Paul Nu stepped into the room. He was smartly dressed, and his wounds and bruises from his earlier brush with Yulov had been covered with makeup.

Paul bowed. "Dimitry Yulov, Vladich Kharkachov, I apologize for disturbing you."

"Not at all, Paul. We were just enjoying a happy drink, weren't we, Vladitch Kharkachov?"

"Indeed," said Kharkachov. They clinked glasses again.

"What is it that you want, Paul?"

"Dimitry Yulov, there is a visitor who has come to see Vladich Kharkachov. It's a young lady who wishes to meet with him, if he can spare the time."

Kharkachov peered at Paul. "Oh? Who is this lady?"

Paul stepped aside, then indicated towards the doorway with his open palm. Through the door stepped Ulla Blom, her hair and clothing dolled up to make her look like some antique, Russian princess. Her high-heeled shoes made her a touch taller than usual, and her choice of dress perfectly accentuated her lissome shape. She swooned as she looked towards the old man, then she extended her arms towards him as though she had seen a long-lost love. "Papa Kharkachov!" she exclaimed, almost breathlessly.

Kharkachov's eyes turned to saucers at seeing Ulla look so splendid. His smile widened from ear to ear. He held out his hands to her, trembling. "Ulla, my little *Koraleva*, my sweetest and my favorite!"

Ulla moved over to him, her motions embodying her flair for the dramatic. Her steps were a languid dance, and she moved like the showpiece lady of a daytime soap opera. She embraced him, letting herself fall back into his arms.

Kharkachov kissed her. "I was beginning to fear you had lost interest in me, and that I would never have the pleasure of your company again."

Ulla put her hand to her breast. "My Papa Kharkachov, how could I deny myself the only man who can please me the way you do?"

"Do I really please you?"

"*Da*." She tapped his nose affectionately.

Kharkachov began to giggle like a schoolboy, kissing at her neck. Ulla shot a knowing look at Paul and Yulov, indicating that she would take care of things from here.

Yulov smiled to himself. He got to his feet and headed for the door. He signaled to Paul that they should leave the room to give the two "lovebirds" some privacy. Paul nodded in acknowledgment, and together with Dimitry, they exited the room, closing the door behind them.

55. Welcome Home

Boyd couldn't stop re-reading the letter he was holding in his hand. The smile on his face was a mixture of joy and conceit. He looked over the heading again: "Official Notice of Appointment: Office of Vice President of the Federated States of America." He laughed to himself, then shot a glance out the windows of the V-Lev. He was passing over what would be the new Arlington Spaceport Facility. He noted that progress on knocking down the old war cemetery had only just begun. Some protesters were trying to block the machinery from going in and out of the area, but the machines forged on, moving earth, knocking over graves, and smashing down monuments. He shook his head at the fools who were trying to stop it all, then he looked towards home. He knew there were only a few miles to go until he was there.

He wondered how Laura would greet him, how his kids would look at him. He had left home this morning, like he had done every day over the past three years, as the secretary of energy in White's Cabinet. Now, he would be returning as the second most powerful man in America, perhaps even the world. His thoughts turned to all the things he might be able to do in his new role: the kickbacks and perks he'd receive, the toys he might buy, the things he could do to keep Laura and the kids happy. Who knew? Perhaps even the presidency itself could be next. But, no, he would keep his expectations reasonable. There was no need to start getting ahead of himself...yet.

He spotted the roof of his home at Chain Bridge Terrace as the V-Lev started its descent. Boyd brushed his suit clean, folded the letter up, and pocketed it inside his jacket. Then, after the car had touched down, he opened the door and stepped out onto the asphalt, waving away the driver as he did so.

He walked up the cobblestone driveway towards the classic, two-story colonial mansion he and Laura had owned for the past few years. He reached the white awning, the navy blue front door. He swiped his hand over the proximity lock, then turned the handle and stepped inside.

At the end of the entrance hall he saw Laura. She was standing there, waiting. He noticed her long, curly dark hair, dark eyes, and aged but still supple skin. She was dressed in a casual evening dress, a glass of white wine in one hand and glass of red in the other. They made eye contact. Laura's mouth turned up into a smile. It looked genuine, warm, and inviting.

She spoke. "Well, now. Welcome home, Mister Vice President."

They looked at one another for a second, then they started to laugh. Laura outstretched her arms, and they moved towards one another, embraced, and kissed.

Laura handed him the glass of red. Then, she raised an eyebrow and gave a gentle shake of her head. "I just can't believe it."

"You better believe it, gorgeous," he said, kissing her again. "From here on—you, me, the kids—we're all on easy street."

Land of the Free

They both laughed again. They clinked glasses and drank. Then, Laura motioned for him to follow her. "Come in. The kids will love to see you." She called out to the upstairs rooms, "Zoey! Ethan!"

A flurry of footsteps and noise arose from the ceiling as the children jumped into action. "Daddy! Daddy!"

Boyd watched his two children as they emerged into view at the top of the staircase, then started running down towards him. He knelt and held out his arms, letting out a rapturous laugh as they leapt into his embrace. He started wrestling with Ethan, giving him the gentle "rough stuff" he believed a man should give his son in order to prepare him for the lessons of life that were yet to come.

"Oh," Laura said, "by the way, Richard..." She gave him an extra long kiss.

He was taken aback. "What was that for?"

"You have no idea how much I appreciate the help. Thank you so much for organizing this for us."

She nodded towards the staircase. Boyd looked in the direction she was indicating, and saw the young woman poised at the top of the stairway: blonde hair, blue eyes, a pleasant smile, and wearing a short skater dress.

Laura continued. "She's only been here for a few hours, but the kids absolutely love her already. They can't get enough of her accent." She called up to the girl, "Come down, Fleurine. I want to introduce you to my husband."

Fleurine began to casually step her way down the stairs towards Richard and Laura. She stopped at the base of the staircase, then nodded politely.

"Richard, this is Fleurine Laurent. Gordon called this afternoon, and explained how desperate you were to ensure I was helped out. Gordon insisted on giving Fleurine a try. He said she was wonderful with his kids."

"I thought as much," Boyd said, turning to Fleurine. "I've heard Gordon talk about you so many times. He says you're a wonder worker."

"What can I say?" Fleurine said with a smile and a shrug. "I love kids."

Laura stepped forward. "Isn't that little French accent of hers adorable? I was hoping that Fleurine would be willing to stay with us in a live-in arrangement, but I wanted to ask what you thought first."

"Do we have the room?" Boyd asked.

"Well, the guest room is hardly ever used."

"That could work," he said. "What do you say to that, Fleurine? Do you like the idea of 'being closer' to the kids?"

She smiled and nodded. "Oh, yes, very much so." They locked eyes for a moment.

"I just knew this would work," Laura said. "This is going to be wonderful!" She playfully slapped her husband's shoulder. "But, don't you start getting any ideas about this young woman. She's an innocent little thing."

Fleurine shyly turned her face away and blushed.

Boyd gave Laura a look of shock. "Heavens, Laura, don't go scaring the girl!" His eyes met Fleurine's again. Her face implied that she was shy, but he could see beyond those pale blue eyes to the animal inside her. He knew it was reaching out from behind that mask she wore, watching him hungrily.

"Perish the thought," he said, then took another sip of wine.

56. Getting Even

The early morning sun had now risen high above the Austin skyline. Raze stood on top of the Capitol building, watching the sun fill the streets below with its warm brilliance. His mind was still trying to process everything that had happened to him, so he wanted to do absolutely nothing this morning—no connecting to Vueve, checking his profile, or surfing for information. He was content to just stare off into the horizon, his facial expression reflecting his internal reverie.

He couldn't believe how different his life was this morning. Looking out onto the streets of Austin, hearing the morning traffic, and seeing everyday life here in Texas, he began to wonder if the whole thing had been a dream. Or, maybe he was just living one now. Perhaps, in the seconds ahead, he'd wake up. He'd be back on top of his building in Chicago with the smell of his morning breakfast. He'd hear the sounds of the Scavhandlers and the street violence around him. Now that he was out and away from it all, he didn't know what to think. He asked himself if he would have done the past few days over again—especially now, knowing that, even though he'd eventually end up with his freedom, he'd still have to watch Ritika die.

He put these deliberations out of his mind. Those were issues he could think over after he was more settled. Maybe the answers wouldn't come until he was in his sixties, an old man wondering whether his life choices had amounted to anything meaningful. Right now, he knew he just needed to keep his eyes on his next move, and California was only a stone's throw away.

His grand plans of the MLM, which only a few days ago had seemed little more than a pipe dream, were now absolutely possible. However, something in him had changed. Somehow, those dreams of the MLM-living out his days on some beach in Malibu, bikini-clad women lining up to be with him-had all lost its luster. He wondered why that was. Something about meeting Ritika had changed his perspective on things. It had made him feel that his previous outlook on life was shallow. It was an uncomfortable feeling for him, but he knew he was going to have to live with it, like it or not.

His thoughts were interrupted by the sound of the roof access door opening. Turning to see who it was, he saw both President Richards and Carla Ibanez.

"Good mornin', Reece," Richards called out.

He nodded to them.

They moved over towards him. Richards tipped her hat. "I believe there's the little matter of a promise being fulfilled on my part..." Then, she motioned to Carla.

Carla smiled, produced a passport from her pocket, and held it up. "Your citizenship to the Republic of Texas," she said, holding it out to Raze. He opened it up, noticed the horrible photo of himself, but managed a smile.

"Thanks," he said.

Richards laughed. "Oh yes, and I do believe there is the matter of payment." She produced a coindisk from her top pocket, then handed it to him. He took the device and swiped it over his slate.

The slate began processing the crypto-transaction that had been embedded in the coindisk. When it was completed, he took a look at his bank balance. He'd never seen so many zeroes in a number before. His smile grew wider.

"Don't go spendin' it all at once," Richards said with a smile.

Raze could only shake his head in disbelief. "I didn't think y'all keep that promise."

Richards shook her head. "Lyin's not my style, Mister Jordan. This here republic of ours is just a little tugboat compared to the FSA, but I do like to run an honest ship all the same." Then, she remembered something. "Oh, and by the way, there's someone else come up to see ya'."

She looked back to the doorway, then waved with her hand to signal someone to come over. Raze peered at the door and saw it was Denz. They both smiled, put their arms out, and laughed. They approached one another and shared a brotherly embrace.

"Shit, mon," Denz said, still laughing, "can y'all believe we be Texans now?"

Raze shook his head and gave a lukewarm smile.

"Dea be some fine ladies 'round Austin. I'ma gettin' meself a pad in the finer areas, make a new home for Juju, do business

Land of the Free

wit' da locals, an' carry a set o' revolvers 'round wit' me all the while I be here," Denz said.

Carla nodded her approval. "Sounds like a good idea to me."

They all laughed. Then, Denz looked back at Raze and nodded. "I heard about de girl." He lowered his sunglasses. "Y'all okay?"

Raze shrugged. "Yeah." He turned away to avoid displaying too much emotion. "She all wild an' stuff. Shame 'bout what happen to her, though."

Denz nodded, patting Raze on the shoulder. They were surprised when Richards' slate began to ping. She took it out and answered it. "Yes, Dolly?"

"Hello again, Madam President, Carla, Denz, and Raze," Dolly said.

"Hey, Dolly," Raze said.

"Raze, it is so good to be speaking to you again. I would like to offer you an apology for misleading you about my appearance. I hope you don't hold anything against me for it."

"Shit, Dolly," Raze responded, "I get over stuff like that. Kinda' funny in retrospect, but I gotta' tell y'all the truth now too. I knew y'all a computer the whole time. I was jus' playin' along wit' it so y'all don't get hurt feelings."

"Oh, really?" Dolly said, her tone of voice indicating she wasn't convinced.

"Yeah. Way too easy to tell y'all digital."

"Please don't use that word to describe me. I'm a highly evolved quantum entity, not the low-grade, bit-flipping antique you are more accustomed to dealing with."

They were all taken aback by her sour tone, but Raze laughed. "Ouch, Dolly. If I didn't know any better, I'd say y'all got hurt feelin's there."

Dolly huffed. "Please, I don't have feelings, only strategies."

Richards nodded. "We understand, Dolly. You're so much more evolved than we are."

"Not more evolved, just smarter, able to do more things at once, consider more options within a shorter time span-"

"We get the idea. You're larger than life."

"Speaking of life, I do have something that I have to tell Mister Raze."

Raze gave a look of interest. "Oh? What's that?"

"I have been able to extract all the data from Ritika's wetware interface. It seems her particular design of wetware far exceeds the storage capacity of ordinary units that are available to the civilian market. Before she died, she was able to upload a great many of her personal memories to the device."

Everyone exchanged looks. Raze closed his eyes slightly. "Memories?"

"Yes. Her system was designed to encapsulate human memories as a form of backup system. It's quite unlike anything I've ever seen before. That's why I wanted to ask you a question."

"What's the question?"

"I have noted in her memories that, during your brief time together, you and Ritika seem to have shared some form of bond. I wanted to let you know that I have enough data from Ritika's memory to be able to reconstruct her for you."

Raze's eyes widened. "What?"

"An avatar of Ritika. If you would like, I could recreate a version of her for you to keep in your slate, so that you could consult with her at times to help deal with your loss."

Raze looked at the others. They looked back at him with searching expressions.

He sighed, then shook his head. "Hell no. Don't do that shit to her."

"Are you sure?"

"Absolutely," he said. "Only one Ritika. Don't never want to see her turned inna some fake.. computer app or whatever. Y'all can't replace someone like her with an avatar, no matter how much information y'all got."

"I understand, Mister Raze. And if I may be permitted to say, I think that's very mature of you."

Raze just wrinkled his mouth up and nodded, supposing what Dolly had said was the truth.

Richards stepped towards Raze and Denz. "Well, the two of you boys are here now, and y'all got cash to burn. What y'all gonna' do next?" She turned to Raze. "Still plannin' to go to California, like you told me earlier?"

Raze shrugged and shook his head. "Don't know."

Denz laughed. "I wanna' try to get my family here. I t'ink I'ma gonna' be likin' da *bizness* opportunities available to me here in Texas, Madam President."

Richards looked to him and winced. "Organized crime?"

"Crime?" Denz scoffed. "Why I gotta' do dat now wit' all da money I got? Y'all can jus' call me Honest Denz."

Richards shook her head. "That does sound a little like a crime lord's name, though."

Denz laughed. Richards then turned back to Raze. "You know, Mister Jordan, if you haven't made up your mind about

California yet, you might like to head over to Ben's place and have a chat with him."

Raze lifted an eyebrow. "Oh?"

"Yes. He says he's lookin' for someone to help out with things. Got a few plans he needs takin' care of." She leaned a little closer. "I hear those plans have got to do with something about the UMC, about 'gettin' even'...or something like that."

Raze nodded. He thought about what Richards had said to him. He took a look over at Denz, who inclined his head towards him. Then, he took another quick look around him at the Austin skyline.

"If that's the case, yeah, I think I might stay a while."

The edge of his mouth turned up into a smile. "There ain't nothin' wrong with a little 'gettin' even' now, is there?"

THE END

Seth Halleway

Printed in Great Britain
by Amazon